PRAISE FOR
HEY SUNSHINE

"Romance is ON POINT."

— Brianna's Bookish Confessions

"Not only is this book one of my favorites of 2015, it's one of my new all time favorites."

— Taylor Knight at Bibliophile Gathering

"Hooked from the very first page."

— Monica @NightReads

"Incredible romance and the perfect amount of drama to keep you turning every page until the end."

— Allissa Lemaire @ABookishLoveAffair

Also by Tia Giacalone

NIGHT FOX

HEY
SUNSHINE

Tia Giacalone

This book is dedicated to anyone who ever wanted more and wasn't afraid to reach out and grab it.

PROLOGUE

"**Y**ou can't wear that, Avery. The guy is flying two thousand miles to come home, for God's sake. Show him some cleavage, at least." Heather Wilson shook her head, clearly disappointed by my fashion choices.

I rolled my eyes at my best friend's disgusted look.

"What do you expect me to do, put on a pageant dress? We're meeting him at the *bus depot*, Heather. I know the whole town will be there but it's not exactly a black-tie affair."

I self-consciously smoothed my hands down the bodice of my knee-length cotton dress. When I first bought it, it had seemed breezy, cute, and comfortable – perfect for a hot, late-August night in West Texas – but now I was reconsidering. What did you wear to welcome your former high-school boyfriend home from fighting wildfires?

Heather snorted, an unladylike sound that was totally out of place with her primly styled chestnut hair and petite frame, but I knew better. Snorting was only the beginning.

"As if we'd have any idea what it's like to attend an actual fancy event. Meeting the Greyhound for the hometown hero is as exciting as it gets around here." Surveying my closet, she sighed.

"Seriously, that dress is boring. It's not like you haven't had time to prepare." She crossed her arms and studied me. "I'll run home and bring over a couple options."

"Yeah right, anything of yours will be way too short and tight," I protested. "That ship has sort of sailed."

"Avery Kent, this is your life," Heather admonished me dramatically. "Don't be such an old lady. You're not even twenty-three, remember? If you're going to do this, do it right." And she disappeared out of the room.

I pulled the rejected dress over my head and tossed it onto the unmade bed. The room was stifling, so I opted to stay in my sports bra and shorts as long as possible instead of getting fully dressed. Central air was an unrealistic dream on a part-time waitress, full-time college student salary. Dropping into the overstuffed chair next to my bed, I leaned my head against the cushion and closed my eyes.

CHAPTER ONE

FOUR YEARS AGO

"**A**very! Wait up!"

I turned and saw Chase Dempsey jogging toward me, still in his practice jersey with his helmet in his hands. My cheeks immediately flushed. Why was our state champion quarterback talking to me? Had he seen me earlier, watching the drills in the stands?

As far as I could remember, we hadn't spoken since seventh grade when he had asked to copy my math homework. Before that, I'd given him half of my peanut butter sandwich when we were eight and he'd dropped his hamburger on the floor at lunch. Not exactly life-altering moments but I remembered them. Did he?

I usually steered clear of football, but for senior year I'd been assigned to cover the team after one of the other students on the paper transferred to another school. I knew next to nothing about the game – practically blasphemous in this county – so I'd started watching the practices last week.

"Hi," I squeaked as Chase came to a stop in front of me.

"Hey," he said, giving me an easy smile. "I saw you from the field. Why'd you leave?"

"Um." I wracked my brain for something cool or offhand to say but came up with nothing. "I had to go." *I had to go? Really Avery?* I gave myself a mental head shake.

Chase's smile faltered for a second at my vague answer but he recovered quickly. "I was wondering if you had plans for Friday, after the game? After we demolish them, I mean," Chase added, his grin growing even bigger.

Plans? Is he asking me out? No way. He probably just needed help with his English homework. "I don't know…" I said, feeling my face heat up again. "Why?"

"A bunch of us are going over to Kyle's house for a party, and I thought maybe you'd like to go. With me," he elaborated.

"You're inviting me to go with you to a party at Kyle's? Kyle Hill?" I asked incredulously.

Brancher was a ridiculously small town with a definite hierarchy, featuring the football team and their friends at the top of the food chain. Those parties were strictly for the A-list crowd at our high school, and a shy, serious, journalism club girl like me didn't make the cut. I was the girl with stacks of college brochures and lists of pros and cons for each one; the girl who color coded her notes by class and always turned in her assignments promptly – never the one who flirted in the hallways or led the dance-planning committees. I had friends of course, and even a few dates, but Chase's group typically passed by me like I was invisible.

"Why not?" Chase laughed.

"But we're not– we don't–" I stopped talking before I could sound any more flustered.

"I've wanted to ask you out for a while, Avery," Chase admitted, and I felt my heart speed up a little. He was so cute. "C'mon, come with me. It'll be fun."

"Okay," I said slowly. "Why not?" I looked toward the parking lot and saw Heather standing there, a puzzled look on her face.

"Cool. I'll call you." Chase winked at me and ran off.

I walked over to where Heather was waiting somewhat impatiently. "Hey, sorry I'm late."

"What did Chase Dempsey want?" she asked immediately.

"He wanted… to go out with me," I said, still mulling it around in my head. "Weird, right?"

"I don't know why this is so unbelievable to you," Heather rolled her eyes as we got into her parents' station wagon. "I told you that after that growth spurt this summer added four inches onto your legs and you got your braces off, the boys would come running."

"Shut up," I said, looking at myself closely in the visor mirror. "Since when do legs and straight teeth equal dates with the starting quarterback?"

"Since you combined them with that swishy long hair and the whole smart-girl thing," Heather insisted. "You're pretty. It's your cross to bear; use it wisely."

"Well, you should know," I teased her. "I heard that Brandon cried when you broke it off with him last week."

"Brandon has a sugar sensitivity, poor guy, and I felt guilty every time I baked anything in his immediate vicinity. It wouldn't have lasted."

"Heartless."

She shrugged. "Sugar-free is not my jam. We need to focus on your party attire," she said, flicking a glance at me. "Two days isn't a lot of time to plan the perfect first-date outfit."

"Sorry." I peered into the mirror again. *Chase Dempsey.* I still couldn't believe it.

∽

"Chase, stop!" I squealed. "I have to finish this paper!"

"C'mon babe." He nuzzled my ear. "You can do it later, right?"

Not really, my responsible mind argued, but Chase slid closer and I relented. "I guess so," I said, giggling. I let him gently push

5

the notebook out of my hands and pull me onto his lap. "I have to finish it today, though."

"Sure," Chase said. "Later. Much later."

"You're a bad influence," I complained half-heartedly as he leaned in to kiss me.

"On 'Most Organized'? No way," he teased me. "The yearbook awards never lie."

I laughed. "You *would* say that, Mr. 'Most Attractive.'"

He grinned. "Like I said, they never lie."

It was because of Chase that I was even on the radar for the yearbook committee. Dating him over the last few months had been an instant pass into the inner circle of Brancher's teenage elite. Chase was the prince, the only son of the town's most prominent and wealthy residents, which made me a reluctant princess by default. But he was sweet, handsome, and seemingly unthreatened by my intelligence, so I put up with life in the high school fishbowl.

"You're nonsensical," I told him, but I kissed him anyway.

"I love it when you use SAT words," he murmured against my lips, and I laughed.

"Speaking of SAT words, how are your applications coming?" I asked.

"You want to talk about this *now*?" he grumbled.

Chase was also more ambitious than most people gave him credit for, something I hadn't anticipated when I agreed to our first date. When I told him about my plans to get out of Brancher as soon as possible and go away to college, I was surprised when he told me he wanted the same thing.

"Me too, babe," he'd said. "Football is gonna get me out of here."

Chase's arm was his ticket out of Brancher, while mine was the grades I worked so hard to maintain, but neither one of us was above the daunting reality of the application process. Colleges liked well-rounded students, whether you were an athlete or an English major.

That meant that I was spending my free time volunteering in the children's section at the library, while Kyle and Chase were reluctantly padding their applications with community outreach hours. The local fire station welcomed them into their newbie volunteer ranks last week. Chase hadn't mentioned it aside from expressing disappointment over their lack of a legitimate fire pole.

"Tell me more about the fire station," I prodded him. "Did you like it?"

"Actually, yeah I did," he admitted. His smile stretched over his whole face as he sat back against the couch. "We went out on a couple calls – no fires – but it was really cool."

"That's great!" I said. "See, it won't be that bad."

He shrugged. "Maybe not."

I smiled. "New yearbook category: 'Most Likely to Save a Kitten From a Tree' goes to Chase Dempsey."

"Give someone else a chance, babe," Chase smirked. "There's already gonna be tons of pictures of me in the yearbook."

I swatted him in the arm. "Incorrigible."

"Oooh, say it again." Chase touched his lips to mine before I could say anything, and I gave up on my paper and gave in to his kiss.

∽

The West Texas sun beat down mercilessly as Chase and I strolled toward the parking lot after our last class of senior year. Other students streamed by all around us, shouting and laughing on their way to celebrate the beginning of summer.

"School is over! We're free." Chase tightened his arm around me and tipped my face up so he could look into my eyes. "Out of Brancher, out of Texas."

Free… I could hardly believe it. We'd talked about it all year, getting out of this town and starting our real lives. Graduation was tomorrow – it was finally happening – and then we'd be leaving for college. Chase would be playing football for Ohio State, and I'd be two hours away working on my creative writing degree at Oberlin College.

"Sort of free," I reminded him. "We do have to actually attend college, you know."

"Right, college," Chase muttered darkly. "I know."

"I'm so excited!" I continued. "It's going to be amazing. And we'll still get to see each other every weekend. I won't miss a game, I promise."

"Sure." Chase pulled me closer for a kiss. "I gotta go." He abruptly changed the subject. "I'm on duty this afternoon."

"Again?" I couldn't hide the apprehension in my voice. Chase was still spending a lot of time at the fire station, long after fulfilling his quota for college applications. He loved the rush; he said there was nothing else like it, not even football. He was a full-gear volunteer now, and I worried every time he went out on a call.

"I'll be careful, babe," he said, kissing me once more.

Of course he would. Stop stressing. I banished the nagging voice inside my head that spewed doubt every time something was going well. "Okay."

"I'll pick you up tomorrow morning," he said as he vaulted over the car door into his convertible Mustang. "We're graduating!"

"Finally!" I laughed, and he blew me a kiss.

I smiled to myself as I watched him drive away. Chase and I were on the fast track out of Brancher and into our new lives. It was time to celebrate.

"He's not here." Janice Dempsey's voice was clipped, angry.

"Oh, okay," I said meekly. "I'll try his cell phone."

After the ceremony yesterday, the Dempseys threw Chase a large, extravagant graduation party. When it was over, Chase dropped me off at home and went back to his house to help clean up. It was a late night, and I was surprised he was already up and gone; I figured he'd still be sleeping.

"If you manage to get ahold of him, tell him to call home immediately," his mother demanded. "I do not find this amusing at all, by the way. His future is at stake."

"I'm not sure I know what you're talking about," I said slowly. "What's going on?"

"You expect me to believe you didn't know? That this wasn't part of your *plans?*" I could picture her sneering face as she spit out the last words.

"Mrs. Dempsey, what happened?"

"Chase is gone. He left early this morning."

"Gone?" I could feel my pulse pounding in my head. *Gone where?* Chase couldn't be gone.

"Yes, Avery, *gone.* For a smart girl, you're not following along here." I cringed at the venom in her words. "Chase packed his things and left sometime before I woke. According to his note, he's been recruited for a forestry position in Alaska."

"Alaska?" What about football… Oberlin… Ohio?

"I don't have time for you to repeat my words back to me. If you hear from Chase, you will call me immediately. Goodbye."

The line went dead and I pulled the phone away from my ear in disbelief. I took three deep breaths before I clicked over to my speed dial and pressed the button for Chase's number. After four rings, a recorded message said that the person I was trying to reach was not accepting calls at this time.

On an impulse, I scrolled through my contacts with shaking fingers until I found Kyle's number. They were best friends and I hoped he'd know something about Chase's whereabouts. He answered immediately.

"Hey, Avery. What's up?"

"Hi," I said cautiously. Kyle sounded completely normal, just like this was any other day. "Have you talked to Chase today?"

"Nah," he said. "We're supposed to hit the school gym later though. Wanna come?"

I almost smiled, because Kyle was always sweetly oblivious, but today was different. "No, thanks. Um, Kyle, I don't think Chase is going to the gym with you today."

"No? That's cool. We can go tomorrow. Maybe I'll go for a run."

I sighed. He clearly had no idea that Chase was MIA. "Kyle, Chase is gone. His mom said he left for a forestry job? Do you know anything about that?" My voice cracked on the last word.

"Oh shit…" Kyle exhaled. "He really left, huh? I didn't think he was serious."

"You knew?" I cried. "You knew he was going?"

"No, no," he protested. "He just talked about it once or twice, you know, since that guy from the Odessa station mentioned it. I never thought he'd actually go."

"What guy from Odessa? I need you to tell me whatever you know, please." Getting information from Kyle's meandering mind was like pulling teeth, but I was determined.

"Um, well, we met this old guy from another station on a call a couple months ago, this other firefighter who used to work for the National Park Service. You know – smoke jumping, doing search and rescue and shit. He talked it up a lot, made it sound real exciting. Chase kept asking him all kinds of questions, and the guy said he could get him a job if he wanted."

Kyle paused, and my stomach sank. This was real. Chase loved the adrenaline rush, the praise and glory of being the hero quarterback fireman, on and off the field. Firefighting and emergency work would be the ultimate high for him. We were eighteen, legal adults. Chase was free to do whatever he wanted, regardless of our plans.

"Anyway, Chase mentioned it a few times, and we kinda joked around, like wouldn't it be crazy if he blew off Ohio and ran up to Alaska instead."

My entire body went numb. "Do you know who it was, Kyle? The firefighter from Odessa?"

"No. Sorry, Avery. I can't believe he just left, without telling you. I never thought he'd do that," Kyle said sadly.

"Me neither," I told him.

Kyle kept talking, his voice distant in my ear as I slid from my bed to the floor and rested my forehead on my knees, too shocked to cry.

∾

A nagging beep woke me from what was probably the worst night's sleep of my life. I rolled over and grabbed my cell phone from the nightstand, jabbing at the screen until the alarm finally shut off. The air in the tiny room was stale, and the only light came from the single window where one of the blinds was crooked and broken.

I watched the dust filter through the stream of sunlight for a second before glancing at the phone again to check the date. Exactly seven weeks since Chase disappeared and three weeks since I'd stopped trying to contact him. *What's the point? He's clearly forgotten all about you.*

A wave of nausea crept over me and I jumped up and ran to the dirty bathroom in the corner of the motel room rented to J.D. Warren, the bull-riding distraction I'd kept busy with for the past month. Crouching next to the toilet, I cried as I emptied the contents of my stomach for the third morning that week. Up came the five beers mixed with pizza as I heaved and sobbed.

Damn it, Avery. I can't believe you did this to yourself. I stood up shakily and wiped my mouth, staring at my reflection in the mirror. My behavior and my appearance were both unrecognizable. "Most Organized" in the yearbook didn't wear skimpy tank tops like this, she didn't drink shitty beer and stay out all night, and she certainly didn't shack up with sleazy but charming rodeo cowboys at crappy motels.

And yet.

I rinsed my face with lukewarm water and tried to ignore the paper bag on the counter, but it was impossible. J.D. wasn't around right now, which meant it was the perfect time to get this over with, if there was a perfect time for such an event. I read the instructions carefully, took the test, and settled back to wait for the longest three minutes of my life.

PREGNANT. The results came up seconds later, immediately, unmistakably. My hands shook as I picked up the plastic stick and stared at the word that was changing the rest of my life. My knees almost gave out but I stumbled back to the nightstand and grabbed my cell phone. My instinct said to get the hell out of here, go home and tell my parents everything. We'd argued more lately than ever before in my life, and I needed to fix it.

Pregnant. Suddenly everything was up in the air – Oberlin, my future, all of it. I looked around the dingy room. What exactly was I doing here? And where was J.D.? It was only nine a.m., and he wasn't exactly a morning person. Before I told my parents, I needed to tell my baby's father. As his cell phone rang, I realized that his clothes weren't strewn all over the floor like usual, and my stomach churned again.

For the second time that summer, I sat alone in a room and listened to a recorded voice telling me that a boy I hoped I could count on wasn't coming back.

CHAPTER TWO

FOUR MONTHS AGO

T O: *AVERY KENT*
FROM: *CHASE DEMPSEY*
SUBJECT: *DON'T DELETE THIS*
Hey Avery,
I know we haven't talked in a long time, but I'm leaving here soon and I miss you. If you don't hate me too much, please write back. I don't know where you are, but I want to see you. Tell me where to go.

I sat back in my dad's desk chair and took a deep breath. I tucked my shaking fingers into the pockets of my hooded sweatshirt and stared at the screen. This email was the very last thing I expected today. It had been almost four years since I'd heard from Chase Dempsey directly.

Indirectly, I'd heard plenty about the Hotshot-crew search-and-rescue firefighter, splitting his time between the wilderness of Alaska and the Washington state forests. Chase had passed up a potential shot at the NFL to save people, trees, and cute furry

animals in need. He was the hometown hero, and the Dempseys –
despite their initial disappointment – made sure that no one forgot
about him even though he had never bothered to contact any of
his old friends.

I picked up my cell phone and dialed.

"Guess what?" I said when Heather answered.

"You reconsidered a blind date with the guy in my fondant
decorating class?" she said hopefully.

"The answer to that one is still no, sorry." I laughed in spite of
my jumping nerves. "You'll never guess, actually, so I'll just tell
you."

"I don't know why you always set me up for failure," Heather
grumbled.

"Chase emailed me," I blurted. "Today, just now."

"What?!" she shrieked. "Are you serious? What did he say?"

"Not much. Just that he was leaving Alaska or wherever, and he
missed me and wanted to see me." I stared at the words on the
computer screen again, wondering if I'd misread them somehow.

"Radio silence for almost four years, he never visits or even
calls, and now he misses you? It's insulting, really. Ridiculous!"

"I know," I said slowly.

Tell me where to go.

He has no idea what I'm doing, or what's happened since he's been gone, I
realized. The Dempseys made sure the whole town knew of
Chase's accomplishments, but I doubted they had ever mentioned
me. Typical. And probably for the best.

"Are you– are you going to write him back?" Heather asked,
and I could almost feel her dubiousness through the phone.

"I don't know yet." I bit my tongue at the lie. Just seeing Chase's
name in my inbox made my heart beat triple time. All the feelings
I'd thought were gone or well buried came flying to the surface,
and suddenly I was seventeen again and the all-state quarterback
was asking me for a date.

"Just think about it before you do anything, okay, Avery? I don't
want you to get hurt again."

"I won't," I said absentmindedly, still staring at the computer. But I knew it was too late for that the minute I read his email.

TO: CHASE DEMPSEY
FROM: AVERY KENT
SUBJECT: RE: DON'T DELETE THIS
Chase,
I don't hate you. I wanted to, because I was really hurt, but I can't. I'm not sure what your parents might have told you but I'm still in Brancher... I never left.

TO: AVERY KENT
FROM: CHASE DEMPSEY
SUBJECT: RE: RE: DON'T DELETE THIS
Hi Avery,
Thanks for replying. I've been thinking about you a lot. I'm glad to hear you don't hate me, although I couldn't blame you if you did. If I come home, will you see me, please? Dinner? We can talk. You're right, my folks never told me anything, so I assumed you'd gone to Oberlin. What happened?

Chase was taking this seriously. It took me three days to decide whether or not to write him back, but once I sent my reply he answered within hours. The question remained: how much did I tell him? What did he deserve to know?

TO: CHASE DEMPSEY
FROM: AVERY KENT
SUBJECT: RE: RE: RE: DON'T DELETE THIS
I'm not sure about dinner. Everything is different now. I don't know where to start.

TO: AVERY KENT
FROM: CHASE DEMPSEY
SUBJECT: START HERE
I want a second chance with you. Catch me up, and I'll be in Brancher in

four months.

∽

Spilling my guts to Chase wasn't exactly what I planned to do over the summer, but that's exactly what was happening. After the basic outline of the past four years, we were filling in the blanks with details... and feelings.

TO: CHASE DEMPSEY
FROM: AVERY KENT
SUBJECT: RE: RE: FOUR YEARS PART TWO
It was hard and often terrifying, but I'm really proud of what I've done on my own – going back to school, raising Annabelle, working, all of it. She makes everything worth it.

TO: AVERY KENT
FROM: CHASE DEMPSEY
SUBJECT: RE: RE: RE: FOUR YEARS PART TWO
I'm sorry that happened to you, with the hospital and everything. I hate hospitals. J.D. sounds like an asshole. You're so much better than that. Anyone who walks out on someone who cares about them is an idiot, trust me I know from personal experience. I'm trying to fix my own mistakes now – and you're at the top of that list.

"I was so afraid to tell him about what happened when Annabelle was born, how I couldn't have more children," I told Heather over breakfast. We were sitting in the back booth at The Kitchen before I started my shift, and I was catching her up on the latest emails from Chase.

"But he was fine with it, right?" Heather wrinkled her nose at the croissant on her plate. "I need to use more butter next time. This batch is dry."

I snagged it and took a bite. "Tastes good to me." I swallowed and smiled at her. "He was sweet. Just said that he was sorry I went through all that. Oh, and that J.D. is an idiot."

"Finally!" Heather exclaimed. "We agree on something!"

TO: AVERY KENT
FROM: CHASE DEMPSEY
SUBJECT: RE: ME & ANNABELLE
I still can't believe you have a three year old. Thanks for sending me the picture. She's pretty, she looks just like you. I know you'll get into NYU, don't worry. I'd like to go back to school, pick up that business degree I never got around to. Maybe New York would be a good place to do it.

TO: CHASE DEMPSEY
FROM: AVERY KENT
SUBJECT: RE: RE: ME & ANNABELLE
I'll be on pins and needles until I have the acceptance letter in my hand. It could change everything in the best way, especially if you wanted to be a part of it. To me, New York seems like the place where anything can happen.

Chase and I had something once, something exciting, and nostalgia combined with a heavy dose of optimism made me believe we could make it work the second time around.

That optimist waited like a giddy schoolgirl for his emails, blushed ridiculously at his deep voice during our phone calls – when we were both available, and he had cell reception – and basically just regressed to her high-school-senior self whenever she pictured his tall, handsome silhouette on the football field, waving confidently at her like he had every Friday night for a year.

He took me back to a time when my only worries were final exams and curfew, and for those fleeting moments it felt right, like nothing had changed. My version of feminism didn't exclude the idea that I could have it all: the husband, the family, and the career. I might've gone about it in a less than ideal way, but it was still my dream.

TO: AVERY KENT
FROM: CHASE DEMPSEY
SUBJECT: COUNTDOWN
Just a couple more days, babe. I can't wait to see you. It's been way too long. Our second chance started with that first email, but it starts for real now.

"What are you smiling about?" my mother asked from across the desk.

We were sitting in the diner's tiny office, my mother going through paperwork and ordering forms while I caught up on some studying.

"Nothing…" As hard as I tried, I couldn't keep the smirk off my face.

"Let me guess… that 'nothing' wouldn't happen to be a long-lost brave and handsome man, would it?" she teased. "Sending you emails of love and devotion?"

I rolled my eyes but couldn't hold back laughter. "Stop!"

My parents made their opinion on my potential reconciliation with Chase very clear. A practical option, she said. A solid choice, he agreed. The best of the worst, according to Heather, who had never liked Chase very much to begin with but was determined to be supportive.

My mom rose and patted my hand as she exited the room. "I'm happy that you're happy."

TO: CHASE DEMPSEY
FROM: AVERY KENT
SUBJECT: RE: COUNTDOWN
I'm counting the minutes.

CHAPTER THREE

PRESENT DAY

I heard stirring from the bedroom across the hall and tiptoed to peek in. A little face turned toward me, silky blond curls tousled and sleepy blue eyes blinking me into focus. Annabelle was sprawled in the corner of her toddler bed, one arm wrapped around her baby doll, the other hand up by her face with her thumb in her mouth. When she saw me, the thumb popped out and her face lit up.

"Mama!" she cried, dropping the doll and holding her arms out.

"Hi, baby girl," I said, crossing the room and reaching down to pick her up. "Did you have a nice nap?"

She burrowed her head into my neck, resting her sweet cheek on my shoulder. "Yes, Mama. My sleepy time is all done." Her baby lisp always made me smile. I kissed the top of her head and smoothed her curls away from her face.

Bending down, I picked up her doll before I carried her out into the hallway. At three years old, she could easily walk but I cherished the cuddle time because I knew it was fleeting. Already, her babyhood went by too fast.

"Do you want a snack?" I asked her. "Auntie Heather is coming back and then we're going to The Kitchen, but dinner won't be for a while." Kent's Kitchen, my parents' diner and my place of employment, would be busy all afternoon. Tonight they were hosting Chase's welcome home party and would keep Annabelle with them while Heather and I met the bus. That was best, I'd decided. I was determined to take this slowly, to protect my heart and Annabelle's.

"Okay, a snack!" Annabelle nodded. "Some crackers, Mama? And cheese?"

"Sure, baby. Let's sit here and wait for Auntie Heather while you eat." I wanted to dig into the sample cookies that Heather had made last night from new recipes for her bakery business, but I resisted. Nervous eating definitely wouldn't help me fit into any borrowed dresses. I got Annabelle settled at her little table in the living room and put a cartoon on the small TV in the bookshelf.

I tried to make our tiny cottage as cozy as possible despite its cramped rooms and weathered floors, and I felt like I succeeded with our mix of eclectic furniture, bright throw pillows, and textured rugs. My dad helped out with the more complex handyman chores, and I was proud of my home. It was mine – I'd paid for it, painted it, cared for it, and raised my baby in it. Of course, it lacked the grandeur of the Dempsey family ranch but the warmth was there.

I shuddered inwardly a bit at the idea of seeing Chase's parents again. Living in close proximity to fewer than a thousand residents, not counting the widespread ranching contingent, we'd encountered each other from time to time, but since my email reconnection with Chase I'd gone all-out to avoid running into Janice and Ron or Chase's sister Elise. They weren't the type to frequent my parents' diner, and I wasn't sure how to interact with them without feeling inadequate.

One snide glance from Janice Dempsey was enough to remind me that I was from her idea of the wrong side of an impossibly small town, not fit to date her son, and quite possibly the reason that he had bolted to the Pacific Northwest in the first place. And then there was the part where they'd never told Chase about my staying in Brancher. I was sure I'd proven every one of Janice's theories right when I got pregnant with Annabelle and changed my future.

My parents were kind enough to host an all-town welcome home party for Chase at The Kitchen, but the Dempseys weren't attending. Chase told me that they'd invited some of their business contacts and society friends to a small dinner party at the ranch, and that we were expected to make an appearance there as soon as we were able. I was dreading it, of course, but I knew that interacting with the Dempseys went along with my second chance with Chase.

When Heather returned, I was tidying up my kitchen after making Annabelle's snack, more to keep my hands busy than because it needed cleaning.

"Here." Heather dumped a pile of dresses on the counter. "One of these has to work. Go try them on, hurry up!"

"I really appreciate this. You know that, right? All of it," I said, alluding to the fact I knew she wasn't fully on board the Chase/Avery train.

Heather snorted again, smoothing her already perfect hair. "I know, silly. Now go get dressed."

∽

Forty-five minutes later, Heather and I were standing nervously in a crowd outside the Greyhound station, straining for a glimpse of Chase's bus. At least, I was nervous and fidgety. Heather looked bored and a little apprehensive but she smiled when she caught me actually wringing my hands.

"Avery, relax! It's not like you've never met the guy," she laughed.

I looked down at my twisted fingers. "I know. It's just... everything is different now." My gaze met Heather's, and the knowing look in her pretty brown eyes brought tears to my own.

Sliding up next to me, Heather slung an arm around my waist. "Look, you and Annabelle, y'all deserve way better than him, okay? The way he left, he's lucky you're even giving him the time of day. You don't need him to want you, Avery. Make him work for it. You're a great mama and a smart cookie. Never forget that."

I returned Heather's squeeze, straightening my spine and pulling my shoulders back. She was right. If this had any chance of working, Chase and I needed to start on equal ground. Chase's money, his family's influence, and his near-legendary status in Brancher didn't matter to me anymore.

Shy, naive, high school Avery was gone; she'd disappeared the day of that positive pregnancy test. In her place was the new Avery: strong and maybe a little jaded but still doing it all. I'd proven to myself over the last three years that I could do anything, even when I was bone tired, sick, or beyond discouraged. I could certainly meet this bus and whatever came along with it.

∽

I'd been anticipating this exact moment for a long time. The bus idled in front of us, exhaust billowing in the thick Texas air, rumbling engine all but drowning out the excited twitters from the anxious crowd.

Somewhere on that bus, between traveling ranch hands, returning vacationers, and those just passing through, somewhere in there was a man I used to know. If I believed everything Chase said, he might even be the one for me and that puppy love could turn into something real. I was willing to take that chance on might, willing to believe his earnestly spoken words and promises until he gave me reason not to. We owed nostalgia that much.

The old Greyhound's creaky door eased open and passengers

began to disembark. At five foot seven, I wasn't the tallest person in the crowd but I could see farther than Heather, much to her irritation.

"Do you see him? Do you see anything?"

"Not yet. Wait, is that him? No." I rose up onto my tiptoes, my boot heels sticking slightly to the hot asphalt for just a second before allowing the bend.

I should've known the crowd would alert me to Chase's presence before my eyes did. A huge cheer erupted when he appeared, framed in the bus's doorway, and his usual smirk wavered for a second but then cemented itself firmly in place. We'd Skyped a few times, but with my horrible internet connection it was more frozen pixellation than actual video, so I still felt unprepared.

When we were high school kids, I'd get giddy every time I caught a glimpse of him in the halls, surrounded by the rest of the football team and constantly garnering admiring glances from all the girls. He'd seek me out, wave and wink, and I'd nearly swoon.

When his brown eyes found mine and our gazes locked, I felt my face grow warm and I smiled. Not quite the swoon from high school, but Chase's happy grin was beautiful and contagious, and I was so glad to finally see him in the flesh.

He hopped down from the bus steps and made his way toward me, the crowd parting for him like he was a celebrity. His dark hair was shorter than I'd ever seen it, and his former adolescent leanness had given way to a strong, sturdy build. When he reached me, he pulled me into his arms, lifted me, and swung me around before planting a huge kiss on my mouth. The crowd cheered and I struggled to relax and catch my breath in his embrace.

I was happy to see him but this was too much with the crowd, the applause. I should have known that any public reunion was a bad idea. That was the part of dating Chase I never got used to – the spectacle. The prince of Brancher always had to put on a show to entertain the masses.

"Hey babe," he chuckled into my ear. "Long time no see."

"Hi," I said, pulling away slightly. I'd pictured a much more intimate reunion in my head, but it wasn't Chase's fault that the whole town wanted to see him come home. The emails were romantic and private – this was not.

Give him a minute, Avery, I thought. The boy just got off the damn bus.

Chase drew in a deep breath of West Texas air. "Happy to be home." He kissed me again, on the cheek this time. "Missed ya." Slinging one arm over my shoulder, he waved to everyone before gesturing to a man who came up next to him. In the fanfare surrounding Chase's arrival, I hadn't noticed that he'd apparently been traveling with someone. The stranger moved easily through the thick crowd, taller than most, with a purposeful presence that was subtle yet arresting. I watched as people moved out of his way without even realizing they were doing so.

"This is Beckett Fox – firefighter, medic, search and rescue, you name it. We worked together up in Washington," he elaborated. "Fox, this is my girl, Avery Kent."

I automatically offered my hand to him. "So nice to meet you, Mr. Fox."

He looked at me at the same time his hand met mine. The touch of his fingers sent a jolt all the way up my arm and startled me almost as much as the intensity of his deep green eyes. Thankfully Chase remained oblivious, waving over my head at some of the other people assembled behind us.

After a second or two, I remembered my manners. I was still holding his hand and I dropped it quickly, my palm burning. I blinked twice quickly to clear my vision.

"Um, I– welcome to Brancher, Texas!"

The minute it came out of my mouth, I hated the way it sounded. Eager, and at the same time too sincere. What was wrong with me? One glance from this guy and I was practically genuflecting all over the place? But honestly, the fact that I could even form words when he looked at me that way was a miracle. Let's be real – the way he looked was a miracle, period.

Easily six foot two or three, with dark blond hair, those green eyes, and a muscular swimmer's build, Beckett Fox was beautiful in an almost dangerous way. My eyes raked over him quickly, admiring the way his big shoulders filled out his worn T-shirt, his jeans hanging perfectly off a lean waist and long legs. I took in his broad chest, the muscles visible even under the loose material of his shirt, strong biceps giving way to tan, corded forearms and hands that looked like they were used to hard work.

I wasn't sure if it was the scratchy five o'clock shadow darkening his jawline, the heat from when his callused hand clasped mine, or the way his thick hair fell across his cheek before he pushed it out of his face, but I couldn't look away. My heart rate picked up when he registered my expression and his pupils widened just a fraction. It wasn't just me. He was affected too. My traitor heart skipped again.

He nodded his head once, averting his eyes at first but bringing them right back to mine, almost involuntarily. "Ma'am." He had a rough, deep voice, a bit rusty, like he rarely spoke. His stance was confident and alert, with an edge that seemed wary.

I felt exposed, practically naked, as we continued to hold each other's gaze. His green eyes searched mine like they were looking for an answer to an unspoken question. I had plenty of questions of my own but zero answers. *Was this for real? Where did this man come from? Was I dramatically imagining the desire that palpably radiated between us? And how was I supposed to function like a human being after this?*

Before I could think or say anything else, we were surrounded by the entire football team and cheerleading squad, all clamoring to get close to Chase. The last glimpse I had of Beckett Fox confirmed that his eyes were still on me even as we were pulled farther apart by the crowd.

CHAPTER FOUR

T he Kitchen was packed by the time we arrived. Ron and Janice Dempsey went on to their party without the guest of honor, leaving Chase his welcome home present – a humungous brand-new SUV that dwarfed my ancient little sedan out in the parking lot. After Chase finished drooling over all the optional features and heavy chrome, we were almost late, and I hated thinking of all the people waiting anxiously for us across town.

Luckily, I discovered it's nearly impossible for people to be irritated if you're late to your own party. When Chase stepped through the diner's double doors, the crowd let out a roar, breaking out into the high school fight song as though he'd thrown the winning pass in a playoff game just that evening, not returned from four years of extreme firefighting as a grown man. I could think of a million more appropriate songs, but these folks couldn't.

Smiling, I shook my head. Once the prince, always the prince in Ector County, Brancher specifically. Chase had it so good here, and his abrupt departure had been mourned and dissected for years by young and old alike.

I saw my parents sitting with Annabelle near the back of the restaurant in our largest booth, and they waved frantically, flagging me down. As we slowly made our way toward them, stopping every few feet so someone could clap Chase on the back and shake his hand, I saw Heather slip in the side door, Beckett Fox behind her. Spotting us, Heather grabbed his hand and pulled him with her as she mercilessly pushed through the well-wishers.

"Lord Almighty," Heather exhaled when they reached me. "This is ridiculous. It's like the return of the prodigal."

My eyes skipped right to her companion's face, who was watching us with an aloof but not unfriendly expression. His eyes met mine and I felt that pull again for an instant before I quickly looked away. *What was that?*

"Avery?" Heather waved a hand in front of my face.

"What? Sorry, I spaced out for a minute," I said, my cheeks reddening slightly. I thought I saw Beckett Fox grin for a nanosecond, but I refused to look at him again.

"I was just telling Mr. Fox here about the diner, how it's pretty much the center of Brancher," Heather said slowly, like I was losing it.

My regular personality, "Most Organized," didn't space out and daydream like that. "Most Organized" kept it on the straight and narrow at all times and would never think unfaithful, unrealistic, and potentially impure thoughts about a man she just met. Sometimes "Most Organized" was exhausting. And not very fun.

"That's right! The Kitchen is the ol' greasy gossip hub of this town, for sure. And Heather, just call him Fox. Everyone does." Chase had come up behind us, finally done saying his hellos. His eyes darted from our group to the door like he was measuring the distance, but then he kissed my cheek and gestured for me sit down.

For a split second, the newcomer looked a little irritated that Chase was speaking for him, but his expression relaxed immediately. *Cool as a cucumber, that one,* I thought. And interesting… Fox. Somehow it fit him. Wary, a bit withdrawn, but undeniably sharp. On another note, I was a little annoyed about Chase calling the restaurant 'greasy' when he knew we went out of our way to serve a more modern, eclectic menu that ranged from fruit smoothies to country-fried steak, but I let it go as well.

I slid into the circular booth next to Annabelle, with Chase right behind me and Elise next to him, Heather and Fox following suit on the other side. Even our largest booth was a bit cramped for all of us, but with the rest of the diner so packed we didn't have many options.

I caught Chase's sister Elise looking at Fox with more than a little interest. I wondered why she had decided to drive herself to the diner and not head to the fancy party with her parents, and now I understood. She didn't care that her brother was home – any new guy in town was immediately on the radar for the single girls of Brancher. The fact that Elise was twenty-one with no prospects of matrimony must have irritated Janice immensely. Only here could you be considered past your prime before you could legally drink.

Too bad Elise Dempsey was a spoiled brat with an ego the size of her daddy's acreage. Someone – not me obviously, because it wasn't my place – needed to warn Fox about that girl. But it wouldn't be me. Definitely not.

"Hi Mama!" Annabelle said brightly. She looked up from her coloring book and grinned at me. My mother smiled at everyone from Annabelle's other side as my father reached across to shake Chase's hand first then Fox's.

"Annabelle, this is my friend Chase. Can you say hello?" I felt like all eyes were on us as Chase and Annabelle met for the first time.

Obediently, her little face turned to Chase. "Hello," she said shyly. I hid my smile in my hand. Anyone who thinks a toddler isn't perceptive clearly hasn't been around many.

"Hi there, Annabelle." Chase smiled confidently.

Annabelle looked up at me, her face curious. "And who's that, Mama?" she asked, pointing at Fox.

Color rushed to my cheeks immediately as everyone's attention moved from Chase and Annabelle to Annabelle and Fox. I glanced quickly in Fox's direction, trying to decipher his expression. He was looking directly at me, a ghost of a smile on his lips, and my face flushed even more.

"It's not nice to point, baby," I admonished her.

Fox surprised me by suddenly reaching across the table and offering his big hand to Annabelle. "My name is Fox."

Annabelle looked at Fox, then back to me, and smiled. She grasped Fox's outstretched hand quickly, his long fingers enveloping her small hand and wrist.

"My name is Annabelle," she said seriously. "You don't look like a fox." Her expression was still curious, her nose scrunched, as she surveyed him.

Fox's face split into a beautiful grin. I heard Elise's sudden intake of breath at the transformation and silently willed my own reaction to not be as obvious. His eyes locked onto mine, and I greedily drank in the strong curve of his jaw, the dimple in one cheek, and the shock of dark blond hair that managed to look messy and purposeful at the same time as it refused to stay tucked behind his ears. A wave of desire swept through me, beating in all of my pulse points, especially my upper thighs.

For one second, I imagined reaching across the table and pushing that hair away from his face, so I could look into his eyes and see myself in their reflection. I wondered what I would look like there, who I'd be. A silly, idealistic coed with a baby and a bunch of baggage? Or a woman with ambition, with obstacles and precious cargo, but nothing she can't handle? I hoped it'd be the latter, even as I berated myself for caring about the effect he had on me.

"That's true, Annabelle. Sometimes things aren't as they seem though, right?" Fox asked, his grin almost shy as he looked quickly at me again before turning his gaze back to her.

Annabelle thought about his words for a moment, then nodded. "Like pretend," she said, satisfied, and went back to her coloring.

I watched the entire exchange between them with something pinching in my chest, not entirely unpleasant but definitely unfamiliar. When Fox sat back in his seat, I let out a breath I didn't realize I'd been holding. Suddenly, it was very important to me that this stranger think highly of me and my daughter.

Further introductions were made, pleasantries exchanged, and small talk abounded as we ate. I very deliberately didn't look directly at Fox again, just in case my racing thoughts were as transparent as they felt.

Chase laughed and talked animatedly through the meal, so alive and enthusiastic at my side, where he held my hand under the table and made Annabelle laugh with silly voices and bubble-blowing into his drink.

"See, babe? I told you we'd get along just fine," he whispered in my ear at one point. I nodded and smiled at him. And for a second, I almost thought this could be my new normal. Almost.

Except… I couldn't get Fox's words out of my head. Things aren't always as they seem, indeed. And today was a prime example of that.

∽

After dinner, my parents took Annabelle home with them so Chase and I could head out to the Dempseys'. I was looking forward to being alone with him again, talking and hopefully rekindling that physical spark we had years ago, but first we had to get this stuffy party out of the way. His parents still made me so uncomfortable, even after all these years. I had nervous butterflies in my stomach as we said goodbye to the crowd of our old friends and left the diner.

Heather, Fox, and Elise were the last to go, and we stood outside for a moment, enjoying the evening.

"Are you going to the Dempseys' party, Fox? Or can I give you a ride somewhere?" Heather asked.

Out of the corner of my eye I saw Elise perk up and then frown, and I stifled a laugh when Heather pretended to be oblivious.

"If you wouldn't mind, the motel would be great," Fox said.

"Avery, it was so nice to see you!" Elise gushed suddenly, like we hadn't been living in the same town for the past four years and wouldn't be attending a party at her home in twenty minutes.

Still, I nodded politely. "You too."

"I'm happy to babysit that little darling Annabelle whenever y'all might need me!" Elise said with a quick glance at Fox, and I wanted to roll my eyes at her timing. What a show.

"Um, thank you," I said slowly. *Not likely.*

"C'mon, babe." Chase nudged me. "Bye, everyone!"

I let him take my hand and lead me to his new SUV, mammoth and gleaming under the stars. The street was quiet, the neighboring stores dark, and just a dull glow emanated from the diner as our cook Billy and my "aunt" Joy, our longtime diner manager, cleaned up and prepared to close for the evening.

Chase told me that Fox had declined his invitation to stay at the Dempsey ranch, instead opting for our town's only little motel, which lacked a pool or room service but boasted kitchenettes and a weekly rate. It was an older building, nothing fancy, though clean and well maintained. I wondered why Fox would decide to stay there instead of with the Dempseys and decided he must like his privacy.

I tried to tear my thoughts away from anyone but Chase as he slowly backed me up to the door on the passenger side, his hands resting on the car at either side of my shoulders, caging me in.

"Alone at last. That was a big crowd." He smiled, leaning forward.

I let him nuzzle my cheek and turned my lips to meet his. He kissed me unhurriedly, like I remembered, exploring my mouth as he ran his hands up my arms to cup my face. I leaned into him, willing my brain to shut down and just enjoy the sensation of his kiss. He took my pliantness as an invitation to go farther and slid his hands down my sides to my ass, pulling me against him tightly so I could feel his arousal.

Startled, I pulled back and he laughed.

"Sorry, babe," he said charmingly. "It's been a while."

I laughed too, although a little nervously. We were dancing around each other, trying to find a comfortable spot between a lot of history and a good reason for a future. There were bound to be awkward moments. Chase reached around me to open the passenger door. I let him help me in, and when he carefully closed it to jog around to the driver side, I allowed myself a shaky breath. *So far, so good.*

$\backsim$

By the time we got out to the Dempsey ranch, about twenty minutes outside of town, Chase and I had exhausted most of the usual small talk. Our longer conversations existed almost entirely in emails, and talking in person was a little awkward at first.

"Did you have a chance to read those articles on New York City?"

"You already sent those to me?"

"A couple days ago. You said you'd read them on the flight or the bus."

"Oh that's right," he said. "Sorry, I forgot."

"It's okay," I told him reassuringly. I was a little disappointed, but I brushed it off. *He's had a lot going on and you can't expect him to remember everything, Avery.*

We pulled up to the ranch and my stomach dropped with dread, but Chase was all smiles as he ran around to open my door and usher me up the wide porch steps. A maid greeted us at the door and a server hired for the evening offered us our choice of drinks.

The Dempseys' house looked the same as it had four years ago – beautiful but impersonal. We greeted a few of Chase's family's friends while I kept my eyes out for his parents. They spotted us from where they were deep in conversation with another older couple and immediately headed over.

"Finally!" Janice said, a slight irritation evident in her voice.

"We've been waiting for you."

"Sorry, Mom," Chase smiled at her. "Lots of people to catch up with."

His father patted his back. "Glad to have you home, son. Nice to see you here as well, Avery."

Chase slipped his arm around me and I tried not to tense up. I felt all the eyes in the room on me, and although I was glad that I'd borrowed a nicer dress from Heather, I began to wish I'd worn something other than my boots. My outfit was fine for The Kitchen but I was underdressed for this party. I realized suddenly that the last time I'd been in their home was Chase's graduation party four years ago, the one that they'd held the night before he left. I tried to push that thought out of my mind and I'd barely taken the first sip of my iced tea when Janice focused her sharp eyes on me.

"Avery, tell us. When do you graduate and what are your plans?" Her mouth turned up slightly at the corners in what I'm assuming was her version of a smile.

I cleared my throat before I became dangerously close to choking on my drink. "In May, actually. I can't wait." Chase squeezed my shoulder reassuringly.

Ron Dempsey took a generous pull from his vodka rocks. "That's great news. Congratulations!" He signaled a passing server for a refill.

"What is your major, dear? Accounting, is it?"

I stifled a sigh. That's what everyone thought – that I'd get a "sensible" degree and take over the diner. "No, it's English Literature. With an emphasis on Creative Writing and a minor in Advertising." Was this a job interview? Avery Kent, applying for the position of being good enough for your son.

"Your parents must be very proud. A degree in under five years. Impressive, given your... circumstances." Janice fixed me with a knowing look.

Circumstances? Was she referring to my child? I felt myself start to bristle. Chase sensed my attitude and hurried to fill the silence.

"Avery wants to go to graduate school," he blurted.

"Graduate school?" Janice raised an eyebrow.

"That's the plan!" I smiled thinly. "NYU, if they'll have me."

Chase patted my hand again. "You'll get in, babe."

Janice watched our entire interaction with an inscrutable look on her face. "New York? With a small child? Is that... practical?" she asked.

I was used to this question, but not from someone I was trying to win over. *Why is it you need to win her over? We're adults now, not high school kids.* That little voice popped into my head again, but I ignored it.

"I guess I'll find out." I tried to look confident, but I could feel myself starting to wither under her scrutiny.

"I must've misunderstood your mother when she told me you'd eventually be running the diner. A shame, really. It's so nice to have a family business where everyone participates." Janice remarked.

Nice one. Both of her children worked in the family auto dealership chain, and she obviously couldn't understand why I'd want to do anything else but perpetuate the future that had been so kindly provided for me. My parents were indulgent compared to the Dempseys when it came to choosing your own path. And when had she spoken to my mother?

I pretended to be admiring the art displayed over the fireplace so I didn't have to meet Janice's eyes, and the conversation continued without me. I should've expected this tonight. She knew just enough about me to be curious, and also to inject little pockets of doubt and negativity into my future plans.

Luckily, Chase's parents saw someone else they needed to talk to and excused themselves. A few more distant acquaintances came by to congratulate Chase on his accomplishments before we were alone again.

"This sucks. Let's get out of here," Chase whispered in my ear.

"But this party is for you," I protested responsibly. "Shouldn't we stay?"

He laughed. "Do you really want to?"

I shook my head gratefully, he took my hand, and we snuck down the hallway to the cavernous TV room located in one wing of the ranch. I felt like I was in a time warp and we were still teenagers, escaping to the room farthest away from our parents to make out. Chase went behind the wet bar and pulled out a couple beers before joining me on the couch.

He slid closer to kiss me, his lips warm and soft, and I found myself leaning into his kiss again, eagerly this time. His mouth captured mine gently, his tongue tasting me, and we kissed for long minutes on the couch, the only sound our breathing and rustling as we shifted together. I slid a hand around his back and traced my fingers over his shoulders, the muscles tensing under my touch. Chase responded by turning my head and placing my mouth exactly where he wanted it, a low groan in his throat.

I was pleased to feel some of the same spark that used to exist between us. Not full-fledged fireworks but definitely something. I tried not to dwell on the fact that I was completely aware enough to analyze our make-out session instead of being wrapped up in the moment, but I figured there was plenty of time for passion to build. A few minutes later, Chase pulled back, smiling.

"Okay, babe, we can't get carried away, otherwise I'm gonna need a cold shower." He laughed and draped an arm over my shoulder. "Wanna watch a movie or something?"

I nodded, pleased that he wanted to take things slow, and he cracked open the beers then reached for the remote. After a few minutes of flipping through the channels, he settled on an Adam Sandler movie, and I let my mind wander.

Being here with him was nice. No, it was more than nice. Nice was your grandma, or clean sheets, or a good parking spot. It was more than nice, but I wasn't sure what.

Dangerous. Sexy. Exciting. That's what Beckett Fox was like. My mind flashed to the first time I saw him at the bus depot. I was irritated at myself for thinking of Fox when I should be focusing on Chase, but after rolling it around in my mind for a while, I decided it was out of my control and that I should satisfy my curiosity and be done with it. During the next commercial break, I took the plunge.

"So, tell me a little more about your friend... known him long?" I asked in what I hoped was a casual voice.

"Fox? I don't know much about him, to be honest. I met him on a Hotshot crew in Washington. He ran us into the ground but he's fair. That night – that night, after everything, his leg was in bad shape but he still made the saves, and most of us managed to get out of there and back to base."

Something flickered in his eyes for a moment, but he continued on with a light tone. Chase had only told me bits and pieces about his decision to end his rising firefighting career. I knew a lot of it had to do with the night he spoke of. They were working a fire in the Okanogan-Wenatchee National Forest and came across a few campers. The situation went downhill quickly due to weather and limited resources, and both a civilian and a firefighter had died that night.

"His leg was in bad shape, like I said, so they medevacked him out to a big hospital near Seattle and I hadn't seen him in months. But we ran into each other as I was settling a few things up near the base. His leg is still giving him problems so he decided to take a little time off and get well. We hung out for a few days and he didn't have any big plans, so I thought, why the hell not? C'mon home with me and see how we do Texas!"

My mind raced at this new information. Fox was really hurt. Or at least, he had been. He looked to be in perfect physical shape when I met him tonight, but once again, apparently looks were deceiving. An injured wilderness firefighter with no real ties to anything, friends with my new/old boyfriend, and an intense look that made my heart skip a beat. Great. As if my life wasn't complicated enough.

Chase sprawled back on the couch, tipping his beer into his mouth. He looked so at home in his parents' living room, like the years hadn't changed everything three times over. But that was

Chase. His carefree nature wasn't a front, that was him. Even four years of emergencies and infernos would have a hard time changing that.

"He doesn't have any family? Where is he from?" I pressed, surprising myself. *Real smooth, Avery.* And also... why did I want to know so much about someone I'd met for three seconds? *Because he looked right into your eyes and something shifted,* I admitted to myself. But that can't happen again.

"Um, he told me his brother and his folks live in California. His dad is a retired General. I think he graduated from UCLA, then headed to CAL FIRE, paramedic training, and on from there." Chase lowered the beer bottle, his expression curious. "Why so many questions about Fox?"

I laughed nervously. "I'm just trying to figure it all out! You know we don't have very many new people in town, and he's your friend, so I want to make sure he feels welcome."

"Sure babe, that's nice of you. I saw him talking to Heather, but I'm sure he's not good enough for Her Highness," Chase snickered.

Wonderful. Apparently, Chase's attitude toward Heather hadn't matured in the last half-decade. In high school, Chase and my best friend had never clicked. He typically wanted to avoid Heather, calling her stuck up and bitchy. I tried to run interference, but Heather hadn't seemed to mind. "Whatever. He's just jealous that we spend so much time together when you could be worshipping his throwing arm," she'd laughed.

Chase shifted on the couch, drawing my attention back to him. He moved his beer to the coffee table and reached for my hands, setting my bottle aside as well.

"I know I've been gone for a long time, Avery," he said seriously, his chocolate eyes looking earnestly into mine. "And I'm real sorry about how I left. I wanted to tell you, but I didn't know how. You understand, right?"

"Um." Chase had never addressed this in any of our emails aside from just repeating how sorry he was, and I didn't push it.

"I felt like everything was happening so quickly, you know?

College, football… it seemed all planned out already, like I didn't have any choices left." He paused and looked away. "Then I met that old smokejumper and he told me I had potential, that I could be something else, something unexpected, on *my* terms. So I left the only way I thought would work, without telling anyone."

Coward. The word sprang unbidden to mind. I pulled away slightly, trying to temper my reaction. He hadn't known how to tell me that we were breaking up, that he was dumping every plan we ever had, so he just didn't. And now he expected me to say it was fine, when my life had been turned upside down the day he left, and I'd spent the last four years reevaluating everything.

The real answer was yes, it was okay. If Chase had never left, I wouldn't have Annabelle. She was worth a million heartbreaks, a million desertions. If everything happens for a reason, then Chase would've left no matter what, even if he wrote me a hundred goodbye poems or tattooed my name over his heart, because Annabelle was supposed to be here, exactly as she is.

And if Chase is supposed to be my endgame, the love of my life, then he would be, no matter what stupid things came out of his mouth in the meantime, or how many sleepless nights he'd caused me, or all the weeks I'd spent crying after he left. Right?

"It's okay," I said softly. I didn't mean it and it didn't sound genuine, but Chase didn't notice. Or maybe he did, and one of us was just better at pretending than the other.

CHAPTER FIVE

Despite my best intentions, over the next few days I found myself looking for Fox when I was out and about. My curiosity was at an all-time high but I couldn't ask Chase any more questions without drawing suspicion.

Honestly, my own motives were fuzzy at this point. I wanted to see him and yet I dreaded seeing him again. No man had sparked that reaction in me... well, ever. *Those feelings are highly inappropriate and completely one-sided*, I told myself sternly. It wasn't even a crush, it was just a silly hormone thing. Chase was the guy in my life, and he deserved my undivided romantic attention. But that still didn't stop me from craning my neck around while I ran my errands, hoping for a glimpse of that blond hair.

The first time it happened, I was caught completely off guard, despite my hyper-vigilance. Heather had asked me to help her load and deliver an order for The Kitchen, and we were placing the last boxes of cookies in the backseat of my car when I spied a lone figure loping along the other side of the road toward us.

There was something about the runner's gait that made me notice him – it wanted to be strong and fluid but there was just a slight hesitation every few strides.

"Is that Fox?" Heather asked from beside me. She shaded her eyes with her hand to get a better look.

My face flushed immediately with recognition. Of course it was. The runner's sleeveless shirt was damp with sweat, sticking to a well-muscled chest and torso. He had his unmistakeable blond hair tied back, but a bit of it escaped and fell down around his eyes. I tried not to stare as he got closer.

"Hey, Fox!" Heather called, elbowing me in the ribs when I just stood there mutely. It was just as well because even though he barely spared us a wave and a small smile as he ran by, my face flamed a shade of red that had Heather teasing and cackling for what seemed like a solid fifteen minutes.

"What is wrong with you, Avery? Fox got your tongue?" she laughed.

I gave her a half-hearted shove. "Very funny."

"He sure is cute, and polite, and has that broody dangerous thing going on… Did Chase bring home some competition?" She raised an eyebrow at me.

"Shut up, Heather, and let's just deliver the damn cookies, okay?" I grumbled.

After that, Fox was everywhere. I saw him running most mornings when I dropped Annabelle off at preschool, and when I picked her up in the afternoons he was doing pull-ups and stretches on the old playground equipment across the street. Brancher didn't have a proper gym except at the high school, so that seemed reasonable, but it was definitely a hazardous distraction for any passing motorist. I tried not to stare at him while he worked out, but the image of his tanned, defined arms effortlessly lifting and pulling his body weight stuck in my mind the rest of the evening.

When I went past the laundromat on my way to work, I saw him through the window, working on a fancy laptop while he waited for his clothes to dry. I spent half of one waitressing shift wondering what he was doing on that computer instead of filling my orders correctly, prompting Billy to ask me if I was feeling okay. I managed to put Fox out of my mind and finish my tables, but just barely. When Chase came into the diner that afternoon, I lavished affection on him to assuage my guilt then felt guilty about that too.

After a week of seeing Fox around and pretending like I didn't, I gave in and waved at him outside the coffee hut. He looked surprised at first and then lifted his to-go cup in my direction and smiled. That smile emboldened me, and suddenly I was cramming a lid on my vanilla latte and heading in his direction.

I approached his table cautiously, taking in his laptop, tablet, and smartphone spread out on the surface. The man had every brand-new toy available, apparently. I was suddenly self conscious of the very outdated flip phone in my other hand. Heather was always complaining about my lack of technology; I could barely even text with my old dinosaur.

"Hello, Avery." Those eyes. Every time with those eyes.

"Fox, hi," I said shyly. My sudden surge of confidence left me as quickly as it came, and I shifted awkwardly from one foot to the other.

Fox quickly cleared a space on my end of the table, shoving his laptop and tablet in his backpack and pocketing the phone. "Would you like to sit?"

"Um, okay. Thanks." I perched on the edge of the chair opposite him and fiddled with the cup in my hands. I could feel his eyes on me, observing in that quiet way he had.

"What are you drinking?" he asked politely after a minute went by and neither of us had said anything.

"A vanilla latte?" It came out as a question, and I laughed at myself. His mouth quirked up on one side, showing a dimple. "A vanilla latte," I repeated, firmly this time. "You?"

"Just coffee. Black." That dimple was still showing, and I wanted to dip my finger in it.

"I don't usually drink this. I mean, I drink coffee. But not this coffee. Not a latte, or coffee from here. Not that this place is bad, it's just that I can drink free coffee at the diner, so…" I realized I was babbling and trailed off. Great, I went from mute to word vomiting. *Really smooth, Avery.*

The dimple deepened. "Got it. No to expensive lattes, yes to free coffee."

"Right." I took a deep breath and asked a question I'd been wondering all week. "Are you working on something? On your laptop?"

An indecipherable expression crossed Fox's face, and then the dimple was back. "Sort of."

I waited a beat to see if he'd elaborate but he raised his cup and took a drink instead. Okay then. His expression remained pleasant so I decided to press my luck.

"Are you thinking of staying around Brancher for a while?" There was that boldness again.

Fox looked right into my eyes before he answered. "I hadn't planned on it, but I think I've changed my mind."

"Oh. Oh, well, that's great," I mumbled. "Really great."

"It was nice running into you," he said, standing and shouldering his backpack. Something over my shoulder caught his eye and I thought I saw his face pale slightly. I glanced over my shoulder but didn't see anything, and I turned back to him curiously. I watched as he looked down uneasily, then shoved his hands in his pockets.

"Are you okay?" I asked, concerned. His self assuredness had all but vanished within a few seconds, and for a moment I had a glimpse of someone very different.

"Yeah," he said, the carefully guarded expression back in place. "See you, Avery."

We went our separate ways after his comment about his plans to stay in Brancher, but our impromptu coffee date broke the ice and now we waved and said hello whenever we saw each other in town. Over the next couple weeks, I found myself replaying my brief conversation with Fox at the coffee hut. I still couldn't get his momentary character break out of my head, but as time went on, I convinced myself I'd just imagined it.

Annabelle was particularly excited any time she spotted Fox in our travels.

"Look Mama! Fox is running!" she'd say from the backseat. Or "That's a big sammich! Will Fox eat it all?" when we saw him leave the barbecue place. One time we saw him in the grocery store, buying fresh fruit and salad ingredients, and I practically had to restrain Annabelle from running up to him to ask fifty questions about the contents of his basket. There was no question who Annabelle got her curiosity from; I wanted to know more about him too.

∽

My daily routine needed a facelift now that Chase was part of it, and fitting him into the already hectic schedule was proving to be harder than I anticipated.

Between school, work, and Annabelle, I'd forgotten what it was like to have a social life outside of family obligations and play dates. I'd just started Annabelle in a new preschool program so I could work a bit more and have a little time to myself, and on her days off we had dance class and always lots of errands. Chase was busy at the Dempsey car lot and we didn't get as much time together as we would like but, honestly, most nights I was too tired to even miss him.

"C'mon babe, can't your parents babysit?" Chase pleaded one evening. For the second night that week we were sitting in my tiny living room watching TV. I was exhausted and not in the mood to argue. My afternoon had been a disaster between Annabelle's dinnertime tantrum over the veggies in her pasta and a leaky pipe in the bathroom. I put Annabelle to bed before Chase arrived and lit a few candles to give a semblance of a real date, but his patience for movies and takeout was wearing thin.

I sighed. "I'll ask. Maybe Friday?" The football team had an away game on Friday and I knew the diner would be slow. Usually one or both of my parents were on hand for weekend nights because they were our busiest, but football season threw everything off.

Chase didn't understand why I didn't ask my parents to watch Annabelle more often and, admittedly, it probably seemed strange. When Annabelle was an infant there were times when I was scared out of my mind, alone in my little house while she screamed with colic or cried hysterically as she cut a tooth. But "Most Organized" needed to feel like she could do it on her own, without anyone's help. I appreciated the fact that my child had loving, doting grandparents, but I brought that baby into this world, she was my fiercest joy, and I wanted to experience all of it.

My deepest anxiety came when I imagined graduate school in New York, a city I was unsure of, where I really wouldn't have a soul to turn to if Annabelle needed something. Doing it on my own now was good practice for next year. But in the meantime, it probably wouldn't kill me to loosen the reins just a little, for the sake of my relationship.

"I finished my final paperwork today," I told Chase, changing the subject. "Now I just have to send it in and wait for NYU to tell me my fate." I snuggled closer to him while he scrounged for the last pieces of popcorn in the bowl.

"That's great," Chase said absently, his eyes on the television.

"Have you decided on a major? Business?" I pressed. I was so excited when Chase expressed a desire to give college a try. He had passed up lucrative football scholarships when he joined the Forest Service, but he had savings or he could enroll at a community college just about anywhere.

"What? No, I'm still thinking." He grabbed the remote and started flipping channels.

When I first told Chase about my decision to apply for the Dramatic Writing MFA program at Tisch School of the Arts at NYU, his support meant the world to me.

"We'll kick New York's ass, babe," he had said. But lately, it seemed like higher education was the last thing on his mind.

He was making good money already at the car lot – everyone in the county wanted to buy a car from the hero firefighter. I was more than a bit worried that he would forego the idea of school entirely, and then I didn't know what would become of our budding second chance. If Chase stayed in Brancher, would he expect me to do the same?

My parents tried to be encouraging, but they thought NYU was a pipe dream and that I should do something sensible, like change my major to accounting and set up a little business and maybe also take over The Kitchen for them so they could open a second location. But numbers and spreadsheets weren't exactly my forte, and I couldn't picture myself behind a desk with a calculator and produce order forms.

Chase was obliviously caught up in an auto-restoration episode and didn't notice the shift in my demeanor, so I let myself brood a bit. I couldn't stay in Texas. I wouldn't. I wanted more for myself and for Annabelle. School was the answer. Even if I ended up writing commercials for cat litter, it got me out of this town and away from the idea of settling. The Kent's Kitchen chain was my parents' dream, not mine. I would take my degrees and my ambition and pound the pavement until someone hired me. I might get a thousand no's first, but I knew someday I'd get that yes.

And in the meantime, I'd wait tables, or park cars, or do whatever I had to do so Annabelle had whatever she needed. I hoped Chase wanted to be a part of that, but if he decided he didn't, I would go ahead on my own.

CHAPTER SIX

I spent the beginning of my diner shift distracted and feeling uneasy about my quick dismissal of Chase's intentions the night before. He hadn't said he wasn't going to college, and I needed to give him the benefit of the doubt.

Don't create problems where there aren't any, dummy, I reminded myself as I cleared plates and refilled iced teas.

The lunch rush was just slowing down when Fox came into the diner and took a seat at the counter. He grabbed a menu off the rack and flipped through it quickly. My watch told me I had about forty-five minutes before I had to pick up Annabelle, so I signaled to Joy that I'd take him and headed over.

"Hey," I greeted him.

"Hello, Avery." His dimple popped out immediately. The way he said my name sounded different than I'd ever heard it. I wasn't sure why, I just knew I liked it.

Fox closed the menu and rested his elbows on the counter. His simple white T-shirt deepened his tan and made his green eyes stand out. Since he'd been in Brancher, his hair had gotten even longer, almost to the nape of his neck. I was used to seeing it tied back when he ran, but today he wore it loose, casually tucked behind his ears with a few strands in disarray. I'm not sure what was so appealing about this man, besides his obvious physical attractiveness. My usual style was the clean-cut type, and I honestly thought J.D. had soured me on all rough-around-the-edges, mysterious men forever. But maybe all those late-night Netflix binges were changing my mind, because there was no comparison to any man I'd ever met in real life. If Jax Teller and Tim Riggins had a brother, it would definitely be Beckett Fox.

"Can I get you something to drink?"

"Just coffee, thanks." His dimple was extra deep today.

I smiled. "Black, right?" I turned to get a coffee mug and his voice stopped me.

"Is your father around?"

"Um, I think he's in the back…" I trailed off, wondering where he was going with this. As far as I knew, he'd met my dad one time at Chase's welcome home party.

"Could you please tell him I'm here? He's expecting me." Fox took the coffee cup I offered.

My dad was expecting him? This was news to me, but I tried to keep the surprise off my face when I knocked on the office door and announced Fox's arrival. My dad got up from his desk immediately and made his way out to the counter, leaving me to trail cluelessly behind him.

He shook hands with Fox and got his own cup of coffee before the two of them settled in a booth and started talking. I cornered Joy in the kitchen but she had no idea what was going on either.

"I don't know, darlin'. Your daddy didn't mention anything to me." Not surprising, as this conversation with Fox was probably on record as the longest chat my dad ever had. She glanced through the swinging doors to where they sat. "That boy sure is good lookin'. Where's he from, again?"

"I don't know. California or something," I said impatiently. I grabbed the coffee pot and went out to refill their cups, but when I got to the table they were discussing the price of beef so I returned to the kitchen with no new information.

Twenty minutes later, I cashed out and grabbed my purse to go pick up Annabelle. Fox and my dad were still talking away in their booth, and I waved as I walked to the door.

"Avery, wait up," Fox called.

I turned and saw him jogging toward me, the pause in his step only slightly noticeable today. My dad was already headed back to his office with his coffee cup. Fox held the door open for me and we stepped out onto the scorching sidewalk.

"Are you in a hurry?"

"Well, I have to go pick up my daughter at school but I have a minute, I guess." My curiosity was on overdrive – there was no way I was missing whatever Fox had to say but I tried to appear nonchalant.

"I wanted to tell you that your father offered me the open cook's position."

When Tiny, our breakfast cook, decided last month he was going to pack up and go live with his brother in Austin, it put my parents in a real bind. Billy worked overtime, my mom pitched in, my dad manned the grill a few times, and we made it work, but we're open seven days a week and finding a new cook proved harder than anticipated. I knew my dad was stressed about it, and I was glad that problem was solved. But Fox? Cooking at The Kitchen? Did that mean he was staying in Brancher permanently?

My face must've been a spectacle because Fox laughed. I wasn't sure I'd heard it before, but it fit him. Deep and rough but genuine. I decided I'd try to keep doing things that would spark that reaction from him just so I could hear it.

"Okay." I didn't know what else to say.

"I can cook, you know." Fox's dimple was back in full force, and he looked amused at my incredulity. "Billy doesn't want to work all nights anymore so we're going to switch it up a bit, and I guess your mom likes cooking so she's going to keep a few shifts."

"That sounds good." I was really winning today in the conversation department.

"There's more," he said. More? Really? Was he my estranged

cousin or something?

Oh please God, do not tell me we're related.

"The apartment upstairs," he continued. "Your dad said it's available, so I'm moving in."

The Kitchen had a tiny apartment above the restaurant. My parents used it for storage and occasionally to crash for the night if they closed late and had to open again early.

I had very briefly considered living there before Annabelle was born, but it was more of a studio than a one bedroom, and certainly not big enough for a baby and all the things that went along with that. And of course "Most Organized" was determined to be independent, so I scraped together everything I had and mortgaged the rest to get my little house.

The old flat wasn't in the best of shape from what I recalled the last time I was up there, but it was probably better than the motel. There was a separate entrance around the back and a tiny patio off the living area, which was actually private as it also faced the back of the building.

All of these thoughts resulted in one big realization: I would be seeing Fox a lot more. And I didn't hate it. He was waiting for my reaction, and I smiled. "I think it's great. Welcome to The Kitchen."

"Thanks." We stood looking at each other for a few seconds, and with the sunlight streaming through his hair and caressing his tanned skin, I had an almost hallucinatory moment brought on by his ridiculous beauty and felt a little lightheaded.

Jesus, get it together, Avery. Clearly, a handsome new coworker, too much sun, and not enough sleep will all interact to make you loopy. He looked curiously at me when I laughed at myself, but he didn't comment. I'd learned over the last couple weeks, even with limited interaction, that nothing much could ruffle Fox. Even though he was probably the only person in the last thirty years to voluntarily move to Brancher, the oddities of this particular small town and being the under-the-microscope new guy didn't seem to bother him in the least.

"Let me know if you need any ideas for fixing up the studio. I'm pretty good with small living spaces." Before I knew it, the words were out of my mouth. I was full of bold moves when it came to this guy.

"I appreciate that. Have a nice day, Avery." The dimple. And then he was gone.

⌒

After more not-so-subtle comments from Chase, I decided to finally give in to his request for alone time. My parents happily agreed to watch Annabelle so we could go out on a real date. They offered to take her to their house overnight, but I declined, saying it was easier to get her off to preschool in the morning if she was home. I appreciated their willingness, but my mom was a little obvious with her intentions.

"It's no problem. You know we love to have her."

"I know Mom, but really, it's fine. Just hang out here and I'll be home early." I finished putting Annabelle's clean laundry into her dresser drawers and straightened up.

She speared me with a knowing look. "It's okay if you stay out late."

"MOM! Stop." I rolled my eyes.

"I'm just saying, Avery, it's perfectly normal to have a life outside of your child." She picked up one of Annabelle's stuffed animals from the floor and placed it on the bed. "Go have fun with Chase."

I sighed. "I need to get dressed. He'll be here any minute."

Suddenly, getting ready seemed like an obligation. I thought of the sixty billion other things I had to do, and sitting around a mediocre, overpriced restaurant while I listened to Chase ramble on about MSRPs and test drives was basically last on my list.

But I knew he was really looking forward to this, so I threw on a brightly patterned cotton dress, shoved my feet into my boots, and looked at myself in the mirror. My skin was cooperating nicely even with the dry weather, and my hair settled back into smooth blond waves after I brushed it out. *Not bad, Avery,* I complimented myself. A little blush, lipgloss, and mascara to bring out my blue eyes, and I was ready to go. I grabbed my lightweight jean jacket and headed toward the kitchen, where my father and Annabelle were molding Play-Doh animals at the small table.

Annabelle smiled. "Mama, you look pretty!"

"Thank you, angel." I looked toward my dad. "And thanks for watching her tonight, Daddy."

He nodded. "Have fun," he said, then regarded me thoughtfully. "Did Fox speak with you yesterday?"

I felt my face start to flush. Why did the mention of Fox always evoke some weird reaction in me? *Because you like him, duh,* a tiny part of my brain teased. "Um, yes. He's the new cook, right?"

Another nod. "He's going to be a big help. Smart man."

Sometimes, the fact that my father was not usually a talker was incredibly inconvenient. "Oh really?" I said, trying to appear mostly uninterested. "Why do you say that?"

"Hard worker. Knows a lot about different things. He'll be setting up a kitchen computer system for us as well." He took the can of dough that Annabelle offered and began to roll a small ball. "Bring us into this century." A small smile appeared on his lips as he repeated the words I'd said so often to him. I might be lacking in the technical department of my personal life but I knew it could be a huge asset to the restaurant, and I'd been pushing my parents to look into it.

I tried to conceal my surprise. "That's great, Daddy."

A horn honked outside and I looked out the window and saw Chase's huge SUV in my driveway. "That's Chase. I have to go."

My father frowned. In high school he had insisted that any boy who wanted a date should come to the door and pick me up like a gentleman. Chase always abided by that rule, apparently until now. My dad's reaction stirred up my own lingering irritation about Chase's insistence on tonight's date, but I put on a smile as I kissed

Annabelle goodbye and headed out.

Two hours later, Chase and I were finishing up dessert in a back booth at a little Italian restaurant in Odessa. My bad mood from earlier had mostly vanished with the help of a glass of wine and copious amounts of cheese. I'd actually enjoyed myself, even though my prediction of the conversation leaning toward the auto dealership proved true.

Still, I smiled when Chase came around and slid into my side of the booth. He put an arm around me and I leaned into him.

"So… what do you want to do now?" he asked in a low voice.

Go home and put on my pajamas, I thought immediately, stifling a yawn. I didn't know what my problem was or why I couldn't muster up some enthusiasm for this date, but I hoped it wasn't too evident to Chase.

He pulled his arm tighter around me and started nuzzling my neck, sliding his other hand up my leg to the top of my thigh. The restaurant was mostly deserted but I still didn't feel right about this level of PDA while other people were eating. I tried to pull away a little bit, hating the look of disappointment on his face but at the same time not caring enough to remedy it.

"I'm pretty tired," I said apologetically.

"C'mon babe," Chase whispered in my ear. "We can go for a drive, take a little detour on our way back." His hand slid farther up my leg.

Because I was waffling and he was an obviously attractive male, my body responded automatically to his touch, softening and stirring at the same time. Even though the idea of a cramped, quick fuck in the back of Chase's SUV left a lot to be desired, I almost caved. But then my brain fought through the fuzz, reminding me to take it slow, there was no hurry, and that I'd decided I needed to actually love the next person I slept with.

And I just wasn't there yet with Chase.

"Sorry." I gently pushed his hand back down to my knee and reached around him for the check.

"Okay, okay." Chase sighed heavily and grabbed the bill from my hand. "No, babe, my treat." He kissed me on the cheek and retreated to his side of the booth.

❦

After Chase dropped me off and I put on my much-anticipated tank top and pajama bottoms, I paced the kitchen for a few minutes while I reviewed the evening. Annabelle was fast asleep, my parents had gone to help close the diner, and I usually did my best thinking late at night when the cicadas' song died and everything was still.

Chase wanted more. At the restaurant, I was proud of myself for standing my ground, for not going through the motions of something I didn't really want to do just to please him. Now I was second-guessing myself. What was I holding out for? A down-on-one-knee proposal? I wasn't exactly a virginal school girl anymore, but I hadn't been out with anyone else for more than a casual meal in more than three years. Maybe this was how dating in your twenties worked. I grabbed my cell phone and dialed.

I blurted it all out immediately after Heather picked up the phone. "Am I ridiculous? He's good, right? Chase? Good for me? For Annabelle?"

"Avery? It's kinda late. Are you okay?" Heather's sleepy voice had an edge of concern.

I glanced at the clock. "Shit. I'm sorry. Go back to sleep."

"I'm awake, I'm awake. I just wasn't expecting deep thoughts after eleven, so you caught me a little off guard." Heather yawned, and I could hear her rustling around on the other end of the line, most likely arranging the multitude of pillows on her immaculate white duvet set. "Where is all this coming from?"

"We went out tonight. He's handsome and charming and pretty much everything I should want but…"

"You don't," Heather said matter-of-factly.

"I didn't say that!" I exclaimed.

"You didn't have to. Listen, Avery. You know I'm not Chase's biggest fan. I think he's selfish, arrogant, pretentious, and nowhere near good enough for you. But I can overlook all of those things if he treats you well and you're happy." She paused. "Truly happy. Deliriously, can't-live-without-him happy."

I hesitated.

"Are you?" she pressed.

I shook my head.

"Are you shaking your head right now?" Heather laughed.

"Yes?"

"Oh, sweetheart," she said, her voice sad. "Shouldn't he be on his best behavior, pulling out all the stops for your fresh start? If it's not rainbows now, imagine how you'll feel in a few months."

"Am I expecting too much, though? Any girl in this town would love to have Chase Dempsey pay attention to them. What if it's just me?" I slumped down into a kitchen chair and rested my chin on my hand dejectedly.

"That's my point, Avery. It *is* you, and your life, and Annabelle's, and you deserve whatever it is you have your heart set on."

"I'm not sure what my heart wants anymore," I admitted. My mind quickly jumped to Fox and how he looked standing in the sunlight in front of the diner, before I shook my head to clear the image away.

"You'd better figure it out, girl. Before whatever it is passes you by." Heather yawned. "I love you. Call me in the morning, I'll bring donuts."

"Love you too. Goodnight." I flopped back onto my bed, my head echoing Heather's advice to figure out what my heart wanted. When I finally closed my eyes, my dreams were full of green eyes and hot coffee.

∽

Chase called me early the next morning on his way to work.

Annabelle and I were having a leisurely breakfast in front of the TV, where I was using a cartoon marathon to mask my guilt over her sugary cereal and my late night.

"Hey babe," he said, his voice somewhat distorted by his car's bluetooth connection. "I'm sorry about last night. Are you mad? You know I'm not trying to push you, right?"

That was the thing about Chase. Every time he disappointed me, he'd follow up with exactly what I wanted to hear to reel me back in. I remembered it well from our high school days.

"I appreciate that," I said slowly, swirling the remnants of my soggy cereal in the bowl.

"Anyway, I know it's last minute, but I wanted to see if you were free for dinner tonight." His voice was almost apologetic, like he was already expecting me to protest.

"Chase, I can't go out again tonight. I don't have a babysitter and besides, I don't want to leave Annabelle two nights in a row." I explained, wishing he could really understand.

"I knew you would say that, babe. But I want it to be the three of us. One of the customers at the lot got us a reservation at a great steakhouse in Odessa."

"The three of us?" I echoed uncertainly.

"Me, you, and Annabelle. What do you think?"

I took a deep breath. If our relationship were to progress, nights like this were essential. "Okay. Sounds great. Where should we meet you?"

"Meet me?" he asked, puzzled.

"You don't have a car seat, Chase," I reminded him gently. *And when I mentioned you might need one, you turned as pale as a ghost and expressed deep concern for your car's custom leather interior.* I sighed, remembering that conversation. I knew Chase liked Annabelle, but sometimes his offhand dismissals made me wonder if he would ever be ready for a full-time stepchild.

"Oh, right," he laughed easily. "I'll find out the details and give you a call in a bit, okay? See you later, babe!" The bluetooth disconnected with a click and I stared at my phone, wondering what I'd just gotten Annabelle and myself into.

∽

Later that evening, I parked my car on a quiet side street in Odessa and surveyed myself in the rearview mirror. It was a moderately priced steakhouse and, although I'd never been, I was fairly certain Annabelle and I were dressed appropriately in short sleeves and pretty floral skirts.

I glanced into the backseat and smiled when I saw how earnestly Annabelle scribbled into her coloring book.

"Are you ready, baby?" I asked her.

"Yes, Mama. I'm hungry!" She pushed her crayons aside and looked around.

"Remember what we talked about, okay? Best behavior tonight and mind your manners." My fingers fumbled a bit as I unbuckled her seat belt. The unpredictable nature of toddlers, especially in a restaurant with cloth napkins, was enough to make me sweat.

"Okay." Annabelle smiled at me, and I shoved my worry away. I was incredibly lucky to have such a bright, darling child, and anyone who didn't agree could take a hike.

Armed with this new attitude I felt ready to take on the world, or at least a dinner reservation. I clasped Annabelle's hand tightly and we made our way into the restaurant.

We were early, but Chase was already there, waiting for us. He smiled and stood up when we walked into the restaurant lobby, pocketing his phone.

"Hey, babe!" He kissed me on the cheek and ruffled Annabelle's curls quickly. "It's great here, right?"

I nodded. The restaurant was very nice but not stuffy. Dim lighting and comfortable booths made the atmosphere cozy and warm, and huge Texas landscapes decorated the walls, lending authenticity and charm. We were immediately led to our table, and I busied myself getting Annabelle settled.

I could feel Chase's eyes on me as I navigated the booster seat and arranged the crayons within Annabelle's reach. A waitress appeared to take our drink order and after she left, I turned to him and smiled.

"How was your day?" I asked.

He shrugged. "It was okay, you know how it goes–" His sentence was abruptly cut off by his ringing cell phone. "Sorry babe, I gotta take this," he said, glancing at the screen. "Chase Dempsey," he said into the phone. "Yes, Mr. Johnson, I got your message." Chase gestured at his phone and then pointed outside, and I nodded. He got up quickly from the table and I picked up my menu.

"Where did Chase go, Mama?" Annabelle asked me.

"He had to take a phone call, baby."

"Is he coming back?"

"Soon," I told her.

Five minutes later, I wasn't sure about the answer I'd given Annabelle. Another ten minutes after that, and I was even less sure but definitely irritated. I glanced at my watch again. At this rate we wouldn't eat before eight, which was practically Annabelle's bedtime.

I was getting ready to ask the waitress if we could just go ahead and order when Chase made his way back to our table.

"Hey," he said, sitting down.

"Is everything okay?" I tried to keep the annoyance out of my voice.

"Oh, sure," Chase said. "Just business stuff." He picked up his menu.

I stared at him in disbelief. He'd been absent for almost twenty minutes and then returned with no apology or explanation, as though leaving us sitting there was no big deal. *You can either start an argument with him now, or you can brush it off and feed your hungry child*, I thought.

The waitress approached our table again and I smiled brightly. Too brightly. "Everything looks delicious. Let's order!"

Over an hour later, I was struggling to my car under the full weight of a nearly sleeping Annabelle and my big purse filled with her toys and books. The meal had been interrupted twice more for Chase to take phone calls but neither lasted as long as the first. I picked my way through the large steak and potato I ordered and tried to listen as Chase talked, but the evening's mood was stilted and awkward. What was the point of him inviting us? He was gone from the table more than he was sitting there, and he was on edge the entire meal, fidgeting with his napkin.

I hefted Annabelle up on my hip again. She'd been an almost perfect angel tonight, so polite and sweet even though I knew she was hungry and probably bored. As we were leaving, Chase ran into a dealership customer at the bar and decided to stay and have a nightcap, so Annabelle and I said our goodbyes and left.

I shook my head as I finally reached my car. After I buckled Annabelle, I sat down heavily in the driver's seat. If tonight was any indication of how we could fit into Chase's new life, I wasn't sure I could take it. *Chalk up one more disillusioned dream for the Chase Dempsey scrapbook.* I let down my hair and pulled off my heels for the half-hour drive home.

CHAPTER SEVEN

I'd never been more grateful in my life that Kent's Kitchen didn't require some horrible retro diner uniform. My parents had banished the awful polyester mini-dresses when they'd rebranded the old restaurant twenty years ago, and I think every waitress we'd had since then deeply appreciated that, myself included.

My personal work outfit of choice usually consisted of skinny jeans, Converse, and a black v-neck shirt, with our signature red half-apron over the top. Sometimes I wore a skirt or shorts, and sometimes I forgot my name tag, but I rarely varied from my usual ensemble. And the name tag didn't matter anyway because everyone already knew me.

It normally took me approximately seven minutes to get ready for work but this would go down in history as The Day I Primped For An Hour, because today I would work my first shift with Fox.

My ponytail was extra bouncy, my lips matched my red apron (which I'd ironed), and I actually ran the lint roller over my black shirt before I slipped it on. Checking myself out in the mirror, I decided I looked perfectly casual. Ridiculously excited, but casual. An entire five hours with Fox... I had no right to be so happy about that, and yet here I was.

Just a new friend, I reminded myself. That's all he could ever be. *Something to distract you from the low-grade uncertainty of your relationship with Chase. Fox has never shown a lick of interest in you anyhow. Watching you carry plates and refill iced teas isn't going to make him suddenly fall in love.*

Fall in love? I blinked halfway through my mascara application, creating a smudgy mess underneath my right eye.

"Get it together, Avery." Sure, now that I was speaking my inner monologue aloud, I was the very vision of sanity. A wayward stuffed bunny that Annabelle had left perched on the bathroom counter eyed me skeptically.

"Oh, nobody cares what you think." And now I was talking to toys. If I made it through these next five hours without Fox questioning my mental stability, I'd be thrilled.

I quickly cleaned up the mascara mess as best I could and grabbed my purse to head out the door. The drive to the diner seemed like it took forever, but just a few minutes later I was walking through the glass doors.

"Good mornin', my dear!" Joy greeted me as I stowed my bag. "Slow so far, but I'm sure the lunch rush will pick up." She glanced over her shoulder. "The new cook seems to be finding his way." Her eyes twinkled as she took in my appearance.

"Oh, is it Fox's first day? I totally forgot." I ducked my head, busying myself with the all-important task of rearranging my pens in my apron pockets.

"Mmmhmm." Joy gave me a sidelong look before she grabbed the coffee pot and headed over to one of the only occupied tables.

Okay, so maybe I wasn't as subtle about the Fox fascination as I'd previously thought. But then again, Joy made it her business to know my business, even more than my own mother. The fact that she was on to me just meant I had to pull it together before Fox noticed.

Fifteen minutes later, I found out that I had little to worry about when it came to Fox noticing anything about me. I approached the window with my first order ticket, all set to deliver a cheerful, nonchalant greeting.

"Hey Fox! Good morning," I said brightly, sliding my ticket into the spinning order wheel. "Order up."

"Thanks." He grabbed the ticket from the wheel and turned his back to pull some items from the walk-in. I stood in stunned silence for a moment at his quick dismissal before I spun on my heel and headed back out to the front counter.

Perceptive as always, Joy felt the shift in my attitude as I returned the menus to their shelf, and I caught her small smile out of the corner of my eye.

I blew my long bangs out of my face in exasperation. "What?"

She patted my hand. "Not a thing, darlin'."

I huffed the rest of the way through my shift, my irritation growing. What was the point of Fox going out of his way to tell me he'd be working at the diner if he was going to basically ignore me once he started? Sure, he was pleasant enough, but there was little-to-no eye contact, no smiles, and certainly not a single dimple. After two or three orders with the same result, I stopped making any effort and instead just rang the bell whenever I dropped off my tickets.

When I picked up my last table's order, Fox called after me. I almost dropped my tray but I managed to turn smoothly and respond. "Yes?" My voice came out a little frosty but I didn't care.

Fox's mouth turned up on one corner, enough to show a hint of his dimple. His green eyes flashed with intensity, drawing me in, and I barely noticed when he reached across the pass-through and set a ramekin on my tray.

"You forgot your tartar sauce."

I glanced down at the little dish and when I looked up again, he'd walked away.

∽

"Are you even listening to me, Avery? You've been stirring that damn pot for ten minutes."

I jumped a little bit at the impatient edge in Chase's voice. "Sorry." Glancing down at the noodles, I realized he was right. I quickly turned off the stove and grabbed three bowls from the cupboard.

Annabelle came padding in from the living room and climbed into her booster seat as I placed the filled bowls on the table, along with a platter of cut apples and oranges.

"I don't want this. Do you ever make anything but kid food?" Chase pushed his bowl away.

Annabelle looked at me, her eyes wide. In her world, macaroni and cheese was the best thing to ever happen, period. She was just about to open her mouth, likely to ask me why Chase wouldn't want to eat her favorite dish, when I cut in.

"I usually make one meal, and Annabelle and I eat together. Sorry if it's not up to your standards. You're welcome to cook something yourself next time." My annoyed words had the desired effect because Chase looked sufficiently abashed. He grabbed an orange wedge from the platter and stuck it in his mouth.

"Sorry, babe," he muttered around the peel.

Annabelle giggled. "You have an orange smile."

Chase turned to her, the orange rind covering his teeth. "I do? How did that happen?" His words were muffled but Annabelle shrieked with laughter.

I relaxed back into my chair. Chase could be so irritating in one moment and then completely endearing the next. His moods seemed to be all over the place lately, and it was beginning to wear on me. At the end of each day I never knew which Chase I should expect: the smiling charmer or the impatient brooder.

After Annabelle was in bed, Chase pulled me onto the couch and into his arms. We'd made it through the rest of the evening without any friction, and I felt my muscles softening as he kneaded my back. I could feel his warm breath on my neck as his hands slowly moved up and down my spine. The lulling sensation had me closing my eyes and leaning into his touch as I let myself drift.

"Are you fucking sleeping?" Chase pulled away and my eyes snapped open.

"What? No. I'm just relaxing," I protested but he was already pulling himself into a standing position.

"You've gotta be kidding me with this shit, Avery. I know you have a hard life and whatever, but you just fucking fell asleep on me in the middle of our date. Is this how it's always gonna be? You're too tired to even spend time with me?" Chase shoved his feet into his shoes and grabbed his jacket.

I shrank back into the couch, shocked by his bitterness. "I'm sorry," I said slowly. I realized then that it was the third time I'd apologized to him that evening, and I wasn't actually sorry. I worked all morning, wrote a paper and cared for my child all afternoon, and then cooked dinner and tried to engage with my selfish boyfriend all evening.

"You're sorry, you're sorry. That's all you ever say. I don't feel like I'm a priority to you. This relationship isn't a priority to you." As Chase's voice took on a lecturing tone, my patience ran out.

While part of me realized he was right, that I wasn't making our relationship a priority, I also knew that he never took into account all of the responsibilities I had as a mother, a student, and a person who paid her own bills. This wasn't high school, when I could sit for hours on end in the bleachers and watch him toss a ball around. This was real life; it was messy and imperfect. And it wasn't changing anytime soon.

But instead of recognizing that, and at least trying to understand, Chase continued to bitch and moan about where he fit into my life. *Find yourself a place*, I wanted to scream at him. Be the man I can't live without, instead of the man I'm not sure I can live with.

Chase stared at me, waiting for a response, but I had none. Anything I could say at this point would be colored by my building annoyance, and I knew too well that once words were spoken, there was no going back. Chase and I would have no hope for survival if I unleashed on him today.

I stood and walked over to where Chase was standing by my front door.

"You know that's not true. Please don't leave upset. I'll call you tomorrow." Maybe by then I'd figure out what to say. Part of me hoped he'd hug me and say he overreacted, but the rest of me just wanted him gone.

Chase sighed. "Goodnight, Avery." He shut the door behind him, and my immediate feeling of relief drowned any remorse I might've felt for the way the evening ended.

∽

My mood was still affected the next day when I showed up for work. I couldn't get Chase's words out of my head, about how I wasn't making him a priority, and his sarcastic tone when he said he knew 'my life was hard.'

Joy noticed my funk, of course, but wisely chose to stay out of my way and not pry. I was in the middle of viciously scrubbing one of my vacated booths when I felt someone behind me. Figuring it was a customer waiting for the table, I plastered a smile on my face and turned. I couldn't conceal my surprise when I saw Fox standing there. Flustered, I dropped my dishrag, and he leaned down to grab it just before it hit the ground.

"Thanks," I muttered. The man had superhuman reflexes.

His brow creased with concern. "Are you okay?"

"Yeah." I really meant no. Or yes. Or I'm not sure, how much time do you have? I took the dishrag from him and started to turn away.

"Avery, wait." He put a hand lightly on my bare arm to slow me, and I stopped dead in my tracks, both out of automatic courtesy and the tingly electric feeling of his skin on mine. "I'm sorry about yesterday."

"Yesterday?" I looked down at my arm where his fingers still rested. Yesterday seemed like a lifetime ago. *What happened? Did he do something to me yesterday?* All I knew about yesterday was that Chase had hurt my feelings, and today I didn't want Fox to move his hand, ever.

"I've been told I have a rather intense work ethic. That's probably putting it lightly," he conceded after a moment. "It was my first day, and I don't like to make mistakes."

I wasn't sure where he was going with this. It was just food, and certainly not the most important job he'd ever had, but I understood wanting to take pride in your work. "Okay."

"You're kind of... distracting." He smiled then, my favorite Fox grin, complete with dimple. I found myself grinning back at him before I could help it.

"Am I?" And suddenly, I was flirting.

"Yes. In the best way." He dropped his hand from my arm but his eyes blazed with something that lingered on my skin just as strongly. "But that's my problem. And if I was rude, I apologize."

My grin widened at his sincere words. "Apology accepted."

"Great." He gestured over his shoulder to the kitchen. "I'm going to get back to work." He quickly filled a coffee mug and headed back through the swinging doors.

I returned to setting the empty table with a little smile on my face. For the rest of my shift, Fox was friendly and open, efficiently handling the lunch rush and asking me questions about my orders to ensure he got them correct. Joy and I passed on the compliments from our regulars, who insisted they'd never had a juicier burger or such perfectly crisp fries.

Fox nodded and acknowledged all the praise, never ceasing in his rhythm and prep movements. He wasn't kidding about the work ethic. As far as I could tell, Fox put his entire focus into whatever his job happened to be at that minute. We were lucky to have him. For how long, I wasn't sure.

That thought nagged me that evening as I brushed out Annabelle's hair and got her ready for bed. Chase was out with some of his friends, and I was looking forward to nothing more than taking a long, hot bath and turning in early. But once again, I couldn't get Fox out of my head. I knew I wasn't imagining the look in his eyes, or the electric current that shot out of his fingers when his skin met mine. He must feel it too. And he'd apologized sincerely for his brusqueness yesterday, admitting that he was distracted by me. *In the best way* – a tingle ran through me when I remembered his exact words.

I shoved the light sheets farther down on my bed and plumped my pillow, trying to get comfortable. The bath hadn't helped me to relax; I felt more antsy than before as I replayed our conversation in my head. All I wanted yesterday was for him to notice me, and now that he'd admitted he did, I wasn't sure how to react. I was with Chase, and although that wasn't going spectacularly well at the moment, I felt I owed it to him to see it through.

Why was that, again? That doubting voice crept up on me and had me struggling to a sitting position amidst my tangled sheets. What exactly did I owe Chase, and why? The more time we spent together, the more I felt like I'd built our past into a fairytale love that was a far cry from the present reality. The storyteller in me loved the romanticism about the passionate reunion with the handsome football-player-turned-firefighter, but high school was long over. Maybe it was time for me to take Chase off the pedestal and reevaluate.

CHAPTER EIGHT

E ar-splitting 80's hair band rock woke me from my restless sleep the next morning. I lunged over to slap my ancient alarm clock and almost squished Annabelle, who had burrowed herself into my bed around three a.m. after a bad dream. Glaring blearily at the numbers, I cursed softly. Too early. I rarely remembered to adjust the alarm for weekends. We would both be zombies today, which was unfortunate because I'd promised to take her to the park to have a picnic lunch.

I lifted one of her little hands and let it drop limply down to the mattress. She grumbled something unintelligible and rolled over, tucking herself into an even tighter ball. Not even Def Leppard could rouse Annabelle when she was tired, so I decided to let her sleep in while I made breakfast.

After perusing the contents of my refrigerator, I was just about to settle for cold cereal when I heard a knock on the kitchen window and saw a shiny brunette head whiz by. Heather let herself in the front door using her emergency key, which most often came in handy for wardrobe crises rather than accidents involving life and limb. This time she was holding a pink bakery box, and I wasn't complaining.

"Good morning!" she trilled. "I'm so glad y'all are awake!"

"'Awake' is a relative term," I said, yawning. "Take it down a notch though, because Bells is still sleeping."

"Oh, sorry," Heather apologized in a stage whisper. "Want muffins?"

I gave her a skeptical look. "Who doesn't want muffins?"

"Here. Freshly baked." She shoved the box at me and twisted her hands excitedly.

I opened the lid and peeked in. The aroma of delicious blueberry and cranberry muffins poured into the kitchen and my knees almost gave out with bliss. I started to thank Heather and noticed her huge grin. No one got this excited about muffins. Something else was up.

"What's going on?" I asked warily.

Heather's eyes twinkled. "I'm in! I'm going to be featured at the expo!"

She pulled out a glossy program, open to a spread of decadent-looking desserts and an elaborate fondant wedding cake. "Heaven by Heather" spanned the top of the ad, along with her smiling picture. Two months before, Heather had applied to be a preferred vendor at a huge bridal expo in Dallas. Wedding professionals from around the country would be there, and the potential exposure was huge.

My eyes welled with tears and I dropped the bakery box on the table to hug her.

"I'm so happy for you!" I pulled back and noticed she was crying as well. "This is your dream, and you've worked so hard for it." She nodded and reached for a tissue.

I thought about all the hours each week Heather spent driving to restaurants and coffee shops in the county, delivering her orders of cookies and pastries. Even just two or three special events per month would practically double her income.

Another thought occurred to me as we stood there crying and grinning at each other. "Will you move to Dallas?"

Suddenly, the idea of Heather moving on seemed like an

immediate reality. We'd planned our escape from Brancher for years, exchanging ideas countless numbers of times, far apart in our ideal locations but always leaving together. Chase had been a part of those plans for a while, but lately he seemed content to stay where he was, on edge with his back to the wall.

Heather laughed at my stricken expression. "No, silly. Not yet, anyhow." She smiled. "But it's a good start."

I smiled back. "You'll dominate Dallas and move on to the Big Apple."

"That's the plan. Now can I go wake up my little sweet potato? I need to love up on her extra before I leave next week." Heather wiped her eyes daintily.

"Sure." I thrust a muffin into her hands. "But bring this. She's cranky when she's hungry."

"Just like her mama," she said, laughing.

I opened my mouth to retort, but changed my mind and took a huge bite of muffin instead. "Mmmph." Heather would kill it at the expo. This muffin was potentially the best thing I'd ever eaten.

"You're welcome," she sang, heading off down the hall.

Heather stayed most of the morning, playing dress-up with Annabelle while I got some chores done around the house. She left around lunchtime, but not before she helped me whip up a few treats for our picnic.

"Do you want to come? We could make it a girls' day. Annabelle would be so excited," I said as we packed up the basket.

"I'd love to, but I have so much to do. Do you think your parents would let me borrow the refrigerated van? It would just be four days, tops. Oh, and I need to decide on my tasting menu and..." she trailed off as she grabbed a pad of paper from the counter and started scribbling furiously.

I put a hand on her shoulder. "Calm down, crazy lady. I can

help you. And of course you can borrow the van. I'm sure all my dad will ask in return is one of your peanut butter cup pies to hoard all to himself." And maybe share a slice with Annabelle. His heart wasn't made of stone, after all.

Heather looked up at me, and then added "PB pie" to her hastily jotted list. "Done."

⁓

I was still thinking of Heather and the bridal expo when Annabelle and I pulled up to the park by her preschool and got out of the car.

"Can I go on the playground, Mama?" Annabelle asked, swinging our joined hands excitedly.

"Sure, baby," I said, shading my eyes as I looked around. For a weekend day, the park was fairly deserted, with just a couple kids Annabelle's age playing in the sandbox while their mothers sat nearby.

I watched Annabelle run off and stop just before she got to the other children. She looked back at me for reassurance and I nodded encouragingly. "I'll be right here," I called, gesturing to our blanket and cooler. I recognized the other moms vaguely from the preschool, so when they looked over at me and smiled, I waved and felt more at ease. I settled our things a reasonable distance from Annabelle and her little friends, close enough that I could reach her in a few strides but far enough away to give her a small sense of independence.

As an only child myself, I realized how important it was for Annabelle to have the social interaction that can only come from her peers, and I tried to facilitate that as much as possible. I hadn't been sure if I'd ever want to have another baby, but once that choice had been taken from me after Annabelle's birth, I knew I had to make sure she had lots of opportunities to make friends because she'd never have a sibling.

Heather had laughed at the stack of parenting books on my nightstand, but "Most Organized" wanted to have all her bases covered. Motherhood at a young age wasn't in my original plan, but it still deserved my very best.

I watched Annabelle play with her friends for a few moments, and once I felt sure that she was happy, I opened a book and tried to lose myself in the story. On the somewhat rare occasions I got to read for pleasure instead of school I usually went for my old favorites, but today I was trying a recommendation from Joy. The long-haired warrior and heaving-bosomed maiden on the cover left little to the imagination.

"There he is again!" I heard a hushed whisper from one of the mothers to my right. Glancing up, I saw them staring across the park. I followed their gaze and felt my cheeks and neck start to flush before I registered who they were talking about.

Fox stood on the outskirts of the park near the old metal pull-up bars and climbing structure, where I usually saw him working out when I took Annabelle to school. His back was toward us as he stretched first his quads, then his shoulders and arms, before dropping to the ground and starting a set of pushups.

I raised my book a bit higher so I could watch him but still appear to be reading. When he worked his upper body like this, there was no evidence of his previous injury. Only when I saw him running could I detect a smidgen of that career-halting wound that had brought him to Brancher in the first place.

As I watched, my book moved lower and lower until it rested on my lap, all pretense of reading abandoned. Seemingly unbeknownst to him, Fox had a captive audience in the three of us. In one fluid motion, he rose to his feet and swung up onto a pull-up bar to begin reps. The bare muscles of his back glistened as the midday sun beat down mercilessly, but he seemed unaffected by the heat and instead doubled his efforts. The other moms gasped in appreciation, but I felt suddenly antsy and turned away.

Tossing my book aside, I stretched as I rolled onto my back to look at the sky. I wasn't sure how I felt about Fox these days. We'd progressed from barely acquaintances to coworkers, which was a big change. I was undeniably and inappropriately attracted to him, and he'd basically admitted the same a few days before. But it was more than that. It was a sudden feeling of excitement, an electric charge that swept me up into his eyes and his words that made me feel alive, like the possibilities were endless. And it was noticeably lacking whenever I was with Chase.

I closed my eyes for a moment, remembering the look on Fox's face when he told me I was distracting him, and a tingle swept through me when the sun was suddenly blocked by a looming shadow. I vaguely heard the buzz of the moms in the distance but that was just background noise, because when I opened my eyes I was overwhelmed by Fox.

He stood over me, his bronzed torso gleaming and beaded with sweat. A pair of bright blue basketball shorts hung low off his narrow hips, just under an incredibly impressive set of abdominal muscles that I'd previously only seen in a Calvin Klein ad. Was that stomach for real? It was perfectly sculpted without being overly muscled, and I caught myself ogling him before I could manage to look away. My face reddened as I looked up at his grin. And then that dimple. Well, sue me for staring. I'd be willing to scrub away my shame on his washboard abs.

I mean, if it wasn't for Chase. Of course, I can't touch Fox's positively edible stomach because I'm in a happy and fulfilling relationship with *Chase*.

My body sagged as I closed my eyes again, and I sighed heavily. Even in my head that didn't sound true.

"Avery?" Fox's voice caused me to jump, and I realized that since he'd been standing there I'd stared, wilted, and sighed, all without saying a word.

I struggled to a sitting position. "Fox, hi," I said cheerfully. "I didn't see you there."

His grin widened at my lie, and he ran a hand through his sweat-darkened hair. "Sorry if I startled you."

My peripheral hearing picked up a few fragmented statements

from our audience. I registered *know each other?* and *so lucky!* as I watched Fox pull a white tank top over his head. With his chest mostly covered, my head cleared a bit.

I debated only a second before my next sentence. "Would you like to sit down?" I gestured at the blanket. When I glanced over my shoulder to check on Annabelle, she looked up and waved. Fox waved too, and her smile hit megawatt status.

"Hi Mr. Fox!" she called. Her playmates' mothers watched the entire exchange openly, not even attempting to conceal their curiosity.

Fox made a move to sit down on the edge of the blanket, but then hesitated, hovering in a half-crouch. "I'm sort of… damp," he said apologetically.

I laughed at his unexpected awkwardness. "It's just an old blanket, Fox. It's fine." How was it possible for someone so sweaty to still smell so good? I breathed in his unique combination of fresh air, cedarwood, and soap. His proximity usually made me slightly nervous in a heart-racing, adrenaline-junky sort of way, but after the initial shock of his bare chest, I relaxed easily.

We sat in comfortable silence for a moment, watching Annabelle play with her friends. The day was quiet, a languorous breeze rustling softly through the small trees. The children's laughter blended with the faint sound of birds chirping, and suddenly the old park seemed idyllic and serene. Fox turned to me, his eyes a brighter green than the grass beneath the blanket.

"I saw you when you pulled up," he admitted. "I was finishing my run and your car has a distinct sound."

I rolled my eyes. "Yeah, I guess my 'new' muffler wasn't such a great deal. Chase won't even ride in my car, he's so embarrassed."

As soon as the words came out of my mouth, I wished I could take them back. Mentioning Chase meant acknowledging reality, where Fox and I were only ever meant to be casual friends and whatever spark existed between us needed to be extinguished permanently. And honestly, after the week I'd had dodging Chase's feelings and demands, that reality pretty much sucked.

Fox looked mildly surprised when I referenced Chase, but he recovered quickly, quirking his mouth up into what I'd come to think of as his trademark half smile.

"So, what are you ladies up to today?" he asked, stretching out on the blanket. I wasn't sure how he managed to look so indifferent when I knew for certain that something in the air had once again shifted between us, all due to a statement I couldn't erase.

"I promised Annabelle a picnic lunch today, so—" My explanation was interrupted by a loud growl from my stomach. It broke whatever tension remained and we both laughed. "... here we are," I finished lamely, indicating the cooler on the edge of the blanket.

Fox sat up, crossing his legs underneath him, and I watched a fleeting grimace flash across his face as he moved. The leg must still be bothering him. You would never guess unless you knew; he hid it well.

"Would you like to join us?" Surely there could be no harm in an innocent lunch in public, with witnesses.

He hesitated, and I realized how much I wanted him to stay.

"There's plenty of food," I assured him after he still hadn't responded. "Heather helped me, so it's even sort of fancy."

Annabelle came running up, leaving a trail of sand in her wake. "Hi Mr. Fox! I'm hungry, Mama!" She plopped down next to Fox and looked up at him. "Are you hungry, Mr. Fox?" She peeled off her sandy shoes and socks and wiggled her toes on the blanket as she surveyed him. "We have sammiches! Do you like sammiches?"

I held my breath, unsure of Fox's response. If you weren't used to being around a preschooler, the incessant questions and chatter could be a little overwhelming. Fox didn't strike me as a big talker, but he seemed to have a lot of patience, so I was curious how he'd react to Annabelle in all her three-year-old hyper glory.

"I do," he told her. "What kind is your favorite?"

She scrunched up her face in thought. "Um... the bread ones."

I smothered a laugh, and Fox caught my eye and winked. This was the part of co-parenting that I often missed: having someone to share in the funny moments. The retelling to my parents or Heather just wasn't the same as witnessing one of Annabelle's frequent gems.

"Those are my favorite too," Fox said seriously.

"If you ask my Mama real nice, she'll give you one. And probably a cookie too," Annabelle told him in a loud whisper, like I wasn't sitting right there.

Fox turned to me as I pulled out a variety of sandwiches, Heather's famous potato salad, fresh fruit, and enough cookies to feed a football team. "Thank you for inviting me. Can I help with anything?"

I handed him a paper plate. "Yeah, help us eat all this! Heather packed enough for five days." I smiled as he took a huge scoop of the potato salad and plopped it down on his plate.

A thought occurred to me as I made a plate for Annabelle: After I'd told her we were picnicking in the park, Heather had insisted on putting more than enough food in the cooler, even providing an extra box of cookies from her daily orders. She'd made an oversize batch of the potato salad as well, though it was only supposed to be the two of us eating. It was almost like she'd predicted this chance encounter.

Well, *was* it chance? I knew Fox worked out here – I saw him a few times a week. Heather knew that too. Maybe I was unknowingly seeking him out, hoping for more interaction. Great. That's all I needed – my subconscious encouraging my schoolgirl crush.

"Mama? Can I have my food now?"

"Sorry, sweetheart," I said, flustered. I handed her the plate and sat back, watching the two of them compare sandwiches and pieces of melon while I munched on the potato salad. It really was delicious. Heather had outdone herself today.

After we ate, Fox insisted on cleaning up the plates and empty containers, taking everything to the garbage can on the edge of the parking lot. I packed the remaining food back into the cooler and looked around. Annabelle's friends had left with their mothers, and the park was mostly empty with just a few bike riders and a couple children scattered around the playground.

Annabelle helped me shake out the blanket, and I folded it just as Fox walked up. "We should probably get going, it's almost nap time," I said, taking in Annabelle's quiet mood.

Fox nodded, taking the cooler and blanket from me. "I'll walk you to your car."

I scooped Annabelle up, settling her on my hip, and her little face burrowed into my shoulder, a sure sign that she was tired. I was overly conscious of Fox's presence just behind me, but he didn't speak until after I'd buckled Annabelle into her car seat and he stowed our cooler and blanket in my trunk.

"Thanks again for lunch," he said, leaning slightly on the driver's side window frame. He was so close I only had to raise my hand to touch that dimple, but obviously I refrained.

"You should thank Heather, she made most of it," I laughed.

"The company was even better than the food." His voice was casual but my heart skipped a beat. "Bye, Annabelle," he called softly into the backseat. She waved as he straightened up and backed away from the car.

"See you soon, Avery."

I hope so. Wait, what? "Okay." I started the car and pulled out of the parking lot, watching out of the corner of my eye as Fox loped away.

⁓

Annabelle and I were coloring on the floor in the living room after dinner when Chase unexpectedly stopped by. I was beyond surprised when I answered the door and saw him standing there, a small bouquet of wildflowers in one hand.

"Hi babe. These are for you," he said, thrusting the flowers at me. "A peace offering."

A peace offering? But not an apology. "Thanks," I said slowly, standing back and allowing him to enter.

"I'm tired of fighting all the time, you know?" he continued, toeing off his shoes and flopping down on the couch. "Hi Annabelle."

She looked up briefly from her coloring. "Hi," she said shyly.

"I don't want to fight either," I said, looking pointedly at Annabelle. "But maybe we should talk about this another time."

"There's nothing to talk about, really." He shrugged. "I'll forgive you." He patted the couch next to him. "Come sit with me. I missed ya, babe."

My brain nearly exploded when Chase said he'd forgive me, so I excused myself to the kitchen to put the flowers in some water and gather my thoughts a bit. I could hear Chase talking to Annabelle in the living room, asking her if she knew where the TV remote was. She must've unearthed it for him, because a second later, I heard the TV click on and ESPN blare into the room.

I thought back to a couple days ago when Chase stormed out of my house after accusing me of not making our relationship a priority. He wasn't wrong. I felt myself withdrawing a little more every day. I wasn't sure what was going on with Chase, but the more time we spent together, the more I was sure that he was a completely different man than the one who had left four years ago. And not necessarily in a good way. From time to time I caught glimpses of the old Chase, the good-natured charmer who always had a smile and was up for anything. But these days he was moody, his anger quick to spark, and his patience thin. When I tried to ask him about it, he brushed me off, saying he was fine and that I was overreacting. Previously I'd accepted that, but as his habitual irritability escalated, it seemed more and more like something else was wrong.

I brought the vase of flowers into the living room and set them on the mantle. Chase was engrossed in ESPN, so I went back to my spot next to Annabelle on the floor.

"That's a beautiful drawing," I told her. Only my child would insist on coloring a snowman in the heat of early fall.

"Thank you, Mama. He's purple." As Annabelle concentrated on her picture, I picked up my notebook and looked over a few things I'd jotted down for the outline of my next project.

Chase muted the TV and turned to me. "What's that?"

I looked up, slightly surprised because he'd never taken an interest in any of my schoolwork before. "Just some notes for my Fiction in Advertising class," I said. "It's really interesting. We're working on proposals for a series of infomercials. We have to invent a product, create a story behind it, and provide all the literature needed to sell it." This particular class was exciting to me because I knew that having an edge in copywriting and marketing would mean more versatility when I put my resume together.

"Infomercials? Who watches those?" Chase looked dubious.

"Lots of people, actually," I said. "The demographics would surprise you."

Chase shrugged, turning his attention back to the TV. "You're wasting your time with all this school shit. You should just get a real job and be done with it." The TV blared to life again, shocking my system almost as much as his harsh words.

Sudden tears filled my eyes as I looked at the man who was supposed to be on my side, encouraging me no matter what. That's what he'd promised in our emails before his return. Give him another chance, he'd pleaded, and I would see how good we could be together. Maybe I was overreacting, but so far we seemed like oil and water.

I dashed my tears away with the back of my hand and sprang to my feet. When Annabelle looked up at me questioningly, I smiled brightly at her.

"Well, that's your opinion," I said evenly to Chase.

He didn't even glance my way. "Whatever. I'm just saying, you don't need it. If we get married, you'll be too busy to work anyhow, helping my mom with all the family stuff."

There was that exploding-brain feeling again. "It's Annabelle's bedtime now, and I have cleaning to do, so you should probably go. Sorry, but I wasn't expecting you."

Chase clicked the TV off and stood up slowly, stretching. "Sure, babe," he said, completely oblivious to my abrupt dismissal. "Bye, Annabelle."

I closed the door behind him, my shock and disbelief at his words still hanging in the air between us. He was wrong. I knew that all my hard work would pay off eventually, and I was well on my way to making a better life for myself and Annabelle. School was not a mistake. I wouldn't let him convince me otherwise.

Determined to shake it off, I turned to where Annabelle hovered in the doorway. "Let's have ice cream and watch *Frozen*, okay? You can stay up a little later tonight." She cheered and ran toward the kitchen while I willed my head to clear and my shoulders to relax.

CHAPTER NINE

It wasn't productive in healing our rift, but I managed to successfully avoid Chase over the next few days. He didn't really try to spend time with me either, so the days apart marked the longest separation we'd had since he came back to town.

On Thursday, when he popped into the diner during the lunch rush, the sight of his easy grin and cropped brown hair almost made me smile a little. But then I remembered his unfeeling comments about my goals and plans, and my irritation and hurt surfaced again.

"Hey," he said, dropping down onto a stool at the counter. "Where've you been, babe? We keep missing each other."

I faked ignorance. "Have we? I guess you're right." I couldn't infuse the correct amount of normalcy into my voice, and I saw Fox glance at me out of the corner of his eye as he grabbed a couple spoons from the silverware tray.

"What's up, man?" Chase slapped his hand into Fox's for a casual shake.

"Hey Chase," Fox nodded. "Just work, you know. We've been real busy here, Avery hasn't sat down all week."

My eyebrows shot up when he said my name, and I missed

Chase's response. Why was Fox making excuses for me? When I looked over at him, I saw he was looking back at me just as intently. I felt that crackle of energy between us again until Fox turned to walk away, breaking the spell. Chase's attention was distracted by the menu and he didn't notice our exchange or the way my eyes followed Fox's retreating form.

"I'll get a burger, okay? Extra fries," he said.

"Coming right up," I said to Fox's back.

After I took Chase's order, the rest of my section filled up and we lost our chance to chat. As he was settling his bill and preparing to leave, he flagged me over.

"What are your and Annabelle's plans this weekend?" he asked.

My icy wall thawed a bit and I smiled, thinking he wanted to spend time with us. *The new Chase wasn't all that bad*, I reminded myself. He had his good moments, and those always brought me right back in. I could forgive his occasional snide comments. I know he didn't mean to be rude, he just didn't have much of a filter these days. "I'm not sure... Did you have something fun in mind?"

He laughed. "I wish, babe, but me and the guys are going camping tomorrow! Remember?"

My shoulders sagged with disappointment, but I quickly straightened and plastered a fake half-smile on my face when I saw Fox looking curiously at me from the pass-through window. I thought for a moment. Part of my brain maybe recalled a comment about an upcoming camping trip, but I couldn't be sure.

"Can't wait to get away from it all for a few days, you know?" Chase continued.

"Sounds great," I said softly. I suppose I couldn't expect Chase to spend every free minute with me and Annabelle, doing family-type things. But it would be nice if on occasion he wanted to, instead of constantly pressuring me to get a babysitter. The fact that he preferred to come over after Annabelle went to bed bothered me too. We were a package deal, me and Annabelle, but sometimes I felt like Chase just saw her as a roadblock to his good time.

I cleared Chase's plates as I listened to him talk about fishing and beer pong, feeling more distant from him than ever. We were young and Chase wanted to have fun, of course I understood that. But sooner or later he needed to grow up, or I wasn't sure there was a place for him in our lives.

After Chase left and the restaurant emptied out for the afternoon, Fox came out of the kitchen again, refilling his coffee as I started my side work. Rolling silverware and refilling sugars was as tedious as it got, and I was grateful when Fox silently slid the napkins over and started helping.

"Thanks," I said, not looking up. Every time I met his eyes I felt like he saw right into my thoughts, and it was unnerving and exciting at the same time. Definitely not a path I needed to go down when I was already feeling slighted by Chase.

"He's wrong," he said, and my head snapped up involuntarily. He pierced me with his cool green eyes that emoted volumes those two little words didn't say.

"Wh– what?" You'd never know I got A's in my Communications classes, what with my inability to form complete words or sentences around Fox.

He shifted, bringing his big shoulders closer to me as he reached for a fork to include in the roll up. "Everything he could want is already here."

I blinked at him as I processed his words. His head was still down as he rolled the silverware, a few strands of thick honey-blond hair escaping the bandanna he used to keep it out of his face in the kitchen. I loved that stupid bandanna. Not all guys could pull off a headscarf situation and still look like a total badass, but Fox managed. On him, it was not quite pirate but not quite hipster, and it worked.

Everything he could want is already here. Fox had a knack for saying the exact things I wished would come out of Chase's mouth but never did. There were twenty-five ways I wanted to respond to that, ranging from throwing myself into his arms to putting my head down on the counter and crying, but impulsively I picked a happy medium.

Stretching onto my tiptoes, I put my face close to his and kissed him softly on the cheek. I allowed myself to breathe in his cedarwood and soap smell, my hand lingering on his shoulder for a second longer than necessary. At the touch of my lips, he turned his face slowly toward me so our noses almost met, and I reluctantly dropped down off my toes, but not before I noticed his sharp intake of breath and the way his eyes hooded as he looked at me.

"Sorry," I said shyly. "I just… wanted to." My cheeks flushed at my inappropriateness, but I figured it was better than the only other option I seriously considered, which was climbing him like a tree and riding off into the sunset. I shook my head, laughing at myself when Fox's expression turned from surprise to amusement as well.

"Don't be sorry," he said. "I'm not."

He turned to walk back into the kitchen, and I steadied myself with a hand on the countertop. Can dimples wink? Because I felt like his just did.

I am in so much trouble.

⁓

It was way after four p.m. the next day when I realized Annabelle's babysitter Claire was late. The afternoon had gotten away from me like it always did on the days when Annabelle didn't have preschool, and between laundry, princess dress up, bill paying, tea parties, and housecleaning, I lost track of time.

I checked the clock on the microwave again as I called Claire's cell phone. No answer. Did I have the time wrong? No, I specifically remembered asking her to babysit Annabelle this evening because I had to drive to campus for a meeting with my advisor and to turn in a rough draft for a scene I was working on. I didn't trust the electronic submission site anymore after a few botched attempts on my end due to my ancient desktop computer and faulty internet access.

I tried Claire's number again, and it still sent me straight to voicemail. She was one of our younger diner waitresses but usually reliable. My thoughts came quickly as I began to worry. My advisor appointment was at five thirty, and my professor stressed that he would only be on campus until a little after six if I wanted him to read through my script, which gave me about twenty minutes to figure out what the hell I was going to do.

Halfway through dialing my mom's cell number, I remembered that she and my dad were hours away looking at livestock for their breeding venture. And Heather was in Dallas at the bridal convention, so dead end there as well. Maybe Claire was working a mid-shift at the diner and running late, or maybe Joy knew where she was. It was worth a shot.

"Damn it," I muttered, kicking a cabinet with my bare foot. "Shit!" That really hurt, and I hopped around for a minute before walking to Annabelle's room. She looked up from her little chair where she was brushing her Barbie's hair and smiled at me.

"Hey, Bells," I said. "Can you help Mama and put a few toys in your bag, sweetheart? We need to leave in a minute, okay?" She nodded and started shoving her Barbie and assorted doll clothes into her Minnie Mouse backpack.

Worst-case scenario, I'd just have to take Annabelle with me. She was usually cheerful and easy-going, but it was almost dinnertime, and I knew from experience that her mood could shift in a nanosecond. Plus, with the additional joy of potty training, frequent pit stops were our new travel style.

I ran into my room and threw on a different shirt, grabbed my bag, and shoved the folder with my scene inside. Annabelle came out of her room wearing her backpack, and I locked up the house quickly and headed for the diner.

When we got to the parking lot, I didn't see Claire's car anywhere, just Joy's truck and the diner's old pickup, along with a few other regulars. It was looking more and more like Annabelle would be accompanying me to campus.

Annabelle held my hand as we breezed through the double doors. She was always excited to go to The Kitchen, because in her experience, it meant crayons, grilled cheese, and maybe ice cream if she was good.

"Hey there, darlin'!" Joy greeted Annabelle, bending down to kiss her cheek. Annabelle happily scampered over to the hostess stand where we kept the crayons and coloring paper, her backpack bouncing as she walked.

I scanned the restaurant for Claire, but there was no sign of her. Damn it, I was going to kill that girl. Ever since she hooked up with the cute starting pitcher from the community college, her head was in the clouds and she walked around with a dreamy smile all the time. And now, apparently, she also forgot about babysitting obligations.

"Have you seen Claire?" I asked Joy.

She snorted. "That girl? You mean the one who didn't show up yesterday for her shift, and called halfway through to say she forgot? No, I haven't seen her. When I do, she's gonna get a talking-to, though. Nothing good comes of being barely eighteen and losing your head over some boy." We shared an eye roll. "She's scheduled to work two breakfast shifts this weekend, and her skinny behind better get it together, otherwise I'm gonna tell her mama."

"Well, add missing babysitting jobs to her list of offenses, because she was supposed to watch Annabelle for me this afternoon so I could go to my appointments on campus, and she's a no-show." I slumped down onto a stool at the counter and rested my chin on my arms.

"Oh no! I am so sorry, sugar. I would take Annabelle in a minute, but I'm on my own here tonight with Billy, and you know we'll be pretty busy. Did you ask Heather?" Joy looked distraught. She knew I rarely asked anyone to babysit, and that I was in a precarious position with graduation this spring.

"She's in Dallas at that wedding expo. It's okay, Joy. I'll just take

Annabelle with me." I hoped my voice didn't sound as defeated as I felt. It wasn't fair to Annabelle for me to drag her around tonight and expect perfect behavior, but I had done my best to make other arrangements, and there was nothing else I could do.

I wasn't sure if it was amusing or telling that neither of us mentioned Chase's sister as a possibility. Elise's "any time" offer was nice, but I didn't take it seriously, especially when I was fairly certain she'd said it only for the benefit of Fox being within earshot, not out of any desire to get to know Annabelle.

"I can do it." I felt Fox's presence before I heard his voice, but he still startled me.

"What?" I asked stupidly. Joy looked surprised too, but pleased.

"I can watch her for you, Avery. I'm off now, I worked a shift and a half to cover for Billy, but he's taking over for dinner." Fox came closer, a cup of coffee in his hand.

My mind raced. I had to be at my advisor appointment in twenty minutes, which was almost physically impossible because campus was about twenty-five minutes away, and then after that I'd be about another half hour or so with my professor. I really only needed someone to care for Annabelle for two hours at the most, with driving time. This could actually work.

But... I still didn't really know Fox. After our impromptu lunch in the park, I felt closer to him, and he was great with Annabelle, but in reality he was practically a stranger. And then there was the surprise kiss... my cheeks burned every time I thought of how bold I was yesterday.

Sure, I'd googled him a couple times, as would any normal person who had an undeniable yet completely inappropriate attraction to her boyfriend's friend, but the description of his work history and college background didn't tell me enough to determine if I should trust him with my child. There was still so much of the unknown about Fox, and he wasn't exactly forthcoming with personal information. And it was a Friday night. Didn't Fox have something else to do?

Fox sensed my hesitation. "I want to help you. I give you my word, Avery, she will be safe with me." My heart thudded a bit at the serious look on his face.

He paused. "We can sit right there in that booth the whole time, and Joy can keep an eye on us." He gestured to the table closest to the kitchen. "She needs to eat, right? I think I can handle that," he said.

I looked at the booth, to Annabelle sitting at the counter coloring obliviously, and back to Fox. Joy caught my eye and nodded almost imperceptibly, and I relaxed. My gut was telling me that Fox was sincere, and with Joy's approval and watchful eye, I was suddenly certain that Annabelle would be in good hands.

"Okay," I said slowly. "Thank you. Two hours, tops."

Fox sipped from his cup again and nodded. "No problem."

"Annabelle, Mama has to go to school for a little while, okay?" I crouched down so I was at her level where she sat on the stool. "But you're going to stay here with Auntie Joy and Mr. Fox, and have some dinner."

Annabelle looked up at Fox and grinned. My heart thumped its staccato beat when he smiled back at her. "Okay, Mama. Can I have a grilled cheese sammich? And apples?"

"Sure, baby. I'll be back in a little bit, be a good girl. Tell Auntie Joy if you need to use the potty." I quickly moved her coloring paper and crayons to the booth and got her situated. Fox slid in next to her, and Annabelle immediately handed him a crayon.

Time was ticking along, but I couldn't tear my eyes away from the handsome, rough-around-the-edges man coloring so intently with my little girl. He said something quietly to Annabelle and she giggled, her little face lighting up. My heart was doing that funny thing again when Joy nudged me.

"We've got her. Get a move on, darlin'. You're gonna be late." She winked.

"Okay. Right. Thank you," I looked to the booth. "Thanks again, Fox," I said, blushing slightly when he turned his steady gaze to me.

"Drive safe, Avery," he replied, and Annabelle waved.

I ran out to the parking lot and jumped in my car, intending to obliterate the speed limit the entire way, but I kept hearing Fox's voice in my head and my foot eased off the gas pedal just enough to keep it respectable.

∽

Almost exactly two hours later, I pulled my car back into the diner's parking lot. I could see a few occupied tables through the window, but the place looked about half empty, typical for after the dinner rush.

I had made good time; even taking seven minutes to stop quickly at the grocery store because I found myself done with my meetings earlier than planned, and solo grocery shopping was a luxury I didn't take for granted. Seeing as no one had called my cell phone while I was gone, I assumed everything went smoothly and tried not to worry.

But I still wasn't completely prepared for seeing Annabelle and Fox sitting together in the same booth where I left them, a mostly empty dish of melted vanilla ice cream with two spoons on the table, and my baby girl cozied up into Fox's side while he showed her something on his iPad. Her dolls and crayons were long forgotten in favor of Fox's sleek tablet, and she giggled as she tapped the screen happily.

Joy spotted me from across the diner where she was taking an order and gave me a thumbs up, which I took to mean that Annabelle and Fox had hit it off the whole time.

I walked toward them, and Fox noticed me first. He nudged Annabelle, and when she looked up, her face split into a huge smile. They were both grinning at me, and my heart skipped again. I either needed to lay off the caffeine or consider getting that checked. It was getting ridiculous.

"Mama, Mr. Fox has all the games! All the good ones!"

"Oh really?" What were the odds on Angry Birds?

Fox looked a little sheepish, an expression I wasn't used to seeing on him. "They're, um, school-related." He turned the tablet toward me to reveal a letter-tracing app, and I tried to conceal my surprise. "She told me about her preschool, I thought it would be fun for her."

I was well aware of all the great learning programs available out there, and it was on my never-ending wish list to get Annabelle a tablet someday so she could use them. But every time I scraped together enough money, there was always something more imperative that came along, like car repairs or winter electric bills.

"Thank you for showing me, Mr. Fox." Annabelle surprised us both by kissing him on the cheek with her ice-cream covered lips. Apparently us Kent girls were big on the sneak attack when it came to random affection.

"It was my pleasure, Annabelle," Fox said. "Anytime."

Annabelle considered this carefully. "Okay," she agreed. "But I need my own ice cream."

~

Fox insisted on carrying Annabelle to the car for me when we left. It was quickly approaching her bedtime, and she made no protest as he scooped her up and led the way out to the parking lot. After settling her in her car seat, I saw him eyeing the grocery bags that filled the rest of my backseat.

"I stopped at the store really quickly," I said, feeling suddenly guilty. What if he was mad that I hadn't come straight back? "I hope that was okay."

"Of course, Avery. I told you it wasn't a problem for me to hang out with Annabelle." He looked at the bags again. "That's a lot for you to carry and get her out of the car."

We both looked over at Annabelle, who was fighting sleep and losing, her tired eyes half closed.

"I do it all the time," I said, trying to keep my voice bright.

Annabelle's mouth opened and shut with a little sigh and it took everything in my power not to succumb to the contagious yawn syndrome.

"I'm sure you do," he said. "You could probably use a break."

I shrugged, not sure where he was going with this. "It's not a big deal."

Fox chuckled a little, a sound that made me think of velvet and waves crashing, or something equally as corny. I blinked dazedly as he continued to speak. "You really don't make it easy, do you? I'll make a formal request, then. May I follow you home and help you carry your groceries, Avery?"

Every time he said my name in that rough, deep voice, like the word was important and sacred, something happened in my body. It started in my gut, and spread upwards into my chest, constricting my lungs in the best possible way until I wasn't sure if I could stand to breathe if I never heard it again.

And then when he looked at me in that certain way, another feeling originated much farther south, causing me to clench my thighs together and reach out a hand to steady myself against my car so I wouldn't give away the shakiness of my legs.

In a perfect world, he would be oblivious to his effect on me, but I was certain that almost nothing went unnoticed by Fox.

He volunteered to babysit your kid, and now he wants to help you unload groceries? My mind was on overdrive. Was this guy for real? For a brief second, my thoughts flashed to Chase and the last thing he'd said to me before heading off on his boys' weekend.

"Babe, don't forget to pick up my dry cleaning while I'm gone, okay? You're the best."

I rolled my eyes when I remembered his light, happy walk as he strolled to his SUV, eager to get out of town and drink beers with his buddies at the cabin. He was completely unconcerned with anything I had going on or obligations he might be piling on top of my already stacked load. He knew 'my life was hard,' as he'd so delicately put it, but he still didn't seem to care. And now here was Fox, not only noticing but wanting to help.

I felt a familiar wave of uncertainty and defensiveness wash over me. *I must look so stupid to him, trying to keep all these balls in the air while my immature boyfriend is off gallivanting with his high-school pals.* "Most Organized" didn't need anyone to help her. The idea of him pitying me was unbearable, and I couldn't allow it.

"No thank you, I'll be just fine," I said, my voice clipped.

Fox's brow furrowed as he took in the change in my demeanor. One second I was practically melting into a Fox-sicle, and the next I was giving him the brush-off. He probably thought I was a lunatic, but I'd be damned if I'd take any more of his sympathetic aid.

Fox cocked his head to one side, studying me. "Did I say something wrong? I'm just trying to—"

"I know, I know, 'help me out.' But I don't need it, so thanks anyway." I turned quickly and moved to open the driver's side door, but Fox shot his hand out and held it shut.

All I wanted was to get in my car, slam the door, drive off, and never have to see that concerned look in his eyes again. It reminded me of things I couldn't help, of actions I couldn't undo, and choices I couldn't remake. I felt tears pricking the corners of my own eyes and I squeezed them shut, both to block out the sight of his beautiful, confused face, and also to try and hold back the emotions I apparently couldn't control. With my eyes closed tight, I took a deep breath and counted to three before I opened them, hoping I'd suddenly be alone in the parking lot with Annabelle.

No such luck.

"Shit, Avery. I'm sorry." Fox lifted his hand from the door, allowing me access. Even though I wanted nothing more than to get the hell out of there and go feel sorry for myself in a pint of ice cream, I hesitated.

"I didn't mean to imply you couldn't handle it. I know you can; you do. I've seen it." Fox spoke cautiously once he realized I wasn't going to run, his voice low and full of palpable sincerity. He dragged a frustrated hand through his hair.

I slumped against the car. "I know you were just trying to help me. I'm sorry I overreacted. I–" *I don't want you to feel sorry for me,* I continued in my head. *I want you to think I'm self-sufficient and smart and amazing. I want you to wrap your arms around me and make me forget everything that isn't you.*

But I didn't say any of that. Instead I just stood there with my ice cream melting in the grocery bags, my baby snoring softly in her car seat, and my oblivious, self-centered boyfriend forty miles and ten beers away. I shook my head at myself in disgust. *Who wants all of this? Why was he bothering?* A crazy girl with a toddler and an unfinished degree in dreaming probably didn't top most guys' wish lists.

Fox shifted uncomfortably, bringing my focus back to him. "I have something I want to show you, okay? So I'm going to ask one more time. Please, let me follow you home and help you get settled in tonight. I know you don't need it, but it'll make me feel better." He opened my car door slowly, like I was a frightened deer about to bolt.

What was I doing? Fox obviously wanted to be my friend. Since when had I decided there were too many people in my life who cared about me, about Annabelle? *Put your ego aside, Avery, and let the guy be nice to you.*

"Okay," I said.

Fox looked surprised but pleased, which made me feel horrible for doubting his intentions. "Okay? Okay, good."

When we reached my house, Fox pulled the diner's pickup behind my car and started unloading groceries while I carried Annabelle inside and put her to bed. She was exhausted and limp, barely stirring as I changed her into pajamas and tucked her in.

I came back into the kitchen just as Fox was unpacking the last of the bags. "You didn't have to do all that," I said, hiding a smile as I watched his big hands carefully placing apples and oranges in my fruit bowl.

He turned at the sound of my voice. I stood very still, conscious of his eyes on me. I'd swept my hair into a messy bun and kicked off my shoes in Annabelle's room, and one side of my shirt had slipped down over my shoulder, exposing the thin strap of the tank I wore underneath. I felt his gaze zero in on that exposed skin, and a flush crept up my neck to my cheeks.

Nervously, I cleared my throat and the moment was gone. Fox smiled neutrally and shrugged. "Your ice cream was melting."

I crossed purposefully to the fridge, trying to shake the feeling of those eyes on my bare skin. "Do you want a soda or something? I didn't have dinner, so I'm starving. But maybe you ate with Annabelle…" I trailed off, realizing I was rambling. His intensity was unnerving in a crowd but alone it was magnified times ten thousand. It would take a lifetime for me to get used to that.

He won't be here that long, I remembered. *He told you that himself, he wasn't here to stay, he's just passing through.*

"No thanks." Fox looked at me curiously, like he could imagine everything I was thinking.

Lord, I hoped not.

"Make yourself at home." I gestured to my little kitchen table and he sat, snagging an apple out of the bowl.

I quickly finished making my turkey sandwich and sat across from him. My eyes automatically admired the big, even bites he took from his apple before I caught myself and awkwardly looked away.

Fox reached into his messenger bag on the floor and pulled out his tablet. Propping it on the table, he tapped the screen a few times and turned it toward me.

"I made this tonight."

I wasn't sure what to expect when Fox said he had something to show me, but this definitely wasn't on the list of possibilities I'd considered.

The screen went dark then brightened slowly to focus on a small hand that I recognized as Annabelle's. Only her little fingers gripping the crayon were visible, the surroundings blurred, and then the scene flashed over to Joy, smiling warmly, her pen behind her ear. Then a long-distance shot of Billy's profile, singing in the kitchen, just a snippet of his voice carrying out to the tables. Back to Annabelle, her face hidden almost entirely by a huge glass of milk, her eyes visible over the top. Then a french-fry castle, held together with toothpicks, and ketchup for the moat.

From there it went to a quick shot of the darkening sky from the window of the diner, the sun low and the clouds on fire, and skipped quickly to a perspective right over Annabelle's shoulder, her blond curls resting against her cheek, and her sweet laughter as she looked back at whoever was holding the camera, which must've been Fox.

The entire video lasted probably only twenty-five seconds, but it took my breath away. The timing, the angles, the filters were all so beautiful, and it looked professional. The ebb and flow of the scenes and the careful editing turned a few moments in a rural Texas diner into a piece of art.

Fox was watching me carefully for my reaction, and when I just sat there, he made a move to reach for the tablet. That jolted me out of my shock, and I waved his hand away and played the video again. And then once more after that. Only after watching it for the third time did I feel like I could form a coherent thought.

"Fox, this is amazing. I don't– I'm not–" So much for coherency. I should just stop trying.

He sat back in his chair, a relieved look on his face. "You like it?"

"Like it? It's wonderful." I searched my brain to remember the phrase one of my professors had used for a certain photojournalist he admired. "It's extraordinarily ordinary."

A strange expression passed over Fox's features, and then he smiled at me. "Exactly."

We stared at each other for a moment longer than what would be considered normal, and I was the first to look away, like always.

Fox cleared his throat. "I was a little concerned about filming Annabelle without your permission. I can delete the clip if it bothers you at all."

That thought had never even occurred to me while I watched Fox's montage. I pondered it for just a moment before I realized I already knew my answer. "No. I trust you." And I did, intuitively. It was so unlike me to feel that way – constantly waffling between the logic of the situation and my own instinct. But I really thought Fox was probably the most honorable person I'd ever met.

"Thank you. I appreciate that," he said.

I wanted to analyze his response but I went ahead with my other thought instead. "Will you give me a copy? I'd love to have it." *And play it a couple hundred times over and over, wondering what was going on in your head when you basically made a movie montage of my life.*

Surprise and then pleasure flashed over Fox's features. "Of course. I can email it to you?"

I glanced into the hallway where my ancient desktop computer perched precariously on a small end table. The screen saver flickered in the semi-darkness, mainly because I was afraid if I turned it completely off, it would never power back up again. I hated using that thing; with my ridiculous dial-up internet connection and plodding processor speed, it took forever to get anything done. Usually I did most of my research and paper-writing at the diner, using my father's newer PC and actual cable internet.

As a primarily online student, I was severely in the minority with my shoddy equipment, but I made it work. A (likely used) laptop was on my list of things to buy when money fell out of the sky, along with about a bazillion other items deemed pure luxury.

Fox followed my gaze with a raised eyebrow. That one eyebrow could stand for about fifteen different sentences, and I'd seen him use it a lot. This time the eyebrow signified something along the lines of "I'm not sure why this is a complicated question."

Oh, Fox. You should know by now that "Most Organized" is nothing if not a complicated girl.

I smiled sheepishly. "Sure, you can try."

Fox pointed over to my computer. "Do you mind if I take a look?"

I made a gesture indicating that I did not. He rose from his seat smoothly and ambled his way over to the monitor with his usual big catlike grace. He spent about twenty seconds poking around before he raised his head and grinned at me.

"You need a new computer."

I rolled my eyes. "No shit."

Fox straightened up and returned to his seat at the table. He pulled his phone out of his pocket and tapped the screen a few times before handing it to me. "Here, give me your email address."

Taking the phone from him, I was pleased to see that he already had me listed as a contact with my phone number. *Probably just for diner stuff,* I told myself. *Don't get too excited.* I typed my email address in quickly and handed the phone back to him.

Fox glanced at the microwave clock. "I should probably get going," he said, but he didn't move from his seat.

The glowing numbers indicated we'd been sitting together in my kitchen for almost an hour, but it felt like just a few minutes. I didn't want him to leave either, but I wasn't sure how long it was appropriate for him to stay. He'd done what he came for – helped with groceries, showed me the video – and now it was late and he was right, it probably was time for him to go.

"Or you could stay." The words were out of my mouth before I realized it. "I was going to watch TV for a while before I went to bed. You could join me," I rambled. Then I realized what I'd just said. "Watching TV, I mean. Of course. Not in bed." The amount of time I spent blushing around this man was truly staggering.

"Of course." The dimple taunted me from across the table.

A minute later we were sitting a few feet apart on my couch while I nervously flipped channels to find something that might be interesting to Fox. The extreme proximity to him was unsettling as usual, but at the same time I found myself missing it when he wasn't nearby.

Not good, Avery, I reminded myself. *He's not your boyfriend. Don't forget that.* As if I could. Lately, my actual boyfriend left a lot to be desired.

I finally settled on one of the *Rocky* movies – the second one, if I wasn't mistaken. Definitely the first or second, because Stallone looked young and relatively unscathed.

"Is this okay?" My usual late-night go-to was *The Notebook*, but I felt it wasn't especially applicable to this situation.

"You like *Rocky*?" Fox turned to me with an interested expression.

"Sure, who doesn't? I'm not a super-fan or anything, but my dad loves these movies. 'Yo, Adrian' and all that. In fact, I narrowly escaped being an Adrian instead of an Avery, but my mom intervened," I admitted.

Fox regarded me thoughtfully. "I can't imagine you as an Adrian," he said. "I can only see Avery."

His last sentence made my body tingle and the little hairs on my arms stand at attention. Unconsciously, we'd leaned toward each other. His hand rested a few inches from mine, the heat radiating off it and urging me to move the short distance to find out how his fingers would feel in mine. His pupils were dilated, his gaze intent. The familiar electricity that was always present between us crackled and snapped in the air. His green eyes caught me and held, and my breath hitched. I pulled away slightly, overwhelmed with the energy, but he didn't move.

Fox had a way of not only looking at you, but looking through you to everything that was underneath, like he was doing right now. It was unnerving and exhilarating and downright fucking scary. *Damn right you can only see Avery,* I wanted to tell him. *Sometimes I think you're the only one who ever has.*

~

My body jolted awake, and I lurched into a sitting position on the couch, pushing a throw blanket to the floor. *What the hell?* I glanced around, completely disoriented, and saw that I was alone in the living room. The thrift shop cuckoo clock told me it was four thirty in the morning.

My first instinct was to run immediately to Annabelle's room to check on her, and when I got to her doorway I saw that she was sleeping peacefully, cocooned in her pink comforter. I sagged against the wall for a second, trying to get my bearings.

At some point during *Rocky*, I'd fallen asleep on Fox. Well, hopefully not *on* Fox. But maybe. I imagined a semi-NSFW scenario for about twenty seconds until I realized how horribly inappropriate last night – tonight? – actually was. I fell asleep with a virtual stranger in the house. Making my way back to the couch, I slumped down and put my head in my hands. What was I thinking?

You were thinking that he is kind, and generous, and not at all a creep, I reassured myself. Still, it didn't rank up there with the best parenting decisions I'd ever made. Yes, there was something about Fox that made me feel inherently safe. Lately my gut had been telling me all kinds of things, and I wasn't listening to half of them. Maybe now was a good time to start.

I started to pick up the blanket, and a folded sheet of computer paper fluttered to the floor. I picked it up and recognized Fox's bold scrawl.

DIDN'T WANT TO WAKE YOU. CLOSED UP THE HOUSE, CHECKED ON ANNABELLE. SEE YOU SOON (TOMORROW?) I HOPE — FOX

He hopes. I hope. Hell, Annabelle probably hopes too. I tucked the note into my pocket, checked the front door lock, and headed to my bedroom to undoubtedly toss and turn for a couple hours while I replayed the evening in my head. Trouble doesn't even begin to cover what this was turning into.

As soon as it was socially acceptable to call Heather – thank God she was an early riser – I picked up the phone and dialed.

"When are you coming home?" I might've sounded slightly frantic, but Heather knew me well enough to filter.

"Oh Lordy. What happened now?" Heather's amused voice had

not a hint of sleep to it. She'd probably been up for hours frosting things.

"Nothing. Everything," I sighed. "Fox."

"Mmmhmm. I thought so. Do you want to tell me about it now, or can it keep for a couple days until I get back?"

"He babysat Annabelle for me."

"What? You let him watch her?" I knew she'd be surprised but if I wasn't mistaken she also sounded pleased.

"Well, kind of. It was at the diner. Claire bailed, and I was in a bind... They really hit it off." I smiled, thinking of the two of them hunched over Fox's tablet.

"Mmmhmm," Heather said again. The amusement was still clear.

"You think I'm ridiculous," I accused her.

"No, sweet pea. Not ridiculous." She paused. "Just guarded. And you have a right to be. But this man, he's different, and you know it."

"Different from Chase, you mean," I said. I'd come to terms with the fact that Heather might never fully warm to the idea of me and Chase, but that didn't mean I liked it. However, if I was being completely rational, I knew that any time your friends or family didn't like your boyfriend, it was a pretty big red flag to be heeded.

"That too. Probably from anyone we've ever known," Heather said.

"He *is* different," I admitted. "And I think I like it."

"Look, Avery, we all know that Annabelle is the most important thing in your life, as she should be." Heather's voice thickened with emotion as she spoke. "You trust him with your baby. Think about that."

I didn't need to consider her words long to know they were true. "But I still don't really know him," I tried to protest.

"You keep insisting that. What are you afraid to find out?" Heather asked.

What if he's too good to be true? What if I get attached and then one day he up and leaves? I had about a million responses to that question but I went with a blanket fear. "What if I'm wrong?"

"Get to know him, then. And try not to do anything stupid. I'll be home in two days."

CHAPTER TEN

I decided to take Heather's words to heart and, over the weekend, Annabelle and I spent time with Fox. Of course, it was all at the diner when he happened to be working but, just the same, I definitely felt like I knew him better after the weekend was over. When any thoughts of Chase crept into my head, I quickly banished them, reminding myself that while my motives might not be especially pure, my actions were innocent.

Besides, Chase was still away on his long camping weekend, and I hadn't received so much as a text from his general direction. I refused to feel guilty when I was so obviously an afterthought, if I even entered his mind at all.

After our almost-sleepover, Annabelle and I popped in for lunch while Joy and Fox worked the mid-shift. The day was warm but not too humid, and the diner was slow with just a couple tables occupied. After we settled into our usual booth near the kitchen, Fox came out to say hello.

"Ladies," he said, smiling shyly. "I was hoping you'd come by today."

Well. There it was. If I had concerns about awkwardness after our movie night, I needn't have worried. Fox was putting his cards on the table.

"Sit down with us, Mr. Fox!" Annabelle grabbed his hand and tugged. Apparently they were both just going to say whatever they felt today.

"Annabelle," I admonished her. "Mr. Fox is working. Don't pull on him."

"Sorry," Annabelle said, releasing his hand. Fox's shy smile turned into a full grin with dimple.

"I'd love to sit with you, Annabelle, but who would make your grilled cheese?"

Annabelle thought about that for a moment. "Okay. But you'll come back, right?"

"I promise," Fox told her seriously. "BLT, Avery?"

I smiled, secretly pleased that he knew what I usually had for lunch. "Yes, thanks. With–"

"Avocado. I remember." Fox speared me with one of his knee-wobbling looks before winking at Annabelle and heading back into the kitchen.

When our plates appeared a few minutes later, Fox sat down as well with his coffee cup in hand. I looked at Annabelle's food and smiled. Fox had cut her sandwich into triangles, which never failed to amuse her, and along with her apples he'd added a side of bright green broccoli. *Good luck with that,* I thought. I'd been trying to get Annabelle to eat visible greens for the last year with little progress.

When he saw me eyeing the veggies, he raised his eyebrow at Annabelle. "I'm trying something new with our vegetable of the day, and I figured who better to sample them than our most *selective* customer?"

Admittedly, I got a little distracted whenever Fox spoke for longer than a couple words, and his full sentences nearly sent me over the edge. I blinked a couple times before I registered his entire speech.

"Any foray into food groups that don't include cheese will count as a win in my book," I laughed.

Annabelle poked at the broccoli before looking up at me.

"Mama, I don't think I like this."

Before I could respond, Fox interjected smoothly. "Annabelle, I was hoping you could do me a favor. I made some magic broccoli, but I don't know if it's working."

She regarded him dubiously. "Magic?"

She had reason to be skeptical. I'd tried just about every trick I could think of to get her to eat her veggies, and so far nothing had worked. If she even managed one bite I practically threw her a party. These days I resorted to hiding them in sauces or other foods so she didn't realize what she was eating. Fox was pretty ballsy to try this broccoli idea, especially since I had no clue if he completely understood the iron willpower of an unconvinced preschooler.

"Magic," Fox nodded. He didn't say anything else, simply sipped his coffee, but I could tell Annabelle was intrigued. She peered at the broccoli a little more closely.

I think we were both holding our breath when she selected a piece and popped it into her mouth. Frankly, I was a little surprised she gave in that quickly. Maybe Fox's nonchalance was the key. I gripped my napkin tightly in my hand, ready for her to spit it out. *Please don't let it be into Fox's coffee*, I prayed. *I don't think he's ready for that.*

Annabelle chewed it slowly, swallowed, and smiled. She glanced around and immediately looked disappointed. "I don't see any magic," she said sadly.

"You don't?" Fox asked. His dimple peeked out from around his cup as he smiled into his coffee. I hoped he had a good plan in mind, because otherwise the fallout from this experiment could be detrimental to our budding relationship.

I mean, his and *Annabelle's* budding *friendship*.

"No," she said, giving the broccoli a distrusting glare.

"Well, did it taste good?" Where was he going with this?

"Yes," she admitted. "Like lemonade!"

I deduced that Fox must've put some sort of citrusy sauce on the broccoli, but it looked fairly plain. I don't really care what he used. Rainbows, unicorns, pixie dust... I'd season it with anything if Annabelle would eat it.

"That's the magic," he said. "Here, let me take your picture. Sometimes it's hard to see at first, but then once you know what to look for, you can find it anywhere."

Mystified, I watched him pull his phone out of his pocket and snap her picture. A couple taps to the screen and he turned the phone so we could both see. Annabelle's face smiling out at us, surrounded by slightly transparent sparkles and swirls of all colors. Fox winked at me while Annabelle exclaimed over her picture.

"Look Mama! Look at all the magic!" Her little face was beaming as she grabbed another piece of broccoli and stuck it in her mouth.

Of course. Want your kid to eat her vegetables? There was an app for that. Or a guy who would make you one. I looked over at Fox, sitting comfortably on the other side of the booth while Annabelle ate broccoli and chattered a mile a minute about what other kinds of magic she could now see with her own eyes.

He met my gaze and shrugged slightly, quirking up the side of his mouth in his half smile. *Once you know what to look for, you can find it anywhere.* Or maybe where you least expected. Wasn't that the truth.

We sat with Fox until his shift was over. He excused himself a couple times for quick orders from the kitchen but largely, we had the place to ourselves until Billy came to relieve him. Joy took Annabelle to the counter and let her color to her heart's content on the printable coloring pages, so in between admiring Annabelle's handiwork and Fox fulfilling his orders, we talked.

At first, it was mostly small talk – school, the diner. We had an easy rapport, and I finally felt comfortable enough to voice some of my curiosity.

I flexed my hands around the coffee cup that Fox brought me. I had to be careful how much I admitted I already knew about him, but I don't think he was fooled.

"So, you're from California?" I asked casually.

The eyebrow. "Mostly. With the Army, you move around a lot. My parents knew they wanted to end up out west, so when my dad retired, we put down roots."

"How old were you?" I had him all to myself, and I was going to ask everything I wanted to know.

He thought for a moment. "High school. My brother Lucas was a little older, ready to start college."

A brother? Sensory overload. "Did he go to UCLA too?" As soon as the words were out of my mouth I realized my flub. Fox had never told me he went to UCLA. I'd learned that from Chase – and the internet.

"No," he said with a hint of a smile. "Stanford."

I laughed. "I think I've heard of it. What does he do now?"

"Personal security."

What? Like a bodyguard? I waited for him to elaborate, but when he didn't, I pressed forward and changed the subject.

"Are you looking forward to going back? To the Forest Service and firefighting, I mean." I wasn't sure what I wanted to hear. The truth, probably. Even if it was that he would be leaving soon.

Fox's expression changed, all amusement gone, his eyes softening as he looked at me. "Not today."

Before I had a chance to respond, Annabelle ran over with her latest drawing. "Look Mr. Fox! It's you!"

I loved my child very much, but her artistic talents were definitely that of a three year old. Like, for example, I wouldn't ever be letting her illustrate my wedding gown and veil a la Angelina Jolie – crayons and couture do not mix. The portrait of Fox looked like a cross between a large watermelon and an abstract jack-in-the-box, but we praised her anyway.

"Can I keep this, Annabelle?" Fox asked her.

"Yes, Mr. Fox," she beamed.

"Will you sign your name on it for me?" Fox handed her a crayon and indicated the corner of the page.

Annabelle screwed up her face in concentration as she "signed" her name on her drawing. She'd mastered the letter A fairly well but the rest was open to interpretation. Poor baby, I'd saddled her with a long and romantic name for a preschooler.

After she scooted back to her seat at the counter, Fox cleared his throat, tapping his fingers on the tabletop. The intimate spell from earlier was broken with Annabelle's art show, and in a way I was glad. I didn't want to think about what would happen when Fox finally had to leave Brancher, and it seemed like he didn't either.

And then there was the Chase situation. He was due back the next day, and we had an Annabelle-free date scheduled, but I wasn't really looking forward to it. Honestly, I felt like my disinterest had less to do with Fox and more to do with my growing uncertainty about Chase and the future of our relationship, if there was one.

A tiny freckle of doubt crept into my brain, because I knew I had a very real reason to feel uncertain in the form of a very big crush, and I resolved right then and there to have a serious conversation with Chase when I saw him. Chase had something going on that he wasn't sharing with me, and if we couldn't achieve that level of trust, I needed to prioritize for myself and Annabelle. It was time we were honest with each other.

∽

I prepared for my date with a huge amount of trepidation. I hadn't seen Chase in a few days and my mind was overwhelmed by Fox, but I knew that wasn't especially fair. I owed Chase the respect of having a clear head when we spoke, but it seemed impossible at this point.

Annabelle had been a bit listless and whiny all day, so on top of everything I felt apprehensive to leave her. She picked at her dinner and was lying on the couch watching cartoons when my parents arrived to babysit.

When Annabelle didn't jump up to greet them, my dad expressed his concern. "Is she feeling okay, Avery?"

"Maybe I should cancel," I said nervously. It would be legitimate at this point, and not cowardly avoidance like I'd considered yesterday.

"Nonsense," my mother said dismissively. "She'll be fine. You took her temperature, right?"

I nodded. "Three times. No fever. She's just crabby."

"We'll be fine, sweetheart. Don't worry."

The original plan was a quiet dinner with Chase at our usual restaurant in Odessa, but the day before he'd changed it to a group outing at Lucky's, the local bar. At first I was relieved because it meant a less intimate evening, but then I reconsidered when I realized that I'd likely have no chance to speak with him privately. And we needed to have that solo conversation, like, yesterday.

After I kissed Annabelle goodbye and she grumpily returned my embrace, I headed out. Chase hadn't mentioned who would be joining us, but I had an idea – his football slash camping buddies Derek and Kyle and their girlfriends. Upon walking through the door at Lucky's, I found out I was right about our companions for the evening except for one unexpected addition: Fox.

I stopped in my tracks, my cheeks reddening as I took in the group assembled by the pool table. Why hadn't I assumed Fox would join us? He and Chase were friends, and he didn't know many people in town. Chase was a sociable guy with "the more the merrier" attitude in regard to just about anything.

Unless it came to outings with Annabelle or trying to get into my pants, I amended. Then three was a crowd for sure.

Fox was standing near the door, staring out the window with a strange, intense look on his face, so he spotted me first when I entered the bar and he raised his beer in greeting as I crossed the small dance floor. Was he waiting for me? *Of course not,* I chided myself. *He's just observant.*

More observant than Chase, who was too busy talking to the waitress, a girl named Janie we'd gone to high school with. It was all very interesting – I was looking at Chase, who was looking at Janie, who was looking at Fox, who was looking at me. Derek and Kyle were the only ones actually playing pool, with their girlfriends sitting at a bar top table nearby nursing sad-looking margaritas.

I didn't get out to Lucky's much, but it was always funny to me that people expected anything other than greasy food and domestic beer. You ordered a mixed drink here and rolled the dice on the results.

"Hi," I said, coming up next to where Chase was leaning against the pool table.

"Hey babe!" he said, quickly turning to face me. Janie rolled her eyes and immediately scanned the vicinity again for Fox. I followed her gaze as she located him across the pool table, observing Derek and Kyle in their game. I thought I saw Fox's eyes narrow infinitesimally when Chase grabbed my hand and pulled me toward him, but then my view was blocked as Chase leaned in to kiss me.

I returned his kiss with a neutral amount of feeling, noticing a sharp tequila taste on his lips that told me he'd been at the bar for at least a couple shots.

"Mmmm," Chase said as we broke apart. "That's what I'm talking about. Janie, get Avery a beer, will ya?" he asked before she walked away, no doubt in pursuit of Fox. He pulled me a little closer. "You gotta catch up, babe."

Chase rambled on, but I wasn't paying attention. I had no intention of getting drunk tonight, especially since I wasn't sure what was going on with Annabelle, but I could have a beer or two. I probably needed at least one so I could have the conversation I needed to have with Chase. And maybe some hot wings, for courage.

"Thanks," I said, accepting the bottle that Janie offered a few minutes later. I glanced around quickly, looking for Fox, but he was nowhere in sight. Janie's cleavage, however, was on full display.

"This is great, babe, isn't it?" Chase leaned back onto the railing that separated the dance floor from the pool tables. "Just a fun night out with all our friends."

I wanted to point out that, aside from Fox, these were actually Chase's friends, not mine. I didn't have anything against Derek or

Kyle, but their girlfriends had made no attempt to talk to me when I'd arrived and I wasn't especially disappointed. I'd asked Heather if she wanted to stop by, but she insisted that she was still trying to get organized after her trip to Dallas.

The fact that my best friend would rather scrub cake pans and sort through bridal contacts than hang out with Chase wasn't lost on me. *It was time,* I thought. We'd given this a shot and it just wasn't meant to be. It needed to end before I considered starting anything else.

A loud crack startled me briefly, and I grabbed Chase's arm even as I registered that it was just someone dropping a pool cue onto the hardwood floor. If I was surprised, Chase was downright spooked as he wrenched his arm from mine and spun around, his chest heaving as he looked for the source of the noise.

Concerned, I touched his shoulder. "It was just a pool cue," I said softly, unsure of his next move.

This is what happened every time I was ready to throw in the towel with Chase. He would be moody and rude for days until I lost my patience, then something would put a terrified look into his eye that would remind me that this new Chase, this new attitude, was bigger than us. But he refused to acknowledge it.

Our history wasn't strong enough to build a solid romantic relationship as adults, of this I was sure. We wanted different things and had different ideas about where our futures led. He wouldn't let me in, and I needed that level of commitment to move forward. Superficial wasn't working for me, and it certainly wasn't working for Chase. But he needed a friend and, if possible, I wanted to be that for him.

The panicked look on his face faded after a few seconds, and Chase and I joined the group by the pool tables, catching the tail end of the game. The boys were laughing and joking around as we walked up.

"I play winner," Chase announced, slamming back the shot that Janie brought him. I hoped he hadn't driven here, or at least wasn't expecting to drive home.

"I'll beat you next, then," Derek grinned.

"Hey, I'm still in this!" Kyle protested.

We all looked at the table. Derek had one more ball to put away before he could try for the eight ball. Kyle had five.

Derek shook his head and patted Kyle on the shoulder. "Not really, buddy."

"He has other talents," one of the girlfriends – I'm assuming Kyle's – smirked and everyone laughed. Tonight was looking up, actually, aside from Chase's ever-changing mood. Derek and Kyle kept everyone chuckling, and I think the girlfriends were starting to thaw. Maybe being friends with Chase would actually be possible, if he could acknowledge I was right about our lack of compatibility.

I was trying to casually glance around for Fox when I saw him seated at the bar, his face in profile from where I was standing. A pretty redhead sat next to him, and from the look on her face, she wasn't getting anywhere trying to engage him in conversation. Janie walked by and practically shoved her boobs in his face, which the redhead quite obviously did not like. Fox remained unruffled through it all. I smiled a little to myself, secretly pleased.

A slow Keith Urban song came on and Chase pulled me onto the dance floor. I tried to relax in his embrace, but everything just seemed off. His hands roamed up and down my back to my hips, dipping dangerously close to the waistband of my jeans without actually delving inside. His breath was hot in my ear, and I squirmed a bit.

I tried to disengage a little, pulling back so I could see his face. Maybe I should just talk to him now and get it over with. It wasn't ideal, but this was as alone as we were likely to be all night.

"Chase, I need to talk to you," I started, summoning up all my resolve.

He tried to dip his face into the crook of my neck. "Sure babe, I'm all ears," he mumbled, nuzzling my jaw.

More like all hands, I thought. But whatever. *Just say what you have to say and get on with it, Avery.*

"We need to have an honest conversation about what we want

in life," I began. "I don't think we–"

"Sorry to interrupt." Kyle's girlfriend tapped me on the shoulder. "Your phone has been buzzing for the last couple minutes, I was afraid it was something urgent," she said apologetically, handing me my clutch purse that I'd left on their table.

I realized then that my phone wasn't in my back pocket as I'd thought. "Thank you!" I told her gratefully. I yanked open the purse and checked my missed calls. Three from my dad's cell phone. My heart leapt into my throat. It was almost ten p.m., there's no way he would call unless something had happened.

I shoved my purse into Chase's arms and left him on the dance floor so I could dart outside and call my house. My father picked up on the second ring.

"Daddy? What's wrong? Is Annabelle okay?" I asked frantically.

"Calm down, Avery," he said gently. "Annabelle is doing okay, but she spiked a pretty high fever half an hour ago and we've been trying to get it down. Your mother is giving her a cool bath right now."

"A fever?" My voice rose in a panic. "How high?"

"About 103, sweetheart," my dad answered. "We called the nurses' hotline and they said to give her some medicine and run her a bath. It's dropped a little but she's still pretty uncomfortable."

"I'm coming home right now." I felt around in my pockets for my keys and then realized they were inside in my purse.

"I'm sorry to cut your night short, but I knew you'd want to know." He cleared his throat. "You're okay to drive?"

"Yes, Daddy." I had a half-full beer to prove it. "I'll be right there." I disconnected the call and ran back inside.

"Annabelle is sick," I said breathlessly to Chase. "I have to go."

"Okay," he nodded. His eyes looked a little unfocused and I wasn't sure he completely understood what I'd just told him, but at least he didn't argue because my leaving immediately was nonnegotiable.

I saw movement out of the corner of my eye and suddenly Fox

was there. "I'm coming with you," he said, grabbing the keys from my hand.

If Chase thought that was strange, he didn't comment. Fox guided me quickly out of the bar and then we were in my car headed home. I didn't question his sobriety; I knew Fox would never risk it.

The engine was still running when I jumped out of the car in my driveway and dashed inside. My parents were sitting on the couch with a sleeping Annabelle between them.

"Shh," my mother said as I came in. "She's finally asleep."

I sank down onto my knees next to the couch. Gently, I smoothed a wisp of hair off her forehead. Her face seemed fairly cool to the touch but a hint of rosiness remained in her cheeks.

"How's the fever?" I asked softly.

"Down to 101," my dad replied. "It broke after the bath."

I sighed with relief. "Thank you both. I'm so sorry, I would never have left if I'd known she was actually sick."

I saw my dad glance behind me as Fox slid silently into the room. They nodded to each other casually, as though no one thought it odd that I'd gone out on a date with Chase and come home with Fox instead.

"I think it's just a little virus," my mom said. "I'm sure she'll be fine in a day or two."

I slumped against the front of the couch. Seeing your child feeling poorly had to rank right up there with the worst things ever. On top of that, I felt horrible for leaving her in the first place. What kind of mother was I that I didn't even know she was sick?

"It's not your fault, Avery," my mom continued, reading my thoughts. "She's in preschool, they pick up little bugs all the time." She patted my hand and rose to her feet. "I think you've got this under control. Your father and I will head home. We'll call in the morning to see how she's feeling."

My dad gestured to the sleeping Annabelle. "Do you want me to move her into her room?"

I shook my head. "No thanks, Daddy. I'll do it later. I'm going to stay up for a while and make sure her fever doesn't rise again."

"I'll make some coffee," Fox said quietly. I'd almost forgotten that he was there, but I was glad he hadn't left.

My father nodded in approval. "Okay, chickie. I wrote down what time we gave her the medicine. It's on the pad in the kitchen." He kissed the top of Annabelle's head and stood.

I stayed where I was and let Fox close the door after my parents. The level of familiarity we'd adopted this evening was exciting and alarming at the same time. I wished it didn't have to come at Annabelle's expense, trying to hold back frustrated tears as I watched my little girl sleep.

Fox came back into the room and offered me a mug. "Coffee," he murmured. He slowly lowered himself to the floor and we sat silently for a minute, nursing the scalding liquid.

"Thank you," I said finally. "You didn't have to leave with me."

He took another sip. "I care about Annabelle." Fox turned his gaze on me, and I felt warmth rush through my veins that had nothing to do with the coffee. "And about you."

His eyes were burning softly in the low lighting, and I started to lean forward almost involuntarily. My pulse jumped when I caught his scent, the cedarwood and soap smell mixed with a faint coffee undertone. The dark button-down shirt he wore contrasted deliciously with his tanned skin, and his thick blond hair fell forward carelessly, sweeping down over his forehead. Before I could stop myself, I reached out to brush it away from his face. I felt him tense when my hand touched his cheekbone and traveled down, lightly making contact with his stubbled jaw. I held my breath as he turned his face so my fingertips slid across his full lips.

Annabelle stirred and it startled me so much that I jerked my hand away immediately. I couldn't look at Fox again as I busied myself adjusting her light blanket and checking her temperature with the ear thermometer. It was holding fast at 100, and I allowed myself a moment of relief.

"Better?" Fox asked softly. He was still against the couch but he'd leaned back into his original position after I'd jumped away.

"Yeah, thank God," I whispered. I waited a beat. "You don't have to stay. I mean, you can go back to the bar if you want. I can call you a cab or you can take my car... we're okay."

Even as the words slipped out of my mouth, I regretted them. They sounded ungrateful and dismissive, but worst of all they were lies. There was nothing more I wanted than for Fox to stay and Annabelle to awaken with no fever.

"But if you wanted to hang out for a little while, that would be fine too." Hopefully by now Fox was used to me just blurting things out and then taking them back. The half-smile on his face told me that he probably was.

"I'm not going anywhere."

"Okay." I hoped my cup hid at least part of my grin.

We sat there and drank coffee until almost two in the morning, alternating between small talk and the low hum of late-night television. The intensity from earlier was gone, but I'd be lying if I didn't admit that at times I wanted to climb into his lap and see what happened from there.

∽

After we said goodbye – Fox declined the cab and chose to jog the four miles home instead of taking my car, just in case I needed it – I finally succumbed to exhaustion and curled up on the couch next to Annabelle. I woke the next morning to a horrible kink in my neck and a hungry three year old with an almost-normal temperature.

After a much-needed potty break – one for Annabelle and one for me – I was in the kitchen making breakfast toast when my mom called to check on us.

"She's doing much better, Mom," I assured her. "I think that bath really helped her last night."

"I'm so glad, sweetheart. I'm sorry that we had to take you from your date, but your father and I decided it was best to call you right away."

"Annabelle is way more important, you know that. Thank you for taking such good care of her." My voice cracked just a tiny bit when I recalled the feeling of seeing those missed calls.

"Did Fox stay long?" My mom made every attempt to sound casual, but I knew she was fishing.

"Um, a little while," I admitted, my cheeks flaming immediately. I was glad we were on the phone and that she couldn't see my physical reaction to her question.

"That was very nice of him to bring you home so quickly, Avery," she commented. "Did you run into him at the bar?"

Fishing again. "It was a group of us, Mom," I explained. "Fox heard me say that Annabelle was sick and he insisted on coming."

"Your daddy thinks a great deal of him," she said. "Says he's smart and very accomplished."

I wasn't sure what to say, but I was instantly curious about what else my dad had said about Fox. "That's good," I replied neutrally, hoping she'd elaborate.

"Mmmhmm." She paused. "I just don't want you to get hurt, Avery. A boy like that has nomad in his veins. Can't stay in one place for too long. We all know how that ends."

My face burned again as I realized she was referencing J.D. Annabelle's biological father was nothing like Fox, and I resented her for comparing them. She'd just said my father liked Fox, and everyone knew that my dad had never, under any circumstances, approved of J.D. They were as different as night and day. I appreciated my mother's concern, but she was way off the mark and I told her so.

"Fox is not J.D., Mother." The edge to my voice lent extra emphasis to my words.

"I'm sure you're right. Just remember what I said." She changed the subject. "Give Annabelle a kiss from us and call if you need anything. Goodbye, sweetheart."

I hung up the phone feeling antsy. The conversation with my mother reminded me that I had another important call to make. As much as I hated doing it over the phone, I couldn't allow the Chase situation to go on any longer, especially after my almost-*whatever* with Fox last night. I checked the clock. Still kind of early, but I needed to do it before I lost my nerve.

The phone rang three times before he answered with a muffled hello.

"Chase? It's Avery," I told him, in case he hadn't looked at the caller ID.

"Hey," he said slowly, the word sounding like it was causing him pain.

"Are you okay?" I asked even though I already knew the answer. Chase sounded like he had the hangover from hell. Maybe this wasn't the best time to talk to him, but selfishly I pressed on before he could answer. "Do you remember last night when I said we needed to talk?"

"Um, sort of," he replied.

I figured that much. I took a deep breath. "Look, this isn't the way I wanted to have this conversation, but I'm just going to say it. I think we need to take a step back and stop seeing each other for now. We haven't been getting along and I don't want things to get any worse." Silence from his end. Shit. "Your friendship means a lot to me," I said honestly.

Chase coughed. "Okay, if that's what you want."

The part of me that wanted to be offended by his quick dismissal was overruled by the part that was incredibly relieved that he took it so well. "You're not mad?" I asked timidly.

He chuckled and then groaned a little. Headache, for sure. "No babe, I'm not mad. I'm a little surprised, I gotta be honest, but I think you're right about us not getting along. I really do hate fighting with you."

"It's not very fun for me either," I agreed.

"So, let's just cool it for a while, okay? No big deal. I'll call you next week, I'm gonna be in and out of town in Midland and Lubbock for a while. You know, work stuff." His last sentence was a bit muffled, like he'd covered his head with the blanket.

"Um, okay." I wasn't sure what we would say to each other next week, but I felt like I'd gotten my point across fairly well just now.

"Oh hey, how's Annabelle?" Chase asked like he'd just had an epiphany.

I shook my head, glad he couldn't see me roll my eyes. The way I ran out of the bar last night, you'd think it'd be the first thing anyone would ask me, but no, not Chase. *Be fair, Avery*, I thought. *He's obviously not firing on all cylinders this morning.*

"She's better, thanks."

"Cool. Talk to you later, babe. I'm going back to sleep." His voice had that muffled quality to it again.

"Goodbye, Chase."

CHAPTER ELEVEN

Annabelle and I stopped into the diner for a quick milkshake two nights later. She was back to school and feeling fine, but we hadn't seen Fox in a couple days and that was enough to make me pack us up after dinner and head out. I wasn't sure if he knew I'd cooled things down with Chase, leaving us both free to see other people.

You know, just in case there was someone I wanted to see. Or be seen by.

When we walked into the diner, I glanced around, hoping for Fox's familiar blond hair tied back in his usual bandanna. Annabelle ran straight for the crayons, the novelty of being at the diner still enough to hold her interest. I knew her enthusiasm probably had a shelf life, but my curious mind couldn't stay away from Fox.

Joy waved at us from behind the counter. "Hi girls! Mighty nice to see you tonight. Are you feeling better, sweet pea?" She scooped Annabelle up and planted a kiss on her forehead. Annabelle giggled and scrambled down to start her latest masterpiece.

"Hi," I said, still trying to spot Fox without craning my neck awkwardly.

Joy saw right through me, I knew, but she wasn't pressing for details just yet. The smirk on her face told me that she had at least an idea of what was going on.

"Looking for someone?" Her grin widened, and I rolled my eyes.

"We just came in for a milkshake," I muttered.

"And to see Mr. Fox!" Annabelle sang from her barstool. "He's our new friend!"

Oh Jesus, that little traitor sold me out. Joy could barely contain her laughter as she turned to Annabelle.

"He's gone for the day, sweetheart. Did he know you were comin'?" Joy slid her eyes sideways to me.

"We see him all the time now!" Annabelle scribbled on her paper with a flourish. Joy covered her mouth with her hand, but not before I heard a snort.

Please stop talking, kid. You're killing me.

I saw Joy's eyes shift as she focused on a spot just over my shoulder and dropped her hand to reveal her wide smile. My pulse jumped immediately because I knew there was only one person who could be behind me.

I turned to see Fox striding up to the counter, the sparkle in his eyes indicating that he'd heard everything Annabelle just said. Of course he had. That was just my luck. I was completely incapable of playing it cool with him.

He focused on me with his usual intense stare, but this time it held a little something extra. I couldn't quite put my finger on it, but it almost seemed... relieved? Before I could analyze it too deeply, Annabelle spun her chair around and spotted him.

"Mr. Fox! I knew you'd come!" She launched herself off the stool and clutched his legs tightly in a hug.

Fox laughed that deep, rough chuckle, and I felt it grab my heart and reverberate through my core. I loved that laugh, and it was far too infrequent. I often saw Fox engaged, or even amused, but rarely did he laugh. It made me happy that Annabelle could bring it out in him.

Fox disentangled himself from Annabelle's embrace and

squatted down to her level. "You bet." Gently, he pushed a lock of her shiny blond hair behind her ear. The tenderness in the way he touched her shattered my already overworked heart into a million pieces.

Annabelle grinned at him. "I'll draw you another picture, Mr. Fox," she promised. "Because we're friends."

"If we're friends, then you need to call me Fox. No Mister. Can you do that?" he asked her.

She nodded. "Yup."

"Good girl. Now, what flavor milkshake would you like? Chocolate?" He looked up at me from his position crouching on the floor. "Is that okay, Mama?"

His words combined with the heat in those green eyes made my ovaries hurt, but I managed a nod even as I protested. "Fox, you're off the clock. I can make the milkshake."

He rose to his full height in a fluid motion, gracefully sidestepping around Annabelle until his chest almost bumped mine. I took a step back automatically, but he followed to maintain our closeness.

"Would you like one, Avery?"

One what? One of you? I'll take ten.

"Um," I managed. His eyes bored into mine.

Joy cleared her throat, and I jumped back again.

"I think he wants to make you a milkshake, girl," she drawled, and I shot her a dirty look. I heard Fox chuckle under his breath again as he made his way to the kitchen.

"I'll surprise you," he said.

Oh buddy. You have no idea.

Annabelle and I prepared to leave after chatting with Joy and Fox while downing our delicious milkshakes – chocolate for her, pumpkin cheesecake for me – when Fox caught my hand.

"Can I ask you for a big favor, Avery?"

Dude, you can pretty much ask me for whatever you want. You like my kid, you carried my groceries, you've got that intuitive-hot-guy thing going on, and your skin feels amazing against mine. You're basically my kryptonite.

"Sure," I said. A normal answer in a normal sounding voice. Score one for me.

Fox hesitated for a second before he spoke. "Are you going to be on campus this week by any chance? I had some things come in that need to be picked up near there, and I can't do it alone."

It was like all the stars aligned right then. I was, in fact, heading to my college in the morning, but even if I wasn't, I'd make the trip for Fox.

"Actually, yes, I was planning on heading out there tomorrow around nine. Does that work for you? I'll have to be back before three." I had a pile of laundry, a kitchen to scrub, and a paper to research, but fuck it. Tomorrow after my study group, I'd play hooky from adulthood with Fox for a few hours.

Fox's dimple jumped out at me from a megawatt smile. "That's great. I really appreciate it."

"Should I meet you here?" I asked.

"I can come to you," Fox replied. "We'll need to take the diner's pickup truck."

I wondered what it was that Fox needed to retrieve, but as usual he wasn't exactly forthcoming with information. I supposed I'd find out soon enough. It made me undeniably happy that he was having his belongings shipped here, because maybe that meant that he was going to be around for at least a bit longer.

"Okay," I said, realizing Fox was still holding my hand.

He looked down as if he'd just noticed it himself, and then squeezed. "Tomorrow, then."

The next morning, I had Annabelle ready and out the door in record time.

"I'll be here to get you after school, baby," I told her as we walked up to her classroom. I waved at her teacher and gave Annabelle a quick hug.

"Okay, Mama!" I watched her skip to the back of the class where some of her friends were already engrossed in a very serious watercolor painting session.

I made myself walk at a reasonable pace to the car, but I really wanted to run home as quickly as possible so I would have more than a few minutes to get ready before Fox picked me up.

I'd just finished wrestling a deceptively casual-looking waterfall braid through the front of my wavy hair when I heard Fox pull up. I checked the mirror. Skinny jeans, flat sandals, and a loose-fitting lace-trimmed tank seemed appropriate for the occasion – simple but still cute. I used a light hand on my makeup, highlighting my eyes with a little shimmer and extra mascara, and nude gloss on my lips.

This is not a date, I repeated in my head. *This is two friends helping each other out. The fact that you wore a matching bra and lacy boy-shorts set is completely coincidental and doesn't mean anyone else is going to see it.*

The doorbell rang and once again, I made myself walk. When I opened the door and saw Fox, I couldn't suppress my happiness. For a second, we both just looked at each other, and I felt that gaze said a hundred things we hadn't yet said aloud.

But we would someday. Of that I was now sure.

Maybe I needed more nice underwear.

"Hi," he said, his dimple peeking at me from a small smile. I was accustomed to seeing him in a diner shirt and full apron with his hair tied back, all of which he pulled off with unprecedented appeal. But in regular clothes, it was a million times better.

Today he was wearing simple, well-fitting jeans worn in all the right places. His boots were broken in and loosely tied, and his dark T-shirt accentuated his arms and shoulders. His longish blond hair was dark, still wet from a recent shower, and casually combed back away from his face. Two days of stubble decorated his face and brought out the strong shape of his jaw. He was beautiful and I loved looking at him, especially now that I could do it without feeling guilty.

My guilty feelings were replaced by lots of other feelings now, and those were likely written all over my face. I felt his eyes roam from the tips of my toes to the top of my head quickly but intently, like he was trying to memorize me.

"Hi," I said shyly. There were two choices whenever I was with Fox – tongue-tied or word vomit. Today was the former.

He gestured to the truck. "Are you ready to go?"

I grabbed my bag from its hook and closed the front door tightly behind me. Fox offered an outstretched hand and I took it without a second thought. He laced his fingers tightly through mine as we walked the few short steps to the passenger side of the truck, where he unlocked the door and helped me inside.

He let go of my hand to shut the door and jog around to the driver's side, and I felt the loss immediately. I was fairly certain it was just a chivalrous reflex that coincided with helping me into the truck, but it seemed more intimate than that. If our new friendship step was hand-holding, I wasn't mad about it. I relished that Fox was sitting next to me in the cab, filling it with his cedarwood and soap smell.

Turning to me, he slipped on his sunglasses. "School first?" he asked.

I'd set my bag down by my feet when I got into the truck, and I quickly rummaged through it to make sure I had the folders I needed. "That'd be great, thanks. I have a quick study group to catch."

Fox flashed me his dimple. "You're doing me the favor by accompanying me. I'm yours all day."

How about forever? Wait, what? *Get a grip, Avery.* "Okay," I smiled.

There wasn't much in the way of scenery between Brancher and the campus, but that was fine with me because Fox was much more fun to look at. With my sunglasses on I felt more daring, like I could openly stare if I chose, but instead I snuck glances at him as we bounced around in the roomy cab of the old truck, admiring the way his hand flexed on the steering wheel or the casual slouch of his shoulder as he rested his elbow on the window sill.

"I like you like this," I blurted impulsively.

He took his eyes off the road for a second to look in my direction, his quirky Fox half-smile on his lips. "Like what?"

"I don't know. Relaxed. You're usually kind of intense, you know?" Here comes the babbling. "I mean, you've said so yourself. It's not a bad thing. You're so focused and dedicated, it makes sense…" I trailed off.

Fox laughed once, that rusty chuckle. "I suppose you're right."

"It must be exhausting," I mused, thinking of what it was like for Fox to be constantly on alert. "Is it?"

"Sometimes." He looked over at me again quickly, but his expression was unreadable behind his sunglasses.

When he didn't say anything else, I nodded, leaning my head back against the seat, and looked out the window. The flat, barren West Texas land stretched on for what seemed like eternity, but I knew we were only about ten minutes from campus.

"I like it here," Fox said suddenly, breaking the comfortable silence. "It feels like normal life."

"Boring life, you mean," I laughed.

He shrugged. "Ordinary can be underrated."

I immediately thought about the video he'd made of Annabelle in the diner, how he took regular things and made them look like something amazing. It was a perspective I greatly admired.

"Do you often make video clips like the one from the other night?" I asked.

"I used to. Sometimes it's easy to get caught up in the job and forget what's around you – there's still beauty in devastation, you just have to find it." He glanced over at me and smiled at the way the open windows whipped my hair around in the cab. "I don't have that problem here. There's a lot to pick from."

There was obviously a chance he could be referring to the endless landscape, the colorful sunsets, or even the somewhat majestic longhorn herds that decorated the pastures, but I doubted it. My cheeks reddened slightly, and I was glad I couldn't see his eyes right then, or he mine. For a man who seemingly only spoke when it was absolutely necessary, he certainly had a way with words.

A long strand of my hair drifted close to him, brushing his cheek, and he caught it, sliding it through his fingertips as he turned back to the road.

"Your hair is like sunshine." The timbre of his voice combined with the sight of his fingers tangled in my hair was an emotional overload. From anyone else's mouth, that sentence might not have worked but from Fox it was perfect.

I wasn't sure what to say, so I grabbed his hand after it slipped through my hair. He intertwined his fingers with mine and didn't let go, even bringing my hand with his as he downshifted when we exited off the highway.

Sometime yesterday we'd crossed the boundary between just friends and something more. It was terrifying and exciting at the same time, if my jumpy heart and trembling fingers were any indication.

Quickly, too quickly, we arrived on campus. Fox pulled the truck into a spot near the library and turned off the engine, reaching over the steering wheel so our hands could stay clasped together. I felt like there was a huge neon sign pointing to our hand-holding, and it was blinking and pulsing out of control while we both tried to act like things hadn't shifted in the last five miles of our drive.

"Is here okay?" he asked softly, indicating the library with a nod of his head. His thumb slipped back and forth over mine for an instant, rough but so warm.

"Perfect." *The parking spot, you, today, all of it.*

I was twenty-two years old with a child, and yet holding Fox's hand for mere minutes was undoubtedly the most affected I'd ever been by a man. I'm not sure what that said about my previous relationships – likely that they were crap. Fox had already left his mark on my life in just a few short weeks.

Reluctantly, I released his hand to unbuckle my seatbelt. Fox slid his sunglasses to the top of his head and watched me fumble with the door handle as I tried to exit. Two seconds later, a strong, tan arm reached past my chest, just brushing my tank top. He unlocked the door and pushed it open in a smooth motion.

"Thanks," I mumbled. Maybe having him drop me off wasn't the best idea. I was about to join a Communications study group and I was sort of having a hard time with the communication part right now.

Heather had laughed every time I told her how much Fox flustered me.

"It's good for you," she'd insisted last week.

"How is that possible?" I grumbled.

"You're kind of anal about keeping it all together," she said dryly. "It's refreshing to see you so... unnerved by someone."

After that conversation I'd known I really had to let it die with Chase. And I had, and now here I was, sitting mutely in the truck with the door cracked while Fox looked at me with his half-curious, half-amused expression that I'd come to think of as the one he reserved just for me.

I cleared my throat, an awkward sound in the silence of the cab. "I'll be back in an hour, okay? The cafeteria is right around the corner if you want to grab a coffee or something."

Fox reached under his seat and pulled out a thick dog-eared paperback. "I think I'll just sit outside and enjoy the sun."

He likes to read. He likes to *read*. This new discovery brought fifteen questions to my mind but I didn't have time to ask any of them – the usual ones like "What's your favorite book?" and "What did you read before this?" and the all-important "What's your *least* favorite book?" because you can tell so many things about a person by what they're into in a literary sense.

Fox's big hand was obscuring most of the book's cover, but I made a mental note to ask him all of those questions later. For a brief second I allowed myself to fantasize about a weekend sometime in the hopefully not-so-distant future, where Fox cooked breakfast for Annabelle and me and we spent a lazy morning curled up with books and puzzles. Maybe he would read the paper and pass me the sections he thought I'd like, or even pick a book for himself out of my massive collection and we could discuss it afterward.

Forget the fact that he was super hot, mysterious, and inherently kind. The man liked to read and that was plus eleventy billion points in my book, no pun intended. My inner nerd was jumping up and down while my outer, slightly cooler exterior sat there with a weird expression on her face, still trying to recognize his book from the back cover. No luck.

I realized I hadn't responded. "Okay." Thankfully he couldn't read my mind. If I could condense everything I'd just thought into a reasonably calm-sounding single word then I was doing pretty well. I hadn't met a man yet that could handle the fifty different types of crazy I had running through my mind on the daily.

Maybe this one can, Avery. Don't sell him short. It was too soon to tell, probably. But in the back of my brain, I kept thinking it could be true. And now that I'd just had a complete two-sided silent conversation with myself, I was once again the picture of sanity. Shaking my head, I slipped out of the cab and headed toward the sidewalk.

I gave Fox an awkward wave as I hefted my bag onto my shoulder and turned in the direction of the library. Out of the corner of my eye I could see him leaning casually against the hood of the truck, watching me as I walked toward the three-story brick building. It took every ounce of my willpower not to turn and wave again, but somehow I managed.

Note to self: don't let Fox drive you to any important school events where you are required to use your brain immediately upon leaving his presence. Even in my deepest moments of infatuation with Chase, I'd never had a problem studying or taking exams. Today I had zero focus during a basic study group for a class I was acing. This was not good.

"You okay, Avery?" one of my classmates, a girl named Ellie, asked. "You seem distracted."

"Sorry." I cleared my throat. "Just tired. Annabelle was sick last week and I haven't caught up on my sleep."

Half true, half lie. And so unlike "Most Organized."

Annabelle's brief illness was not what was keeping me up at night lately. The part of me that felt guilty for blaming my kid warred briefly with the part of me that felt embarrassed by my inability to shove Fox out of my head for even an hour. The embarrassed part won, and I decided that was okay because when Annabelle had been an infant, I'd never used her colicky nights as an excuse for anything. She owed me, right?

Ellie made a sympathetic face. "That's hard."

The guilt resurfaced and I shook my head. "I'm fine. Let's keep going."

⌒

Forty-five minutes later, I all but ran out of the library and skidded to a stop a few feet in front of the truck. Fox sat on the tailgate, his back to me, while a couple of pretty coeds I didn't recognize attempted to engage him in conversation. I approached quietly, trying to hear what they were saying.

"So, do you know where that is?" one of them asked. She flipped her long, glossy brown hair over her shoulder.

"No, sorry. I don't go to school here, like I said." Fox's voice was bored but still polite. I stifled a laugh.

"But, you've probably seen it," her friend insisted. "It's close to campus."

"I don't live here, either," he replied. I scuffed my sandal against the sidewalk and he turned his head at the sound. "Excuse me." He reached down next to him and grabbed his book and a couple bottles of water before sidestepping the girls and walking around the truck to meet me. My heart stuttered a little at the restored grace of his long stride and the way his shirt brushed against his flat stomach, but it was nothing compared to the way his face changed when he saw me. Happy, is how I would describe it. Happy and a little eager. I felt the exact same way.

"Hi," he said, offering me a cold bottle. "How was your

group?"

Over his shoulder, I could see the girls whispering to each other with annoyed glances at us before they walked away.

"Hope you can come by the party!" one of them called over her shoulder. Fox ignored her. They seemed completely mystified as to why he'd rather be talking to me than to them, but I was used to that. I knew I cleaned up pretty well but they were in a Dallas Cowboy cheerleader league that was way out of my wheelhouse. I raised an eyebrow in their direction, and Fox just shrugged, looking slightly embarrassed.

"How was your book?" I asked. "Did you have a chance to read it, or…?" I gestured toward the two pairs of retreating cutoff shorts in the distance, a sly grin on my face.

Fox looked taken aback for a second until he realized I was teasing him. In one quick movement he tossed the book and his empty water bottle through the cab's open window and reached out with both hands to grab my hips and pull me closer. Surprised, I lost my footing and crashed right into him, my palms flat against his broad chest. His arms immediately closed around me to keep me upright, and for ten seconds I forgot myself and melted into his embrace.

He hugged me tightly and rested his chin on the top of my head. I could feel his heart beating under my hand, slow and steady as the relentless Texas sun streamed down around us and the idle chatter from passing students faded into the background. All I could focus on was the familiar thump of Fox's heart, and how my own heartbeat calmed from erratic and nervous to match his pace.

Fox leaned back slightly and looked down at me. "Ready to go?" he asked. I felt his voice more than I actually heard it, but I nodded. He opened the driver's side door and all but lifted me into the cab, and I slid along the bench seat to make room for him when he hopped in.

It was somehow freeing to be away from Brancher, somewhere no one really knew us or how we normally interacted with each other. We drove in silence, sitting much closer than before with his arm brushing mine as he shifted gears, a palpable anticipation in the air. The line of friendship that used to be so clear blurred a little more with every mile that ticked by on the odometer.

∽

I'd assumed we were picking up his belongings at the post office a few miles from campus, so I was surprised when we pulled into a commercial truck rental lot. Fox parked off to the side of the main warehouse and turned to me.

"I'll be right back, okay?" He slid a hand over my knee and squeezed slightly. I watched him walk toward the office, his stride easy and confident. The sun shone down on his hair, completely dry now and starting to fall into his face, framing it in thick blond strands. Once he disappeared out of view, I grabbed my bag to check my phone. No missed calls, which was always a good thing when Annabelle was in school. I operated strictly by a no-news-is-good-news policy.

A few more minutes went by and I slouched down in my seat, wondering why Fox had asked me to come with him if he only wanted me to sit in the car. I glanced toward the office again and was shocked to see Fox coming out of the warehouse, coasting sleekly on a big black Harley Davidson. He wheeled it right up to the side of the truck and hopped off, a huge smile on his face.

A motorcycle? Fox had a motorcycle? And not just a motorcycle, but a Harley? I quickly reevaluated everything I'd previously assumed about his cautious nature and steady personality. I knew it was biased, but I ranked motorcyclists right up there with bull riders when it came to making poor decisions. You didn't live in rural West Texas for any length of time and not hear about various horrific accidents involving bikes and semi trucks on long, deserted stretches of highway. My father's best friend in high school had died that way. It was before I was born, but I'd heard the stories.

Fox opened the truck's door and held out a hand for me to exit.

I could see the excitement in his face as he glanced between me and the big black death trap parked nearby. I'd been looking for a flaw and here it was. Heather would hate that I was right. No wonder he'd asked me today. I had to drive the truck home. My stomach dropped. He didn't just want my company, he actually needed a ride.

He told you that, dummy. He said he couldn't go alone. Now I understood. He would drive the bike, so someone needed to drive the truck that would be loaded with the pallet of boxes that a warehouse employee was currently toting on a forklift. And that meant that we wouldn't be riding back together. I wondered if he'd leave me in the dust to play with his toy now that they'd been reunited.

"So, you have a motorcycle?" I said, stating the obvious because I wasn't sure what else to say.

Fox picked up on my tone and gave me a strange, confused look. Obviously, he had a motorcycle. It was sitting right there.

"I do." He grabbed my hands and clasped them both in one of his. "Is that a problem?" He met my eyes and I saw the genuine concern there.

I looked down, suddenly feeling silly. Fox had a motorcycle. So what. That didn't change anything. He was still the same person he was fifteen minutes ago, the one I could barely catch my breath around who set all my nerves buzzing with a single glance.

"No." Except I meant yes. Except I meant that statistically, he was more likely to be involved in a fatal accident than someone driving, say, an SUV. Like Chase. Chase had a nice, safe SUV. Chase wasn't putting himself on a rocket and launching it at 90 miles per hour down a highway with nothing between himself and the asphalt but a fucking leather jacket.

But Chase didn't want his car to be a family car, I reminded myself. He might've had actual seats and doors, but he didn't want them to be used by my child, or by me, really. He didn't want a car seat, or snacks, or a stack of Annabelle's picture books, or anything that could possibly smear his pristine premium upholstery.

Comparing Fox to Chase, especially now, was ridiculous. I'd made my choice when it came to Chase, and I didn't regret it. No gleaming piece of machinery could change the way I was starting to feel about Fox. Could it?

"No," I said again.

Fox didn't seem convinced, but the warehouse worker interrupted us at that moment.

"Mr. Fox, sign here please."

Fox took the clipboard and scribbled his signature, all without taking his eyes off me. He thanked him absently, still focused on my face.

"Avery. Tell me what you're thinking."

"I'm not sure," I admitted. I really wasn't. Everything I thought I knew about Fox conflicted with the motorcycle by his side.

"Okay." Fox turned abruptly and started loading the duffles and boxes from the pallet into the back of the truck. I watched him silently, slightly surprised that he'd given up so easily after he asked me what I was thinking.

He probably doesn't really care. It was none of my business anyhow. I didn't get to have an opinion on Fox's mode of transportation. He wasn't my boyfriend, and he hadn't asked me to climb on the back of the bike. Therefore, my feelings were irrelevant.

Fox finished securing the truck's load with strap-down ties and bungee cords, and came back to where he'd left me standing.

"Are you ready to go?" he asked gently. It reminded me of the night he'd watched Annabelle at the diner and asked if he could follow me home to help with the groceries. This was his 'don't spook her' voice, one that you'd use on a frightened kitten or a skittish horse.

I nodded, still unsure of what had just happened. We had been wrapped around each other, then we drove here, then I saw the Harley and jumped to fifty-five conclusions. That sounded about right. Fox put a hand on my bare upper arm and slid it down until his fingers closed over mine. I let him lead me to the driver's side and open the door.

"I'll stay just ahead, okay?" he said as I climbed in and buckled my seatbelt.

I gave him a small smile and started to adjust my mirrors. Fox shook his head slightly at my non-response and started to walk back toward the motorcycle, then stopped in his tracks and turned back to me.

"You can drive a stick, right?"

I rolled my eyes. "Yes, Fox, I can drive a stick. And a tractor. And even that forklift if I had to." My dad had made sure of that. Being a girl didn't get you out of any chores on the small but highly functional Kent spread.

"The forklift?" Fox's dimple popped. He looked infinitely more relaxed than he had a few minutes ago when my responses were all monosyllabic and vague.

"If I had to," I said loftily, enjoying the way his eyes started to sparkle at my faux smugness. My trepidation about the motorcycle began to dissipate at the sight of the half smile playing on his lips. Bike or no bike, this was Fox. And I liked him.

Heather was right, I needed to stop looking for excuses and focus on the truth that was right in front of me before I screwed everything up.

"Good to know, sunshine." Fox smoothed a few strands of hair off my forehead with his fingertip. "You can never be too prepared for a forklift emergency." He slid his finger down my jaw and slipped it quickly across my bottom lip.

I sucked in my breath at his touch, my eyes locked on his. A moment passed, then two, before I looked away. When he looked at me that way I felt like I saw right into his head and even his heart. Typically I didn't find pet names to be romantic, but when he called me sunshine? Let's just say it beat "babe" any day.

⌒

I was grateful to have twenty-odd minutes alone in the truck to process how I felt about Fox and the motorcycle. True to his word, Fox stayed just ahead of me for the drive home. In spite of myself I admired the way he handled the big bike – assertive yet smooth, like it was something alive under him that only he could control.

When we reached the diner and pulled around to the back entrance of Fox's apartment, I hadn't changed my mind about the motorcycle itself, but I did remember exactly why I was so infatuated with the man riding it. Fox made life seem accessible, even ideas that I would normally be afraid of or at least apprehensive about. He was rock solid and level headed, two things I greatly admired. I didn't like motorcycles, no. But I trusted Fox.

I had to smile when I caught sight of his face after he pulled off his helmet. He seemed exhilarated, relaxed, and most of all, happy. It was a good look on him. I hopped down from the truck and came around to help him as he started to unload the boxes and crates from the bed.

"I can do all this," Fox insisted. "Go inside if you want, I'll drive you home when I'm done." His voice still sounded a bit guarded, like he was remembering our strangely stilted conversation at the warehouse.

I put my hand on his forearm, effectively halting his movements. He turned to me, his brow creased into a questioning look.

"I'm sorry about my reaction to your motorcycle," I said, putting as much sincerity as I could into my words. "This wasn't what I was expecting when you told me you had things to pick up, and I was a little unnerved by it."

He nodded and started to speak. "I'm—"

"Wait," I said, moving my hand from his arm to lay a palm on his chest. "It scares me," I admitted, focusing on my hand where it rested. "It's none of my business, but it scares me." I slid my eyes up to his and was surprised to see emotion burning there. "Please be careful. I don't want anything to happen to you."

Fox seemed at a loss for words. He put his hand over mine and held it tightly to his chest. My body began to relax from his warmth, and I leaned in slightly, wanting to be even closer.

"I promise," he said finally.

Those two words had never meant much to me unless they came from Heather or a blood relative, but I took Fox's statement as truth. "Okay."

I disentangled myself slowly from our half-embrace and reached for what I hoped would be a light box, intending to carry it upstairs.

"Shit," I grunted, earning a chuckle from Fox. "What's in this? Bricks?"

"Close," he grinned. "Books." He grabbed the box from me, stacked another on top, and tossed me a big duffel that must've been filled with bedding or clothes.

Books. That's right, Fox was a reader. I'd almost forgotten in the wake of MotorcycleGate. I followed him up the stairs quickly, my curiosity piqued. Not many people had large book collections on shelves these days, with the e-reader being so popular, but I'd kept all my favorites in their paper and ink form for nostalgia's sake. That, and the fact that my e-reader was a first generation that wasn't always reliable, like much of the technology in my life.

Fox switched on the light in the apartment and it took a few seconds for my eyes to adjust, but I blinked again because I couldn't believe what I was seeing. The rooms were completely transformed – fresh paint, new fixtures, and were those hardwood floors? The tiny, formerly dated flat was nearly unrecognizable.

"Fox!" I exclaimed. "This looks amazing."

He set down the boxes of books on the small breakfast bar and surveyed the space, looking satisfied. "It needed a few things. Your dad gave me a free hand."

I dropped the duffle I was holding and walked through the cozy living room into the equally small bedroom. Sunlight streamed in from the western window, highlighting the crisp white comforter on the platform bed and the gleaming new floors. Last time I saw this room it had been piled high with files of old receipts and produce orders. I couldn't believe what a difference Fox made in such a short span of time.

Well... Couldn't I? He'd made the same difference on me. I spun around and headed back into the front living area. Fox had opened the boxes of books and was beginning to place them on the empty bookshelf tucked into the corner. I quickly scanned the titles and authors as he arranged them.

Vonnegut, Dostoyevsky, and a little Shakespeare. Tolstoy's *War and Peace*, which I expected. Gabriel Garcia Marquez's *One Hundred Years of Solitude*, which I did not expect but should have. A small collection of poetry, including Whitman and Frost. Some Christopher Moore, which made sense, and a few political autobiographies. Hunter S. Thompson, John Updike, Faulkner. Books about war, history, and fire. A Smokejumper's memoir and a few on survival. It reminded me that riding the motorcycle was in no way the most dangerous thing Fox had ever done.

Pushing that thought from my head quickly, I held up a worn copy of *The Adventures of Huckleberry Finn*. "Favorite of yours?" I asked with a smile, noting the tattered cover.

Fox looked over and flashed me his dimple. "Gotta love Twain."

"I might have to raid your collection," I mused, picking through the remaining titles in the last box. "You have quite a few I haven't read."

"Be my guest," Fox said, shelving what looked to be an early edition of London's *The Call of the Wild*. I loved that he had the perfect mixture of adolescent favorites, classics, and mature, masculine nonfiction.

Silently, we finished arranging the books together. I was acutely aware of Fox beside me, like always, but in his apartment, his personal space, it seemed even more intimate. When Fox ran outside to bring up more boxes, I sat down heavily on the futon he had functioning as a living room couch. Looking through Fox's books was the best insight I'd had to him so far. It confirmed that he was just as multi-faceted and interesting as I'd thought. Maybe too much for my own good, especially if he wasn't going to be here long.

But neither was I, I reminded myself. I had an exit strategy already in place. *Take one day at a time and keep your eye on the prize.* Fox had his stuff shipped here, which meant something, for now anyway.

I jumped up when he came through the door with another couple boxes stacked in his arms and the last big duffel strapped across his chest.

"Fox! Is that everything? Why didn't you let me help?" I cried.

"I've got it," he said, easily hefting the boxes up as he walked into the bedroom. I followed him without thinking, intending to help unpack. He stacked them neatly in the corner, dropped the duffel into the closet, and turned to face me. "Can I take you for a late lunch? As a thank-you for helping me?"

A thank-you for what? I thought. *All I did today was give you a hard time about a motorcycle you obviously love, then carry one bag of pillows while you moved a small portion of the New York Public Library up two flights of stairs.*

"Um, sure." I glanced at my watch. Still plenty of time before I needed to pick up Annabelle.

"How about barbecue?" he suggested.

Barbecue meant sticky fingers, sauce on my face, and corn in my teeth. *Abort. Abort.* "That sounds good." I'd just grab some extra napkins and hope for the best.

"Great," he said, taking my hand. I felt the jolt from his touch that was becoming almost familiar or, at least, anticipated. "Let's go."

Fox pulled up in front of my house after the most fastidious barbecue date ever – although if I was being really honest, his presence was so absorbing that I didn't even really think about food on my face – and turned to me.

"What are your plans for dinner?" he asked.

I laughed. "Um, we just had lunch."

He flashed his dimple. "I know."

When he didn't elaborate, I shrugged. "Probably spaghetti... it's one of Annabelle's favorites." That reminded me, I needed to run to the grocery store after I picked her up. Garlic bread with our pasta was a must.

"Can I come by later?" Fox asked. "I'll bring dessert."

My heart stuttered at the hopeful look on his face. Fox rarely gave away his thoughts with an expression, but lately I felt like he was becoming an open book. "Sure."

He leaned toward me, reaching for the passenger door handle. I held my breath as his lips brushed gently over my cheek. "See you soon, Avery."

CHAPTER TWELVE

When Fox rang the doorbell at six p.m., I had everything nearly ready for dinner. The spaghetti was almost done, the sauce – with some sneaky vegetable additions for Annabelle – simmered quietly on the stove, and the garlic bread had five more minutes before it needed to be pulled from the oven. I put together a small green salad at the last second, feeling like the table could use a little more color. And who knew? Fox seemed to have a way of getting Annabelle to eat things, so I was optimistic.

I ran to the front door, Annabelle at my heels.

"FOX!" she cried when she saw him standing on the porch.

"Hello, ladies," he grinned. I took the pie box from his hands – one of Heather's, smart man – and gestured for him to come in. Annabelle hopped up and down excitedly while he removed his boots and stowed his messenger bag near the door.

"Do you want to color with me, Fox? Or see my room?" Annabelle twirled in a circle. "I have lots of dolls!"

I was about to save Fox from being subjected to what would likely be a three-hour tour of Annabelle's bedroom, but the thought struck me that she'd never once asked Chase to play with her, much less show him her toys. Granted, he usually came over when she was already in bed, or getting ready at least, but Annabelle was an unusually perceptive little girl. Somehow, she could sense when someone was merely tolerating her presence rather than enjoying it.

"I'd love to," Fox told her.

I watched Annabelle grab Fox's hand and start to tug him down the short hallway. He glanced back at me with a shrug and a small smile, and I smiled back, shaking my head as I walked into the kitchen to stir the sauce. Every now and then I could hear Annabelle's sweet, high voice piping up and Fox's low chuckle at whatever she'd just said.

I was just about to call them in to eat when my phone rang. Glancing at the caller ID, I saw that it was Chase.

We hadn't spoken since the morning after I'd abruptly left the bar, when I'd told him I thought we should take a break. I knew he'd been in and out of town, but I hadn't heard from him and I was fine with that. I didn't stop to dwell on how hard it was to fit Chase into my life while Fox seemed to blend in seamlessly.

"Hello?"

"Hey, babe!" Chase's voice sounded far away. "How've you been?"

"Fine," I said absently, ladling sauce over the plates of spaghetti. Now without even that small spark of anticipatory excitement I used to get from hearing his voice, I could compartmentalize my feelings much more easily. Chase was firmly in the friend zone, while Fox pretty much monopolized the whole field.

"That's good," he said. "I've been super busy, you know, with work stuff. Sorry I haven't called, but you know how it is."

"No problem," I said, shuttling the plates to the table. I grabbed the bottle of sparkling apple cider I'd picked up at the store and poured three glasses. Annabelle was crazy for fizzy juice, as she called it, and I was feeling festive.

"Okay, well, I just wanted to let you know I'll be gone for another week, but maybe we can get together after that?"

An alarm bell went off in my head. Get together? Why? Did

Chase not correctly remember our conversation from the other morning? I wasn't sure what to say. "Um, maybe?"

"I miss you, Avery," Chase admitted.

Shit. Shit, shit, shit. "You do?"

He laughed uncomfortably. "Well, yeah. Don't you miss me?"

"Chase, we talked about this," I started. "Remember? We decided to cool things off?" *And by cool off, I meant freeze into an unsalvageable glacier?* I sat down at the table, nervously wringing the dishtowel in my hands. I couldn't believe this. It had taken all my courage to break it off with Chase and now he was acting like it had never happened.

"I know, babe, I know," he said, and I felt relieved. My ease was short-lived when he continued. "But I don't want to lose you. So when I get back into town, say you'll see me. Just for dinner or something, okay?"

I thought of Fox, playing with Annabelle in her room, her happy giggles drifting out into the hallway. I thought of the day we'd had together, all of the moments when my heart soared and my fingers trembled. I thought of his voice and the look on his face when he promised me he wouldn't be reckless on the motorcycle. And I had my answer.

"I don't think so, Chase," I said slowly. "I'm sorry."

He sighed. "Don't say no yet, Avery. Just think about it."

"That's probably not—"

"I'm not giving up," he interjected. "I'll call you when I get back."

Now it was my turn to sigh. "My answer will be the same."

"We'll see," Chase said, his vulnerability gone and usual cockiness firmly back in place. "Goodbye, Avery."

He disconnected and I sat for a moment, processing the conversation. Fox cleared his throat behind me and I almost groaned. How long had he been there and what had he heard? When I spun around to face him, the look on his face answered both of my questions.

"Chase?" he asked casually.

"Yes," I admitted. "I'm not sure what he wanted." That was kind of true. I knew what Chase wanted, I just didn't know why. There were plenty of other girls out there who would love to be Mrs. Chase Dempsey and host luncheons and plan charity fundraisers while popping out a football team of children and making sure their lipliner was always perfectly applied. He'd be much happier with one of them.

"I can guess," Fox said dryly, and I laughed.

"It doesn't matter," I told him, taking the garlic bread out of the oven. Fox flicked open the childproof cabinet, selected a knife, and smoothly started slicing the bread. I looked around. "Where's Annabelle?"

He finished with the bread and put it into the napkin-lined basket I offered. "Dressing for dinner."

"Oh, Lord," I laughed, and turned just in time to see Annabelle make her way into the kitchen decked out in full princess regalia. The child had really raided the dress-up box this evening, sporting her favorite pink tutu, green fairy wings, and a sparkling costume tiara. Her neck and wrists were completely covered with plastic necklaces and bracelets, as well as a collection of rings spinning on her little fingers. She reminded me of a tiny elderly woman, wearing all of her jewelry at once to a fancy gala event.

Annabelle was a spectacle, but Fox took it all in stride. "Let me pull out your chair for you, your highness."

"Thank you," she said seriously, settling herself into her booster and arranging her skirt. As soon as she spotted the sparkling cider, all sense of decorum vanished. "Fizzy juice!" she squealed.

"Eat some spaghetti first," I warned her. "Don't fill up on juice."

She spread her napkin across her lap and picked up her fork. I put some salad on my plate and passed the bowl to Fox.

"What about me?" Annabelle asked.

"You want salad?" I asked her skeptically.

She watched Fox serve himself. "Yes. Is it magic?"

"Sure," I replied, sneaking a glance at Fox. He was focused on his plate but I saw a hint of dimple.

Annabelle smiled as Fox scooped a bit of salad next to her noodles. "I love magic salad," she said, taking a big bite. "Do you, Fox?"

"I do," he said. His eyes darted to mine quickly and held. "It's my favorite."

Annabelle chattered on about magic and fairies and princesses while Fox and I just stared at each other across the table. My awkward conversation with Chase was long forgotten, burned out of existence by the heat in Fox's eyes. No one had ever looked at me the way he did. And I was pretty sure no one else could. We were finding our way to each other, every day a little closer.

∽

Two hours later Annabelle went protestingly off to bed, but not before she conned Fox into reading three bedtime stories to her and her dolls. The idea that he could not only accept my child but enjoy her was overwhelming. Part of me worried that she was growing too fond of him, getting too attached before I could navigate the reality of our relationship. There was more between us than some casual hand holding, but we hadn't addressed it yet. I wondered when we would.

Fox and I settled on the living room couch with mugs of tea. I needed to sleep tonight, and while Fox could evidently drink pots of coffee at all hours, I couldn't. I swirled my tea bag around, watching him out of the corner of my eye as he sipped.

"Can I ask you something?"

He raised an eyebrow at me over his cup. "Sure."

"Did you consider other careers besides firefighting? Or did you always know exactly what you wanted?" I'd been thinking a lot about this lately as it applied to my own life, and since I wasn't ready to answer it myself, I figured I'd ask Fox.

He thought for a moment before he replied. "I've always

known I would be in public service. My brother and I both decided that when we were boys. Lucas took another path, but I followed through."

"Was it what you wanted, though?" I persisted. Something in his voice seemed off.

"Sometimes what you want and what you should do aren't the same thing." He paused. "For me, being a firefighter and a medic was both."

His words resonated with me. I felt like I was constantly stuck between what I had to do and what I wanted to do, with no reprieve. What I wanted was to pack up Annabelle and move out of this town tomorrow to somewhere I could breathe, somewhere I could look around and feel excited, like I had a real future. But what I had to do was wait it out, scrimp and save, and try to get a game plan in place that wouldn't put us in jeopardy of not having a roof over our heads or food on the table.

What I wanted to do right now was toss my cup aside and jump into Fox's arms and wrap my legs around his waist. What I wanted was to bury my hands in his thick blond hair, pull him to me and let him kiss me until we were breathless, or at least breathing the exact same air. I didn't just want it, at times I was certain that I *needed* it.

But what I should do, and what I would do, is tread carefully until I was sure where I stood with him. What I should do is not get too attached to a man who had plans to head far away just as soon as he was completely well. Whenever that might be.

"What about the filmmaking? Just a hobby?" I heard myself ask the question, but my mind was still right in Fox's lap with my hands in his hair and his hands... well, never mind.

He shrugged. "Mostly. My mom – did I ever tell you that my mother is an artist?"

"No," I said. "That's amazing. What's her name?"

"She goes by her maiden name for exhibits. Savannah Miller," he said, and I gaped.

"Savannah Miller is your mother?" I couldn't believe it. How had this never shown up in any of my internet searches? His mom was honestly famous. Few living artists were household names, and Savannah Miller's landscapes set her apart from the rest. Her artist's eye spanned the country, from beautiful renderings of West Coast beach coves to rolling Kentucky bluegrass plains. My parents even had a print of one of her Texas scenes in the great room at the ranch house.

"Yes. You know of her?" Fox seemed pleased.

"Um, I don't live under a rock." I shook my head. "Savannah Miller."

"Right. So, my mother encouraged anything artistic, anything out of the box. She sometimes felt like my father pushed his service agenda on us too much." Fox got that faraway look in his eyes again, and I watched as he absentmindedly rubbed the thigh of his injured leg.

"How did you feel about it?" I asked softly.

"The General means well," he said in a neutral voice.

"The General? You call your dad 'the General'?" I laughed.

Fox's lips twisted wryly. "Lucas and I do, yeah."

"What about your mom?"

"Never." His grin was short and quick, but I caught it. "She outranks everyone."

I smirked. "I'll bet."

"I paired Environmental Studies with Computer Science and Engineering for a double major at UCLA. I learned a few video editing tricks and it went from there. From our Hotshot bases, I'd send clips home if I couldn't call." Fox smoothed a hand through his hair, pushing it away from his face. Somehow the mood had shifted to slightly melancholy, and I wasn't sure why.

"Your mom must've loved that," I said, thinking about not seeing my parents every day. I was ready to move on, but I wasn't sure they were ready to let me go. I couldn't say that I blamed them. If it were Annabelle talking about moving two thousand miles away, I'd be a wreck. Fox had gone into the blazing wilderness to face the wrath of Mother Nature.

Fox smiled his half smile. "Yes, she did."

"Do you ever think you'd like to do something further with filmmaking?" I asked.

"I've been considering it."

"Really?"

His face turned thoughtful. "When I graduated and went to the fire academy, my goal was to get my paramedic certification and move up in the ranks as far as I possibly could."

I thought of the few movies I'd seen about firemen. I knew wildland firefighting was different, unpredictable and definitely dangerous. They did search and rescue and evacuated homes that were somewhat off the grid, but mostly they delved deep into the heart of these forest fires, with limited resources. It seemed like a natural environment for someone as serious and steady as Fox, someone who could analyze risk on the fly and know how to proceed. But he had said 'was.' "And now?"

He looked directly into my eyes and my breath caught. "I don't think my career is over. But I'd be lying if I said things haven't shifted."

My brain scrambled at a million miles an hour trying to read between the lines of what he just said, but my speculations were endless.

Fox set his mug on the coffee table and turned to me. "I brought you something."

Surprised at the subject change, I looked around. "You did?"

He nodded. "And before you say it's too much, or you can't take it, just hear me out." He rose quickly and retrieved his messenger bag from where he'd left it when he came in.

Settling himself back on the couch next to me, he opened the bag and pulled out a silver laptop, which he placed on the table. I glanced at him, confused. Did he order me something off Amazon?

"I had this laptop among some of the things that were shipped to me, and I'd like you to have it. For school, for Annabelle, whatever." He reached into the bag again and pulled out a charger.

I sat back, stunned. He was trying to give me a computer? And not just any computer, but a seemingly new laptop? I shook my head.

"Fox, I can't—"

"You said you'd hear me out," he reminded me.

I had not agreed to that, in fact, but I nodded. "Okay."

"It's not brand new," he continued. "But I fully refurbished it and it's all ready to go, installed with whatever I thought you could use, including a 4G wireless card that will solve your connection problem for now." Fox flipped the top open and the screen came to life. A couple swipes on the trackpad and we were scrolling through the available software. I didn't know what to say.

"You'd really be doing me a favor, Avery," he said.

"A favor? By taking a laptop that you could probably sell for hundreds of dollars? How?" I laughed.

"You know the diner apartment is small. I don't have room for it."

I rolled my eyes. "It's a laptop, Fox, not a walk-in refrigerator. It doesn't take up any space. Try again." His dimple was wearing me down all on its own, but I was enjoying the banter.

"Well," he said, sliding a little closer to me on the couch. "It would be much more gratifying for me to send the videos that I've made for you, knowing you actually had somewhere to watch them."

"You've made videos… for me?" *He said videos, right? As in, plural, more than the one I already saw?*

"Yes."

"And you want me to watch them on this laptop?" I felt like we were having this conversation in a language I didn't speak.

"Yes." Fox's eyes held an indecent amount of amusement. He always enjoyed making me wonderfully uncomfortable and confused.

I briefly argued with myself over the impropriety of taking the computer versus the overwhelming curiosity I had regarding the videos. My weakness for Fox won, as I was sure it would every time. My thick skin was nonexistent when it came to him.

"Okay. I'll take it. Thank you. But just as a loaner, until I get one for myself."

Fox's face split into his rarely seen full grin. "That was easier than I thought it would be."

"I guess you make me easy." The words were out of my mouth before I could stop myself. My cheeks flamed into color. "I mean, you make it easy for me to let you... You know. You're easy and I... Shit." I dropped my head into my hands.

Fox snickered and slid a little closer. "You're very pretty when you blush." He paused. "And also when you don't."

I peeked at him through my fingers. "I have to stop doing this."

"Doing what?" His dimple popped and I groaned again.

"Letting you get to me!" My frustration boiled over. "I'm normally a very articulate person! I'm in the top ten percent of my class! My degree is in writing and WORDS, for fuck's sake! And then you come along, and you're all mysterious and perfect and unnerving, and suddenly I can't complete a sentence!"

Fox was silent for a moment, his expression carefully blank, but I could tell he was fighting a smile by the way his lips thinned and it just annoyed me further.

"Oh sure, it's really funny, right? You fluster me and it's hilarious." I sank further down into the couch, knowing that I was pouting over something petty but beyond caring.

"If you think you don't affect me too, you're wrong." His voice was so low, I almost missed it.

"Wh– what?" I stuttered. Seriously, I had to get it together. This was ridiculous.

Fox leaned toward me and whispered a kiss across my cheek. "Check your email." He rose to his feet and was at the door with his boots on before I could fully register what he'd said.

"My email?" My cheek was on fire where his lips had touched it.

"Goodnight, Avery." The door clicked shut behind him.

It took every ounce of willpower I possessed to wait until I'd closed up the house to curl into my bed with the laptop. Within seconds I could see that this new computer was going to make my life a million times easier. The internet content loaded immediately, without any hiccups or false starts.

I logged into my email account and found a few expected items: study group times, reminders about Annabelle's class photos, some junk mail. The last email was from Fox. I clicked it open and hesitated, my finger hovering over the trackpad. What would he show me in this clip? More importantly, what did I *want* to see?

I pressed play and sat back. The screen immediately brightened to an almost blinding white, and slowly color filtered back in, leaves dappled with shadows, birds chirping. The camera panned quickly to the left, now in full spectrum, and focused in on a retreating figure while everything else was blurred.

A delicious shiver licked down my spine. The figure was me, walking away from Fox toward the library on campus. He'd definitely made this today. After a few seconds, the point of view shifted to a cloudless blue expanse, and a few haunting notes from an acoustic guitar slid through the silence. I imagined him lying on his back in the bed of the truck watching the sky as I wracked my brain to recognize the song. The camera jumped to Fox's hand, paging through a book, and focused on a single line – *yet he saw her, like the sun, even without looking. Anna Karenina*, that was the novel he had in the car. An interesting choice, but I knew he liked Tolstoy from my introduction to his bookcase today.

That song kept playing as the scene slid back to empty blue sky, and it finally registered. It was a broken-down version of "Ain't No Sunshine (When She's Gone)." The video faded from blue sky to black and I shut the lid of the laptop with a happy snap.

Sunshine. I smiled. Maybe a little corny, but so much better than "babe." Oh yes, Fox. Things had definitely shifted.

CHAPTER THIRTEEN

The sky was already darkening with heavy clouds when I picked up Annabelle from school. I glanced overhead nervously as I ran from the car to her classroom. Fat droplets of rain started to fall, and I cursed my lack of umbrella. Damn these sudden storms. I was never prepared, even after living in West Texas my entire life.

"Sorry, sorry," I said to her teacher, rushing through the door. Her preschool's aftercare option was essential to my schedule and I tried never to abuse their policies, but today I was late.

"It's okay, Avery," Mrs. Dale said kindly. She gestured to Annabelle, coloring at a little table with a couple other children. "She's just fine."

I let out a big breath. "Thanks." Annabelle wasn't the last child here today, but she had been in the past. Still, it made me feel better to know that I wasn't the only parent who occasionally pushed the limits of the program hours.

Annabelle saw me and jumped up from her seat. "Mama!" she cried, running over.

"Hi, baby," I said, hugging her. "Did you have a nice day?"

"Yes," she said, hopping from one foot to the other. "I'm hungry!"

I glanced at my watch. My parents were in Midland picking up some supplies, and my dad called me earlier to say they'd be home later than they thought. The dogs were outside and with those clouds we'd definitely have some heavy rain, so it looked like I still had to drive out to the ranch to let them in before I could head back into town.

When we'd moved out to the ranch ten years ago, after my grandfather died and left it to my father, I knew my dad wanted to bring back the full glory of the property, but the diner had ups and downs with its profits, and he was stretched thin trying to maintain both the ranch and the restaurant. He just couldn't do it all anymore, which was another reason I was so grateful that Fox had come into our lives when he did.

"I think I have some crackers in the car, baby," I told her. "We have to go to Grandma and Grandpa's real quick, and then we'll go home for dinner, okay?"

"Okay, Mama," she said agreeably. "I can't wait to see Duke and Missy!"

I smiled as I thought of my parents' old Lab/Aussie mix and his mate. Duke was a senior citizen now, and Annabelle had a real soft spot for him. The feeling was mutual, especially since Duke knew that Annabelle was very liberal with her meals and snacks.

I bundled her into her hooded sweatshirt and we made a run for the car. The rain was coming down harder now, but the air was still fairly warm. I navigated the wet streets carefully, half-listening to Annabelle chatter in the backseat. When we turned off the highway onto the main road that would lead us out to the ranch, I heard the first crack of thunder.

"Shit," I said under my breath. I hoped the dogs had enough sense to seek cover on the porch, but Duke and Missy had two half-grown pups from their last litter who spooked easily. The last thing I wanted to do was have to hunt around for them in the rain. Duke was a good herding dog in his time, with a level head. Hopefully the others would follow his lead.

"Mama, what was that?" Annabelle asked suddenly.

"What?" I said, my voice distracted as I peered over the steering wheel. The wind was blowing any and all loose leaves and branches, swirling them into a soggy mess that kept sticking to my windshield wipers as they tried to do their job. One plus side – after the rain, all the dust and dirt would be hard packed for a while.

I heard a thump and a rattle. "That!" Annabelle cried.

The car lurched slightly but kept going. Oh, this was great. "I'm not sure," I said slowly. I eased my foot off the gas pedal and tried to listen, but the rain made it hard to distinguish any abnormal sounds.

I made a split-second decision and pulled into the next driveway I saw. Unfortunately, I didn't recognize the house, but when the windshield wipers cleared a little of the gook, I did see something familiar: Chase's SUV. Relief flooded through me. I thought I remembered Chase telling me he was out of town, but I must've heard him wrong. If he was here, this house had to belong to someone I knew at least vaguely. Maybe it was Derek's, although I was fairly sure Derek lived closer to town. Regardless, I could knock on the door and see a friendly face, which was wonderful since the weather seemed determined to derail my errand.

I pulled up as close to the front door as I could and judged the distance. I couldn't leave Annabelle in the car, but I didn't want us both to get soaked.

I unbuckled my seatbelt and turned around to face her. "Ready to make a run for it, baby?"

Annabelle laughed. As annoying as this was turning out to be for me, to her it was a fun game. "Yeah!"

I reached over and unbuckled her from her car seat, then hauled her bodily into the front seat and threw my windbreaker over her head like a cloak. "Okay, let's go!"

We ran up the porch steps holding hands, and when we reached the door I whipped the jacket off her head as she stomped the rain off her shoes and laughed. "We made it, Mama!"

I shook my wet hair, feeling the rain soak into my T-shirt. I was just about to ring the doorbell when the door opened and a woman appeared. "Can I help you?" she asked.

"Hi, I'm so sorry to bother you," I started. I shoved my straggly hair out of my eyes and focused on her face. Wait a second. I knew this girl. This was the pretty redhead from Lucky's, the one who had been flirting with Fox the night we were there.

"Oh, hi," she said with mock surprise.

Suddenly I was very confused. "I'm sorry," I said again. "Do I know you?"

"You're at *my* door," she said. "Shouldn't I be asking you that?" She didn't seem startled to see me at all, even though I'd appeared randomly on her doorstep resembling a drowned rat.

"Right. Sorry." I couldn't stop apologizing. I glanced over my shoulder at the driveway. That *was* Chase's car, right? "Um, I'm really confused," I admitted. "Is that Chase Dempsey's car?"

"I don't know what you're talking about," she said in a bored voice.

"Chase Dempsey?" I persisted. "He's my– well, he used to be–"

"Babe, who's at the door?" I recognized his voice immediately.

"Mama?" Annabelle tugged on my hand.

My heart was pounding and I heard a buzzing in my ears. What was going on? Chase came up behind the girl, bare chested and clad only in sweatpants that hung low on his hips. His face paled when he saw me and Annabelle standing on the porch.

It was then that I noticed the redhead was wearing a short, silky robe, even though it was just early evening. You didn't need to be a rocket scientist to figure out what I'd interrupted. My face grew hot, and a million thoughts rushed through my head. There were so many details in this situation that I wasn't privy to, but I could imagine.

"Chase?" My voice was barely audible over the rain.

"Avery, what are you doing here?" Chase's eyes darted over to Annabelle, to my car, and back to me.

"Nothing. I'm just– I was– my car..." I trailed off and the redhead snorted.

She looked me up and down disdainfully and flicked a lock of her bright hair off her shoulder. "I thought you two were broken up. I'm not sharing him with you anymore, anyway."

"Not sharing him?" I echoed.

"Stop." Chase's voice had a razor-sharp edge as he addressed her.

She rolled her eyes and ignored him, crossing her arms over her chest. "Did you know about me?" she asked me.

I shook my head mutely. My body felt numb, both from the cold of the rain and the shock of seeing Chase here and what that meant.

"You knew she'd figure it out eventually," the redhead said snidely to Chase. "I guess today is the day."

I started to back away. Chase's eyes were locked on me. "Avery, wait."

"So sorry to have interrupted… whatever." I pulled Annabelle with me as I tried to flee from the porch, but Chase stepped around the girl and called to me.

"I was going to tell you!"

"Oh yeah?" I said sarcastically. "When? At our dinner next week?" I picked Annabelle up and headed down the stairs, not caring that the rain would quickly drench us both.

"What dinner?" the redhead asked.

"The one where he planned to ask me to give him another chance!" I called up to her. I quickly opened the backseat and ushered Annabelle inside before she got too wet. I buckled her in record time and jumped into the driver's seat. Whatever was wrong with the car would have to wait until I got to my parents' house. I needed to get out of here immediately.

～

I took the turn out of the driveway onto the street a little too fast, my tires squealing, and for a second I thought the car would spin out, but I corrected my steering and we were on our way.

Stupid, stupid stupid, I told myself. And reckless. I couldn't drive like a maniac in this rain, especially with Annabelle in the car. I took a deep breath and tried to slow my heartbeat, which was pounding out of control after the revelation on the porch. The redhead's words kept echoing through my head – *I'm not sharing him with you anymore.*

I was an ignorant fool to think that Chase Dempsey loved or cared about me at all, if he ever had. He'd had a girl on the side probably the entire time, and I'd been too blind to see it. A sob hitched in my throat and my eyes filled. So much for being a good judge of character, or having a clear head when it came to relationships. I'd failed miserably on both accounts.

"Mama, where are we going?" Annabelle asked from the backseat.

I blinked twice to clear my vision and peered through the windshield. "We're going to Grandma and Grandpa's, baby," I said, trying to keep my voice even.

"Is Chase coming too?"

"No, Annabelle," I whispered. "Chase isn't coming."

This was okay. This was what I wanted. My raw nerves and leaky eyes had little to do with the actual loss of Chase. That decision had been made before tonight, and I knew it was the correct one. I was upset because of what had almost happened, what I'd almost given him. And what I'd almost given up because of him.

Stupid girl, my brain echoed again. After everything, still too quick to trust. My walls were up from the beginning with Chase, for good reason. The car chugged along through the rain, and I saw the familiar mile marker that indicated we were getting closer to the ranch house. I glanced at Annabelle in the backseat, taking my eyes off the road for a split second.

"Mama!" Annabelle pointed out the windshield.

I flicked my eyes back to the street and my heart leapt into my throat even as I slammed on the brakes. The car screeched and fishtailed a tiny bit before coming to a stop, the tires protesting loudly on the wet asphalt. A few yards in front of us, a telephone pole was down in the middle of the road, wires broken and occasionally snapping in the rain, sending sparks of light into the otherwise dark sky.

"Damn it," I cursed under my breath. *Could tonight possibly get any worse?* The minute the thought crossed my mind, thunder cracked overhead and I winced. I put the car into park and kept the engine running as I contemplated my options.

The most appealing one was to turn around and head back to town, but the thought of Duke and the other dogs cowering in the rain was too much guilt to handle. I rested my head on the steering wheel for a moment, closing my eyes tightly as I shivered. My shirt was still soaking wet, but I couldn't turn the heater on without fogging up the windshield. Thank God Annabelle was mostly dry and bundled in my jacket.

Thunder crashed and lightning flashed through the clouds again and I jumped. Sitting here in the middle of the road, just a few feet from a downed power line, with rain falling and electricity running through the sky wasn't exactly the best plan. I made a move to put the car in reverse so I could turn around and find a different route when out of the corner of my eye I saw a spear of lightning strike an oak tree directly to my right. It sliced right down the center of the huge tree, splitting it nearly in half, and sparked a small fire in the branches that flickered and sputtered against the rain.

I froze, my heart hammering so hard I could hear it above the thunder. The wires from the downed power line were just a few feet from the tree, and I wasn't a scientist, but I was fairly sure this wasn't ideal. In fact, this was very bad and I needed to get us out of here immediately.

"Mama! That tree is on fire!" Annabelle cried.

"I know, baby," I said, fumbling with the gears as I once again attempted to reverse and turn around.

"It's on fire!" Annabelle repeated. "Mama, it's a fire!"

"I know, Annabelle!" My voice broke on her name, and I shoved the car into reverse. "We're leaving now!"

The car finally clicked into gear and surged backward a few feet before coming to a grinding halt. *What the fuck?* I frantically checked the position of the gearshift and tried to rev the engine but nothing happened. Slowly, all of the lights on the dashboard dimmed as I watched, panic filling my throat. I was not stuck out here, in an electrical storm, with a stalled car. I was not. It was not happening.

Annabelle hiccuped from the backseat and I turned around to see her sucking her thumb with tears in her eyes.

"It's okay, Bells," I said, trying to soothe her in a voice that didn't sound like my own. This voice was higher pitched and slightly manic. This was a voice of someone who didn't know what the hell to do now.

"Mama, the tree is still on fire," she said in a whisper, pointing out the window.

I followed the direction her finger pointed and tried to stay calm. The tree was indeed still on fire. In fact, the fire was bigger than it had been before, and I watched as it snaked down the trunk slowly, inching toward the fallen telephone pole. The rain picked now to let up a bit, and the fire was spreading, the wind helping it along. The gusts shook the car, and Annabelle whimpered.

I pulled out my cell phone and saw that I had no service, as expected, but my stomach dropped when I saw the confirmation on the screen. We should stay in the car, I knew. Getting out and trying to go anywhere on foot was a bad option for multiple reasons. But the car was currently too close to the power lines and tree fire for my liking. Maybe I could push it farther down the road? I was already wet.

"Annabelle, Mama is going to move the car, okay? I'm not going anywhere, I just need to get out and push it for a minute so we can get away from the tree." She nodded mutely, and I unbuckled my seatbelt in preparation.

A crack and a loud snap jerked my head to the right and I watched in horror as one of the power lines was lifted by the wind straight into the tree's flames. Immediately, the fire jumped into overdrive and sent sparks into the air while the rest of the lines whipped and snapped freely in the wind. We were too close, too fucking close.

I shoved the gearshift into neutral and leapt out of the car, bracing myself against the door frame while I pushed with all my might. The car started to roll a little and I wanted to cheer. Just twenty feet, that was all I needed. The wind was working against me, and I kept losing my footing on the slick road. I glanced over my shoulder and saw that the fire was still raging. This sporadic rain wasn't helping anything; in fact, it was probably only aggravating the power lines.

I pushed the car another couple feet, and another, until the tires hit a small dip and I didn't have enough momentum to carry them over. My boots slipped and skidded on the asphalt as I pushed with renewed energy, but I wasn't strong enough. Glancing back again, I saw that we weren't far enough from where we had started, and I put my head down on the door frame in defeat.

I wouldn't cry. I had to be strong and upbeat for Annabelle. Her little face was pinched with worry, and she kept looking from me to the tree and back again.

"Mama?" she called, her voice small.

"It's okay, Annabelle," I repeated, even though everything was decidedly not okay.

A flame-engulfed branch split from the tree and fell at that moment, landing on top of a couple power lines. The fire jumped from the tree to the pole, running along the side of the street and snaking out in different directions. The oil from the road must've been fueling it, spread out by the rain and encouraged by the wind. I watched, momentarily entranced, as the tendrils slowly crept closer to the car. I had to get us out of here.

I wrenched open the backseat and fumbled for the second time that night with the child safety buckle. "C'mon, c'mon, c'mon," I chanted under my breath.

Headlights flashed through the back windows, and I heard someone calling my name. "Avery! AVERY!"

My head jerked up and smacked the door frame. Shaking off the pain, I looked through the window and saw a familiar figure jogging toward the car. Fox ran up, breathless.

"What are you doing here?" I couldn't believe it.

Fox glanced around, taking in the tree, the flames licking toward us slowly but steadily, the downed power line. "We'll talk later." He reached into the car, quickly unbuckled Annabelle, and hefted her into his arms. "Let's go."

We ran back down the street to where he'd left my dad's four-wheel drive. I thanked my lucky stars that my parents had taken the diner's pickup into Midland, and that my dad had a car seat for Annabelle in his SUV. Fox left me to buckle her in while he loped back to my car with a couple sandbags, which he split open with a knife from his belt and spread liberally on the road fire and over the power lines. I watched nervously as he navigated the flames, but he was completely in control.

"Get in the car!" he called back to me when he saw me standing there. I obeyed quickly, and in a few moments he was climbing into the driver's seat. He put the SUV in gear and drove it up the side of the road, through some brush, and around the fallen pole on the opposite end from the tree fire. The four-wheel drive handled the off-road terrain easily and quickly, and then we were back on the paved lanes, speeding toward the ranch house.

The weather was still terrible, thunder cracking every few minutes, lightning streaking through the sky, and rain coming down in bursts and fits. And yet, I felt myself start to relax. Fox was at the wheel, a focused and alert look on his handsome face, and Annabelle was safe and dry in the backseat. This was a vast improvement over the events of the past hour.

If only my shirt wasn't soaked through and my hair wasn't a tangled disaster. If only I hadn't found out what a gigantic asshole Chase actually was. If only I didn't get stuck in a storm with my baby while I tried to keep my car from catching fire. I started to laugh and then choked on a sob. I glanced nervously out of the window. The poor dogs were outside in this. Maybe I wasn't as relaxed as I thought.

"Are you okay?" Fox asked me, not taking his eyes from the road. He slipped a hand from the steering wheel and slid it down my forearm where it rested on my thigh, leaving a trail of goosebumps in his wake. "You're ice cold." He cranked up the heater, and the SUV responded immediately. There was definitely something to be said for keeping your defrost mode in working order.

I sucked in a breath and nodded, and then realized he couldn't see me since his eyes remained firmly fixed on the road in front of us. "Yeah."

"Fox came and got us, Mama," Annabelle piped up from the backseat, as if I wasn't present for that particular event. "Wasn't that nice of him? Thank you, Fox. You should say thank you, Mama," she parroted, repeating a phrase she'd heard many times before.

"Thank you, Fox," I echoed.

He turned to me for a brief second, his eyes finding mine in the semi-darkness of the road, illuminated only by the dashboard lights and the occasional flash of lightning. Even in the low light, I could see the flash of green and the intensity within them, stronger than the storm. "Any time."

CHAPTER FOURTEEN

When we pulled up to the ranch house, the rain was coming down harder than ever. Fox got Annabelle out of the car and ran with her up the porch steps and I followed quickly, although I was reluctant to leave the warm sanctuary of the SUV.

I was so relieved to see two of the four dogs huddled on the porch, but my stomach dropped when I realized who was missing – the two older dogs. Missy probably tried to bolt and Duke went after her.

"Fox, I have to find Duke and Missy," I told him, unlocking the front door and urging Annabelle and the animals inside. The dogs darted in and immediately shook their wet coats in the hallway before running into the dining room and curling up under the big rectangular dining table. Thunderstorms always spooked them.

I flicked the hallway light switch a couple times and groaned. No power.

"Where's the generator?" Fox hovered in the doorway, the water dripping off him into a puddle on the doormat.

I frowned. "Out back, but it should've come on automatically."

"I'll go check it out and look for the other dogs," he said. "Stay inside with Annabelle."

I hesitated. I couldn't leave Annabelle alone in the dark, but I was really worried about Duke. He didn't know Fox, and I wasn't sure if he'd come when Fox called him. What if he was hurt?

"I'll be right back, Avery," Fox assured me. "I'll find them."

I grabbed a slicker off the hook by the door and pushed it into his chest. "At least wear this."

The eyebrow reminded me that he was already drenched, but he took it. "Find some candles or flashlights, just in case. I'll build a fire when I come back."

I rolled my eyes. "There you go again, underestimating me."

Fox caught my chin in his fingers and held my gaze, the heat in his eyes enough to start an inferno. "Never."

Okay then. Who needed the generator? I was feeling pretty warm right now. Fox backed away and shut the door, shrugging into the slicker. I turned to Annabelle and saw that she'd made herself at home on the couch in the great room, but I knew she didn't like the dark. I snagged the bin of toys my parents kept for her and dragged it over.

"Here Bells, find something to play with for now, okay? Mama's going to get us some flashlights and we can read books or do shadow puppets until the lights come back on."

Annabelle dug into her stuff and unearthed a few My Little Ponies and a play doctor's kit. Knowing that would keep her busy for a while, I headed into the kitchen to retrieve the flashlights. My dad still kept them in the same place as when I was a kid, in the junk drawer next to the sink, as well as the big torch lantern on the top shelf of the pantry. I grabbed everything, added a box of crackers for Annabelle, and made my way back into the great room.

After I started a fire in the fireplace and firmly locked the childproof grate, we ate crackers and played with her toys for about fifteen minutes before I felt an empty second of silence in the air and then a surge of energy as the generator kicked on and the house buzzed to life.

I jumped up and ran around flicking the light switches in every room on the bottom floor until the downstairs was lit up like a beacon in the darkness. A moment later I heard Fox come in the front door and stomp his boots in the foyer. I hurried over, hoping Duke and Missy were with him.

Fox swiped a hand through his wet hair. "I didn't find them. I'm going back out, I just wanted to make sure you two were all right."

My heart sank at his first sentence. "We're fine," I assured him. "But Fox, you've done more than enough. I'll go. Duke and Missy know me. They'll come when I call them." I could hear the wind beating the branches of the trees, howling down the pastures. It would be hard for anyone to hear a shout, even a dog. But I wasn't going to let that deter me. I grabbed another slicker and shrugged it on, sticking a flashlight in my pocket. "I can't leave them out there."

A crease of worry deepened between Fox's brows. "Ten minutes. Then we switch, okay?"

I nodded and headed out the door and down the porch. When I glanced back, I saw that Fox was standing in the doorway, arms crossed. *Think, Avery, think.* Where would Duke go? If he was trying to herd Missy, and the ranch house was too far, where would he take her?

Suddenly I knew. I ran down the driveway, past the working paddock to the tiny shed next to the main barn, almost a half mile away from the house. This was Duke's favorite spot as he'd gotten older, because he could sit in the awning's shade and look out over the property. I'd almost reached the shed when I saw that the door was slightly ajar like usual. My dad never thought there was a point to locking up a few rakes and lead ropes.

"Duke! Missy!" I called out. I heard an answering bark and relief made my eyes well up. Missy poked her head out of the shed and barked again. I ran inside and dropped down onto my knees next to Duke, who was lying in a corner of the small space. His tail thumped when he saw me and he struggled for a moment, trying to get to his feet.

"Duke! Are you okay?" I ran my hands over his coat and when I got to his left hip, he yelped softly. I pulled my hand away and saw that it was covered with sticky blood. "Oh no, oh Duke," I cried. My eyes immediately filled with tears that threatened to spill over onto his matted fur.

Missy pushed her nose up against my arm and whined. I ruffled her ears with my clean hand. "Good girl, Missy," I told her, sniffling. "Thank you for staying with him."

I surveyed the situation quickly. I'd been gone more than ten minutes already, probably closer to twenty. I could run back to get Fox, but I was afraid Duke would try to follow me and hurt himself worse. I skimmed my flashlight quickly over the wound, but his fur was too thick for me to tell how bad it was. I'd have to wait until I got him inside. I slid my arms underneath him to test his weight. Maybe I could carry him back. I grunted with the effort. He was an older dog but still every bit of sixty pounds. I sat back in defeat, knocking my head on a wooden handle that protruded from the dark edge of the shed.

"Ouch," I muttered. Damn it.

Wait a minute. I spun around and realized I'd bumped into the handle of a rusty old wheelbarrow my dad had stashed in here sometime recently. I stood up to inspect it. It was dirty, but it would do the job.

"C'mon guys," I told the dogs. "Let's get out of here."

The wheelbarrow nearly tipped a half dozen times while I tried to jog back to the ranch house. If I'd thought I was wet before, it was nothing compared to now, as I'd taken off my slicker to cover Duke so he wouldn't get soaked on the trip back. Missy trotted at my heels, never trying to distance herself from us. I wasn't sure how they'd gotten to the shed in the first place, but Missy certainly wasn't leaving without Duke.

I rounded the corner by the working paddock and ran straight into Fox. The wheelbarrow tipped dangerously again, but he grabbed it and righted it just in time.

"Fox!" I cried. "I found Duke!"

The look he gave me was a cross between furious and relieved, but I didn't want to sit out in the rain and analyze it right then. He yanked his slicker off and draped it around my shoulders before he plucked Duke out of the wheelbarrow like he weighed nothing at all, whistled to Missy, and started to run back to the ranch house. We all sprinted up the porch steps and through the front door and I kicked it closed behind me.

"Mama!" Annabelle jumped up and down in the hallway. The other two dogs stood on either side of her like sentries. "Duke!"

"He's hurt, Fox. I don't know how badly," I told him.

Fox hurried into the dining room and laid Duke down in the middle of the table, Missy at his heels. He quickly unwrapped the slicker and started rubbing Duke's fur gently, running his fingers over his legs and back, checking for injuries. When he got to the hip wound, Duke bared his teeth for a second but allowed Fox to explore the cut. I stood at Duke's head with Annabelle next to me as we petted him softly and told him what a good boy he was.

After a moment, Fox raised his head to look at me. The worried look on his face had faded to merely preoccupied. "His hip is sprained, but it'll heal. The cut's not too deep," he said, and I sighed with relief. "He must've snagged it on a wire or a nail. Dogs aren't likely to get tetanus, but he probably needs a shot just in case. If you have a first aid kit, I can fix him up for tonight and then tomorrow we can get him to a vet."

"Yes, I'll get it." I ran into the kitchen and pulled the big white box out from underneath the sink.

"I'll get mine too!" Annabelle said, hurrying over to her play kit. She came back to the table wearing her plastic stethoscope, a determined look on her little face.

Fox fished out what he needed and started to work. I was afraid that Annabelle would be upset, seeing Duke bleeding and in pain, but she calmly stood back and watched with me as Fox clipped away Duke's hair from the wound, cleaned it, and applied butterfly bandages. He finished the whole thing off with a big white dressing that he wrapped tightly around Duke's leg.

"Is Duke going to be okay?" she asked Fox as she followed him into the great room with Duke in his arms. Fox settled him into a dog bed by the fire and crouched down in front of Annabelle.

"Yes," he said. "Your mama found him just in time."

Annabelle nodded, satisfied. "I'll sit right here next to him so he doesn't get lonely." She sat down on Duke's uninjured side and rested her blond head against his dark fur. "Don't worry, Duke," I heard her whisper to him, and Duke's tail thumped on the floor softly.

Within minutes, Annabelle had the three dogs on the floor with her, her head still pillowed on Duke's shoulder as she watched the movie Fox put on the large television. The dogs did their best impression of following along, and I smiled at the unlikely quartet. Maybe Annabelle would be a veterinarian someday.

A shiver ran through me, and I looked over to Fox. We were both soaked to the bone. "I'll find us some dry clothes," I told him.

He nodded, his eyes still on Annabelle and the dogs. "I'll be right here."

I looked around for a second, confused. "Where's Missy?"

Fox scanned the room quickly. "She was under the table when I was examining Duke."

"Missy!" I called softly, not wanting to disturb Annabelle and the other dogs. "Missy?" I walked into the dining room and saw her curled up underneath the table like Fox had said. "Missy! What are you doing in here all by yourself?" When she didn't move or lift her head, my heart jumped. "Missy?"

I crouched down next to her and put a hand on her fur. Her body seemed cold, her breathing barely detectable. "Fox!" I called, trying to keep my voice calm so Annabelle wouldn't notice.

Fox was in the dining room within seconds, obviously not fooled by my faux-nonchalant voice. "What is it?"

"Is she–?" I asked him when he knelt next to us. "She's not responding."

Fox took Missy's head in his big hands gently, first lifting an eyelid to look at her membranes and then sliding a finger into her mouth so he could see her gums. I saw the look on his face and bile rose in my throat. "What, Fox?"

"I'm not sure," he said shortly. Carefully, he rolled her over onto her back and I gasped when I saw a huge jagged cut on her stomach with the glistening of intestine just beyond. Blood stained the carpet where she was lying, and her head lolled to the side as Fox supported her.

"No! She was fine!" I cried. "She ran with us all the way back!"

"She wasn't fine, Avery," he said. "Dogs have a pack mentality, they keep up or get left behind. Missy either injured herself worse when she left the shed or she kept going on adrenaline until she got home."

"Can you help her? You can help her, right?"

Fox put his ear to Missy's chest for a moment and then sat back. "I'm sorry, Avery. She's gone."

∽

I woke up the next morning when the sun filtered through the blinds in my parent's great room, my head in Fox's lap and his arm draped along my body, cradling my torso. My nerve endings were immediately aware of the exact placement of his skin on mine, even through our clothes. I slid my fingers up his arm experimentally, over the blond hairs on his forearm to where his sleeve bunched just below his elbow.

His chest expanded quickly at my touch, and his hand flexed where it rested on my stomach. "Good morning," he said in a low voice.

I looked up into his eyes. "Good morning."

I tried to sit up, but his arm was heavy and he didn't seem inclined to move it.

"Don't get up yet." His hand slid over my stomach in a light caress. Giving in, I snuggled back down, but not before I glanced over at Annabelle on the other couch. She was sleeping in a nest of blankets, with Duke in his bed on the floor at her side. The other two dogs sprawled in front of the waning fire, luxuriating on the rug.

This moment would've been nearly perfect if I didn't have to pee. I glanced up at Fox again and saw that he was looking out the window. The sun continued to stream in from outside, hitting the back of the couch and bathing him in a soft light.

"How does it look out there?" I asked.

His dimple smiled down at me. "Messy, but fixable."

I nodded. "Good." I couldn't take any more bad news. Tears sprang to my eyes when I thought about Missy, and I let them roll down my cheeks for a moment before brushing them away.

Last night, Fox put Missy in a wooden box lined with towels and placed her on the sun porch while I rolled up the rug that was stained with her blood. Fox offered to bury her in the morning, but I wanted my parents to have a chance to say goodbye first. Annabelle was preoccupied with being Duke's caretaker and hadn't noticed that Missy wasn't around, but I'd have to tell her eventually.

We sat in silence for another couple minutes while my bladder screamed but the rest of my body was too numb to listen. I watched as Fox's arm rose and fell with my chest, mesmerized by the way his long fingers looked against the fabric of my thermal shirt.

"How did you know we were out there?" I asked finally. "Stuck, I mean?"

Fox's index finger drew lazy circles on the side of my ribcage. "Your dad called the diner, said he'd asked you to get the dogs."

I nodded. "He didn't realize the storm would be this bad."

Whatever guilt I was feeling over Missy, my father's would be ten times worse. He wasn't an incredibly emotional man, but he loved those dogs like children.

"I was listening to the radio in the kitchen, and they were reporting lightning strikes and downed lines across the county." He looked down at me, the barest hint of anxiety clouding his face.

"My dad must've been panicked," I said slowly, watching his expression. *And you?* I wanted to ask. He came for us, so obviously Fox must've been worried too.

"Listening to my gut has kept me alive so far." His arm tightened around me so briefly, I wasn't sure if I imagined it. "So I hung up the phone and got in the car."

Our eyes locked, and for the first time in the last ten minutes, I forgot all about my need for the bathroom. Slowly, Fox bent his head, bringing his face closer to mine. His thick blond hair fell forward, almost brushing my cheek as he leaned down. He was so close, I could count his individual eyelashes. A warm tingle radiated off every part of his body that was touching mine, sending waves of heat through me to my core.

Sliding my arm out from underneath his, I reached up to cup the back of his neck and pull him to me as his hand slid up my side and rested just below my breast. My fingers tangled in the hair at the nape of his neck, trembling in anticipation.

"Mama?"

Fox sat back so quickly that I thought I imagined our almost-kiss. I craned my neck to the side and saw Annabelle sitting up on the couch with a big smile, her curls a disheveled mess.

"Good morning, baby," I croaked, and I blushed when I heard Fox's soft chuckle. *Well, I guess now is a good time to finally get up to pee.*

∽

"No, I'm serious," I said into the phone. I was talking to Heather, catching her up on the events from the past twenty-four hours.

"I can't believe it. Well, I take that back. I *can* believe it," Heather amended. "You were always too good for Chase, Avery."

"The part I'm most upset about is the fact that I didn't even see it coming." *Because you were so distracted by Fox,* I reminded myself. Any remaining guilty feelings I had about my crush were pretty much wiped away after Chase's cheating revelation, so at least there was that.

"And with that redhead? My cousin Jill's best friend, you know the one with the son who plays the trombone? Anyhow, his trombone teacher said that girl dated her nephew last year and every time she came to the house, she never brought a single dish to share. Who does that? Didn't anyone teach her manners?"

I tried to follow Heather's train of thought and ended up at a loss. "Maybe they really care about each other."

"Always wanting to believe the best about people, that's my girl."

"To a fault, apparently. Whatever, it's in the past now."

Heather laughed. "Mmmhmm… and the future is blond and bright."

"Heather," I groaned, but I laughed too.

"So Fox just showed up in the rain like a superhero and whisked you girls away from danger? Was he all wet and dripping? T-shirt sticking to his chest and stuff?"

"Pretty much," I said, remembering Fox in the storm.

"And then he patched up Duke and saved the ranch?" I heard a blender go off in the background, which didn't surprise me. Heather did her best baking when she was excited.

"Well, that's being slightly dramatic, but basically. I definitely couldn't have done it all myself, especially when we– when Missy…" I trailed off.

"I'm so sorry," Heather said. "She was a great dog."

"I just hope she didn't suffer too much," I whispered.

"Fox said no, right? That by the time her adrenaline wore off she was likely unconscious?"

I cleared my throat and took a deep breath. "Right. Let's change the subject." I didn't want to think about Missy anymore, or the look on my dad's face when I had to tell him that she died.

"Okay. I hope you thanked Fox appropriately for all of his help." I could practically see the smirk on her face through the phone.

I waited a beat. "I tried."

"What? Tell me everything!" Heather cried.

"Not much to tell, unfortunately," I admitted. "Annabelle woke up and interrupted us before anything happened."

"Dang it!" Pans clattered sharply in sympathy with her disappointment.

"Tell me about it," I sighed.

"But there will be a next time, you think?" she asked hopefully.

"Under less dire circumstances ideally, but yes. I definitely think there will be a next time." Sooner than later, if I had my way. The anticipation was killing me.

"I can't wait!" Heather trilled.

"You'll be the first to know."

CHAPTER FIFTEEN

Bored. I was so bored. The diner was empty. Two hours into my lunch shift and I'd made a grand total of seven dollars in tips. The sugars were refilled, the silverware rolled, and I'd even scrubbed out a few dish tubs that didn't need scrubbing. I was just contemplating wiping down all the menus for the second time when Fox walked in through the back entrance.

The minute Billy saw Fox, he had his apron off and his keys in hand, heading toward the front door. "Bye, Avery! Thanks again, Fox."

Fox nodded to him as he tied the strings of his own fresh apron. "No problem."

I watched as Billy all but ran out the door and down the street. Because we'd both been borderline comatose less than five minutes ago, his sudden burst of energy was a little confusing.

Fox caught my curious look and smiled, his dimple like my own personal homing beacon. "I guess he had somewhere important to go."

"I guess," I said, feeling the gravitational pull I still hadn't gotten used to whenever I was in his presence.

"So now it's just me and you." He came closer, reaching past me for a coffee cup.

"Just me and you," I repeated, my eyes locked onto his. His arm brushed mine and he looked down, jolting me out of my trance. I cleared my throat awkwardly and watched him as he filled his cup.

"It's been slow, then?" he asked, not looking up from the coffee pot. His voice was a little uncertain, a little vulnerable, and I liked it. Ever since he admitted the other day that I affected him too, and showed me as much in the sunshine video, I was looking for signs that reinforced his statement.

This was beyond the initial distraction he'd confessed to when we started working together, and more than the new hand-holding and occasional caress. Without the complication of my faux relationship with Chase, we were navigating real feelings that were happening in real time.

"Yes, slow," I confirmed in a soft voice. I took a deep breath while I gathered my thoughts. "Fox, I want to thank you for the other day, coming after me and Annabelle in the storm. I don't know what I would've done if you hadn't shown up," I told him honestly.

That was something that had been keeping me up at night for the past few days. I really *didn't* know what I would've done without Fox that night. Sometimes I took my need for independence a little too far – I was so determined to prove I could handle anything that I put myself into situations that were beyond me. Of course, I'd had no way of knowing exactly what would happen, but I hadn't even told anyone where I was going or why. If my dad hadn't called the diner… well… things could've gone a lot differently.

"I was prepared to turn around and go home if I got to the ranch and your car was there," Fox said.

I just stared at him, surprised. "Why?"

He shrugged, still looking a little unsure. When he spoke again, his voice was a slight blend of sarcasm and sadness. "The department therapists called it hero's guilt. Trying to help people even if they don't need it." He paused. "To make up for the ones I couldn't save." He looked away, appearing startled and embarrassed by his admission.

Those two sentences said more than what lay on the surface. I took a step closer, touched by his sudden vulnerability. "Do you agree with them?"

He shrugged again. "Sometimes."

My heart ached for him just then, for all the things he never said, the internal turmoil he never shared. I hated that this was the first I was hearing of it. And then I thought of something else. "What about that day at the coffee hut?"

"What do you mean?" His words were even, cautious.

"You saw something over my shoulder… something that startled you. It happened again at the bar."

I could picture his face, uneasy as he'd stood there next to the coffee cart, more than just the backpack weighing him down, and then again the night he stared out the window at Lucky's. Those looks stayed with me all these weeks. They were his biggest moments of uncertainty in all the time I'd known him, up until now.

Fox shook his head. "I can't believe you remembered."

I slid a finger up his arm softly. "I remember a lot."

He blew out a breath. "Sometimes things remind me of other people."

"Other people?"

"Circumstances where I wished there was a different outcome."

"What do you mean?"

"It's a never-ending loop – what I could've done differently, what I would do next time. Something or someone will remind me, and then I'm back there."

Another couple sentences that spoke volumes in very few words. My heart skipped a slow beat. He looked lost, extremely uncomfortable, and not at all like Fox. "Oh."

He smiled a wisp of his usual half smile. "Old habits die hard and all of that."

"Fox, I'm sorry." I wasn't sure what to say, but an apology was a good place to start. I was definitely sorry – sorry he felt that way, sorry that I'd brought it up, and sorry that he couldn't possibly be the only one to have a similar experience.

"Don't be." He reached out and brushed a loose strand of my hair behind my ear. "Ghosts aren't always a bad thing." He paused. "Boo Berry cereal, for example."

I caught a hint of the confident, dry humor that I knew so well, and my body relaxed a little. I knew Fox was trying to lighten the mood of this conversation for my benefit, and although I wanted to reassure him that I could handle whatever he wanted to share, I let him steer the topic in a different direction.

I wrinkled my nose at him. "No way. Count Chocula is way better."

He laughed. "Everything okay out at your parents' place?"

"For the most part. My dad found where the dogs got hurt. One side of the south fence was completely down, it must've fallen on them and they had to wriggle out from under it."

"I figured it was something like that," Fox said.

"On the plus side, Duke is doing great, and my dad mended the fence. Other than that, no major damage, just a lot of clean up. Thank you for the rosebush, by the way. My mom planted it over Missy's grave."

For a small operation, there was quite a bit of acreage but nothing my father and his part-time ranch hand couldn't fix. My dad had been spending more and more time out there lately, and Fox was slowly taking over some of the responsibilities at the diner that Joy didn't have time for. I knew they were still hoping I'd change my mind about New York and graduate school to stick around, but the closer I got to graduation, the more determined I was. I wanted options, and I wasn't going to find them around here.

Fox nodded. "I'll give your dad a call, see if I can come out and help."

"Fox, you've been here every day since the storm, working doubles and taking care of the ordering and closing the till so my dad could focus on the ranch. That's above and beyond the call of duty. You're definitely employee of the month, okay?" I teased.

His mouth quirked up on one side. "Is there a trophy?"

I rolled my eyes, suppressing a laugh. "I think it's a plaque. And a gift certificate for a pony ride at the fair."

He turned his full sexy Fox gaze on me, sweeping those green eyes from my beat-up Converse all the way to the fabric flower I'd stuck into my messy bun. "Can I bring a date?"

I could feel my grin split my face from ear to ear. "Depends. Who did you have in mind?"

Fox's slow smile got my blood flowing as he picked up his coffee and turned to head into the kitchen. "I'll let you know."

When he was out of sight, I shoved a silverware tray aside and slumped dramatically against the counter. I wasn't sure what was worse, the anticipation of my graduate school admission or waiting for Fox to finally make his move. At this point, I'd have to say the latter.

༄

Game over. I'd tossed and turned all night, and this was ridiculous. I got up, threw on a sweatshirt over my pajamas and grabbed my keys. The day after the storm, Fox and my dad had gone out to retrieve my car from where it had stalled in the road, and I'd been driving the SUV while I waited for the repairs to finish but I had the old sedan back now, and I crossed my fingers that it would get me to the only place I wanted to go right at this moment.

Ten minutes later, I raised my hand and rapped my knuckles on the apartment door quickly, before I lost my nerve. The thirty or so seconds after that ticked by excruciatingly slowly, and I almost turned around and ran down the stairs to my car to forget the whole thing. Fox opened the door in faded navy blue pajama bottoms, pulling his arms through a white T-shirt, his hair perfectly disheveled and sexy. When he saw me, he stopped short.

"Avery? It's like four thirty in the morning. Is everything okay?"

My eyes locked onto the sliver of bare stomach that peeked out from his rumpled, half-on shirt. "No."

"No? What's wrong? Is it Annabelle?" Fox quickly slipped the shirt over his head and reached down to grab his running shoes from the mat by the door, but I put my hand on his arm to stop him.

"Annabelle is fine. She had a sleepover at the ranch." *Say it, just say it.* "It's me."

"You?" Fox looked genuinely confused. He dropped his shoe to the floor and ran a hand through his hair.

"Yes, me." I took a deep breath. "Well, me and you." I echoed his words from yesterday at the diner.

His expression changed to one of caution, and again I nearly lost my nerve. He leaned against the doorjamb and surveyed me seriously. "Do you want to come in and talk about it?"

This was it. "I like you, okay?" I all but exploded. "And I thought I was making it perfectly obvious, giving you all kinds of signs and green lights, but either you don't like me the same way even though you've hinted at it, or you're taking it slow for some unknown awful reason, but I can't take it anymore!"

Fox's lips twisted. That dimple could coax daybreak out of the darkness, and I could almost feel the sun rising as I stood there, waiting for his response.

"You like me?" He reached out, sliding a hand around the curve of my waist.

"Y– yes." His touch immediately knocked the breath out of me, but I managed to reply.

In one quick motion, he pulled me forward into the apartment and then backward, using the pressure of his body against mine to shut the door. I shifted over quickly when I felt the doorknob dig into the small of my back, and he followed, placing both hands on the door on either side of my face.

"You like me?" he asked again, softer this time.

"You know I do," I whispered.

"Then show me."

Something inside me broke then, all the restraint I'd maintained so virtuously since the day I met him. Fisting his shirt in my hand, I pulled him even closer to me, our lips just a breath apart. With my other hand, I wrapped my fingers through the hair at the nape of his neck and held on. My mouth crashed against his and I wasn't sure if I tasted him or smelled him so much as I felt him, filling me up and rendering my senses totally and completely into one track – Fox.

If I started out bold, he grew even bolder, wrapping his arms around me and sliding his hands up under my shirt, running those long, capable fingers over my bare back. I pressed closer, reveling in the way I was obviously affecting him, feeling his shoulders tense as I released his shirt and ran my hand along the strong ridge of his collarbone.

Every glide of his tongue against mine, every hot breath in my ear, the low groan that built in the back of his throat and came to fruition when I closed my teeth over his bottom lip – it was all perfectly and unmistakably exactly what I wanted when we first kissed.

I wasn't sure if it had been days or minutes when he pulled away slightly and looked down at me.

"Avery," he murmured against my lips.

"Mmmm?" I was floating.

"I like you too."

∽

Six or so hours later, Fox and I were back together at the diner to work the lunch shift. After our impromptu make-out session against his front door, I'd gathered my wits about me and we went our separate ways – me to bang on the door at Heather's house and tell her the minutiae of the morning because, after all, I'd promised her she'd be the first to know, and Fox to take a cold shower.

Or so he'd said. It was still hard for me to tell when he was kidding because his poker face was nearly inscrutable.

"Hi," I said shyly when he came out of the kitchen to greet me.

"Good morning, Avery." His voice was extra deep today and a little scratchy, and just intimate enough to remind me of all the places his hands had roamed while his mouth was on mine earlier.

He raised an eyebrow at the stack of books I'd placed on the back counter. "Homework?"

"Sort of," I replied. "Just trying to get a head start on my graduate program with a few things off the reading list."

My face flushed when I realized his gaze had focused on my lips before he flicked his eyes upward to meet mine. A small smile played across his mouth when he took in my reddened cheeks.

"Graduate school... NYU, right?"

I nodded. "My application is in, I'm just waiting now."

"That's a big move," he remarked neutrally.

"I know... that's kind of the idea," I said. For a moment, nostalgia crept into my thoughts and I considered everything I'd be leaving behind when we moved from Brancher. There were things about this town I would definitely miss, and one of them was standing right in front of me. That is, if he stayed himself.

"And Annabelle? Is she excited?" I thought I heard just a hint of apprehension in his voice but decided I was imagining it.

"I think so," I said slowly. "She doesn't totally understand, but she's always down for an adventure."

"And you're ready for an adventure too." It wasn't a question.

"Yes." My voice was firm. "I'm ready."

"You'll get a spot."

"I'm optimistic about it," I joked lamely. "You know, that whole 'all your eggs in one basket' thing is kind of a bitch."

Almost daily I waffled back and forth about submitting applications to other schools. I'd even completed a few but never sent them in. There was still time, but the application fees added up quickly and I was short on funds at the moment and many foreseeable moments, if the empty diner was any indication. Besides, my heart was set on NYU.

"They'd be lucky to have you. You're smart, focused. Not to mention extremely goal oriented and excessively prepared," he said wryly, gesturing at my stack of books.

I laughed. "Maybe you should've written my recommendation letter." *You and your dimple. If the admissions officer was a living breathing human, they would never be able to resist granting any of your requests.*

"I forgot occasionally impulsive," he said, coming closer.

"Oh?" I murmured as he entered what would definitely be considered my personal space.

"Yes," he said, leaning forward to brush his nose into the crook of my neck.

My eyes darted around the restaurant quickly and I was relieved to find we were alone. The only occupied table had paid their bill and left while we were talking. I clenched my hands at my sides, resisting the urge to wrap my arms around his waist.

"And beautiful," he continued, his lips just skimming my cheekbone as we breathed each other in. "I forgot beautiful."

"Maybe you should make a note," I whispered, my voice trembling slightly as the scruff of his jaw brushed my cheek. "I– I have a pencil you could borrow."

He laughed softly, not retreating an inch. "I'll do that, sunshine." He touched his mouth to mine, gently at first to see how I'd respond, and then more firmly after I slipped my arms up and around his neck.

I forgot completely that I was standing in broad daylight, behind the counter at my parents' diner in a ridiculously small town that thrived on gossip, and I kissed Fox back.

CHAPTER SIXTEEN

I was still kissing Fox, my body pressed fairly obscenely against his for the middle of the day, when I heard the door chime that signaled someone entering the diner, and I jumped back so fast I nearly knocked over an entire tray of coffee mugs.

Fox stayed exactly where he was, with one hip propped against the counter and an amused look on his face, while I straightened my apron and wiped my mouth with the back of my hand like I was seven years old.

"Well, hello there, Avery, Fox," Joy greeted us, looking entirely too pleased with her luck at coming across the two of us in a compromising position. Pleased and not at all surprised.

"Joy, hi," I said, still tugging pointlessly on my apron, which almost exactly matched the flaming red color of my cheeks. "Didn't expect you this early!"

"I can see that, darlin'," she drawled. "Don't mind me, I have some paperwork to finish up in the office before I start my shift, so I'll just head on back."

"Okay," I said, and Fox nodded, his eyes still on me.

"Oh, and Avery?" Joy called over her shoulder as she walked. "If you wanna keep kissing that boy, why don't y'all go into the kitchen? More privacy, less of an audience in there."

Fox half-snorted into his coffee, and I felt like my face was going to melt off. I snuck a glance at Fox and saw his dimple peeking around the mug.

"You're enjoying this, aren't you?" I asked.

His green eyes shot sparks of amusement over his cup, but he didn't answer. I slid closer, reaching to take the coffee out of his hands. He let me have the mug, and I set it aside, feeling the warmth radiate not only from the ceramic but from his body next to mine.

The door chime jangled again, but I didn't look over. Only when I saw Fox's eyes dart toward the entrance and his posture change did I wonder who had just come in.

"Hi, Avery," a familiar voice said behind me.

Chase. I turned slowly, hoping my facial expression wouldn't give away the conflicting thoughts running though my brain. "Hi."

He looked the same as he always did, the same as when I saw him a few nights before, half naked at the redhead's house. The same as when he admitted he'd lied and cheated. Handsome, but not trustworthy. Strong, but not loyal. Confident, but not relaxed.

"Hey, Fox," he said, nodding to him. Fox said nothing, merely returned his gaze evenly and without emotion, but Chase didn't notice.

"What's up?" I said, trying and failing to sound casual.

"Um, can we talk?" he asked. He glanced at Fox again. "Somewhere in private?"

I couldn't look at Fox, but I wanted to. "I'm not really sure what's left to say." Actually, I could think of about a million things I'd like to say to Chase, but it would be a colossal waste of effort and breath, and I preferred to use my time productively.

Chase had the decency to look uncomfortable. "Look, babe, I know you're pissed, okay? I'm sorry you had to find out that way."

Whenever I was with Chase lately, that brain-exploding feeling wasn't far behind. "What way would've been preferable? After you convinced me to get back together with you? Or maybe after we slept together?" Out of the corner of my eye I thought I saw Fox stiffen when I said that, but I couldn't be sure.

Chase shook his head. "It was just a few times. She doesn't mean anything to me, I promise."

"Is that supposed to make me feel *better*?" I asked incredulously. "The fact that you were willing to throw away whatever we were starting for someone you don't even care about?"

"I told you I was sorry! I was bored, you were working a lot, you didn't have time for me anyway," Chase said, trying a new tactic.

"That's your opinion, but whatever. We weren't getting along very well, things weren't clicking, and I valued our friendship. So I decided to break things off, because that's what you do when you respect someone." I could've left it at that, but the words popped right out of my mouth. "You don't go fuck redheaded barflies because you're *bored*."

Chase's eyes widened. "You're right. But listen—"

"I don't have to listen to you anymore, Chase. It's one of the perks of us being broken up, along with you being free to sleep with the entire town if you so choose. Oh by the way, your new girlfriend was aggressively hitting on Fox at the bar just a few nights ago, and she never brings food to share at a potluck. Have fun."

"Avery—"

"Nope." I turned and walked to the end of the counter and started methodically lining up ketchup bottles for refilling.

"I thought we were friends, Fox." Chase's voice was verging on whiny.

"We are," Fox said, crossing his arms over his chest.

"What did you tell her?" he wanted to know.

My head snapped up and I focused on Fox. His guard slipped for just a second and I saw a flash of uncertainty cross his face. "Nothing."

"You must've told her something," Chase continued as though I wasn't standing right there. "Thanks a lot, man."

"The only person you have to blame for this is yourself, Chase." Fox's voice had an edge to it that I hadn't heard before.

Chase looked over at me to gauge my reaction.

I sighed. "Just go home, okay? We're done here."

"Babe, please—"

"She wants you to go." Fox's voice was like ice.

"All right, all right, I'm leaving. See you around, Avery."

Chase walked out, and I turned to Fox.

"I don't believe this! You knew? You knew and you didn't tell me?" This new development was more upsetting than Chase's betrayal, and that illustrated how much I'd grown to trust Fox.

Fox's expression was guarded. "I didn't know for sure, I just suspected, based on a few offhand comments he'd made."

"Your suspicions are more accurate than most people's rock-solid proof," I countered.

"I— it was too complicated. I couldn't let how I was starting to feel for you influence my objectiveness about a situation where I didn't have all the facts."

"This wasn't a fucking Supreme Court case, Fox. You should've told me," I cried. His choice of words – the part about his feelings – wasn't lost on me, but I couldn't focus on that now.

"It would've been biased, coming from me."

"It would've been the truth and something I needed to know."

"I'm sorry, Avery." He did look sorry, but I was too hurt to care.

I shook my head sadly. "Tell Joy I left early."

⌒

For the second time that day, I found myself on Heather's doorstep. After she saw the look on my face and let me in, she went right into the kitchen and came back with a plate of cookies and a bottle of wine.

I grabbed a cookie and took a big bite. "I'll pass on the wine, thanks. I have to pick up Annabelle in a little while."

"What happened? This morning you were practically floating through the door. Now you're slumped on the couch like a pretty blond potato." Heather selected a cookie for herself.

"Ugh," I managed.

"I hope you're referring to something other than these cookies, because they are clearly delicious."

"Fox knew about Chase and the redhead. Like, he knew before I did."

"Uh oh," Heather muttered. She reached for the wine bottle and poured a glass. "You sure you don't want some?"

"While day-drinking is always an attractive solution, I think this is bigger than that, unfortunately." I set my cookie down. "Maybe if you had mimosas."

She started to get up and I laughed.

"Okay, what exactly did he say? He said he knew about Chase's cheating and didn't tell you?"

"No," I admitted. "He said he'd had suspicions but didn't want to tell me because it would be biased coming from him based on his feelings for me."

Heather stared at me. "He said that? His feelings for you?"

I grinned in spite of myself before quickly remembering I was angry. "Yes."

"And the problem is what?"

"What do you mean? He knew that Chase was fooling around on me and didn't say anything! Clearly that is *the* problem!"

"Avery, listen to yourself. You could give two shits about Chase's lying ass. Yeah, sure, it stung a little and caught you off guard. But the real thing that's hurting your feelings is the fact that *Fox* might've lied to you, not Chase."

"So?" I said irritably.

"So get some perspective! You said yourself that Fox essentially overthinks everything he says and does, right?"

"Yeah," I admitted.

"Don't you think he'd have a very good reason for not voicing theories that weren't confirmed? Like the fact that he wouldn't want to upset you unnecessarily? Or influence any of your decisions with his own agenda?" she pressed.

"You think he had an agenda?" I asked hopefully.

Heather threw the wine cork at me and rolled her eyes. "You're so clueless."

I tossed the cork back at her. "What?"

"Avery, that boy had a plan from the minute he laid eyes on you. He waited patiently until you'd gotten Chase and whatever half-hearted second chance you were attempting out of your system, which must've been as excruciating for him as it was for me."

"Point taken, Heather," I muttered. I waved my hand dismissively. "Back to Fox."

"Are you honestly upset about Chase cheating?" she asked me.

I thought about it for a second even though I already knew my answer. "No. It was shitty but probably inevitable. I got caught up in the nostalgia for a while, but I don't think my heart was in it from the beginning. I'm actually sort of relieved that we've had a definitive ending."

"Agreed. Are you really mad at Fox for keeping his suspicions to himself? Maybe he didn't think it was necessary to hurt your feelings since you'd already broken things off with Chase. Ever consider that?"

I paused. *Shit.* "You're probably right."

"Of course I am. Cut the guy some slack." She pushed the cookie plate toward me. "If you're gonna make me drink alone, at least eat the rest of these."

CHAPTER SEVENTEEN

I was cleaning the kitchen after dinner when I heard a car pull up outside my house. I'd spent the majority of the afternoon after I picked up Annabelle in a total funk, and even homemade pizza didn't help. Waiting tables and running around after a three year old were my main forms of exercise, but if I was going to keep indulging in comfort food, I'd probably have to consider actually working out. Maybe Fox would let me tag along on his runs. The thought of Fox and the look on his face when I'd walked out of the diner made me wish I still had ice cream in the freezer.

I heard the mystery car shut its engine off, but when I glanced outside I only saw a large truck I didn't recognize. Must be someone for the neighbors.

Before I could walk into the living room and join Annabelle as she worked on her princess puzzle, the doorbell rang.

"Mama, who's here?" she asked excitedly. "Is it Fox?"

I wish. "No, baby," I told her.

"It might be!" she insisted.

"No, Annabelle, it's not—" I broke off when I opened the door and saw Fox standing on the porch. "Fox," I finished lamely.

"FOX!" Annabelle cried, jumping up and running to the door.

She threw her arms around his legs. "I missed you."

Me too, kid, I thought.

Fox reached for Annabelle and swung her into his arms. "Hey Bells. What's new?"

"I got a puzzle!" she told him. "Do you want to see?"

"Absolutely," he said, setting her down. "I just need to talk to your mama for a second, okay?"

"Okay!" She ran back into the living room.

"Hello, Avery," Fox said in his deep, perfect voice. "I'm sorry to just drop by like this." His words were oddly stiff and formal, and I hated that.

"Stop," I said.

When you told Fox to stop, he practically ceased breathing. The man had stillness down to an art form. He stood there, watching me, waiting for whatever I'd say next.

"I'm sorry," I began.

"No, I'm the—"

"Stop," I said again. A faint version of his quirky half smile appeared on his lips. "I'm sorry that I lashed out at you earlier," I continued. "I was just caught off guard with the idea that you'd known."

"I didn't know, Avery, honestly," he said. "We went out for beers one night after my shift, and he said a few things that got me thinking."

He reached for my hand and I let him pull me closer. His warmth was calling to me, and I decided not to fight it. I wrapped my arms around his waist and tipped my head back to look into his eyes. "I believe you."

"I would never lie to you." His face was so serious, his green eyes staring intently into mine, his hair loose and falling down around his forehead. I felt his heart beating where our chests were pressed together and knew without a doubt that he was sincere.

"I know that too."

"Fox!" Annabelle called from the living room. "Are you ready for puzzles?"

Fox laughed, releasing his grip on me only slightly. "Just a minute, sweetheart. I need to show Mama something. Want to come outside with us?"

I looked up at him questioningly. "Show me what?" I could think of a few things I'd like him to show me, actually, but none of that was appropriate at the current moment.

Fox stepped back, taking my hand in his and opening the door. "Outside please."

I let him lead me out onto the porch, Annabelle at our heels, and when he stopped there, I wasn't sure what was happening. I looked around but didn't see anything out of the ordinary – cars on the street, kids playing in the yard next door, a telephone book on the stoop where whoever delivered it must've left it... Who still used telephone books these days anyway? I had my new-to-me laptop and I was never going back.

"What am I looking at?" I asked.

He pulled me down the steps to the truck parked directly in front of the house. It was then I realized I hadn't heard the motorcycle pull up when he arrived. *Whose truck was this?*

"The other night in the storm made me think," he began. "After I hung up with your dad I tried your cell phone but service was spotty. I needed a way to get out to the ranch, and I could've jumped on the bike, but motorcycles and rain don't mix very well, and they are especially useless when it comes to transporting children."

"Okay..." I said, the light beginning to dawn.

"Luckily, your dad left the SUV at the diner, but I didn't like that feeling."

"What feeling, exactly?" I knew, but I wanted him to say it.

"I didn't want anything to stand in the way of me getting to you and Annabelle again. So the next day I bought this." He pointed to the truck.

"You bought a new truck," I said, shaking my head. "You're nuts. You bought a new truck just in case you had to drive me and Annabelle around?"

"No," Fox said, opening the passenger door. "I bought a new truck because I plan on driving you both frequently. Get in."

I was still shaking my head as I hopped up into the cab and Fox lifted Annabelle in behind me. The crew cab had four full doors and a million buttons on the dashboard, along with what looked to be a top-of-the-line stereo system and, best of all, the new car smell. I breathed in deeply while Annabelle scrambled over my lap.

"Look Mama, a seat for me!" She turned around and pointed into the large backseat where a brand-new car seat was already installed.

I followed her finger to the new, top-of-the-line seat and tears sprang into my eyes. This was too much, this couldn't be happening. We hadn't even been out on a real date yet, but he bought a truck and put a car seat in the back for my kid?

A gentle hand turned my face in Fox's direction, and I saw his eyes narrow worriedly when he saw the expression on my face. "Avery? Did I get the wrong one? The store said I could return it, no problem. Just tell me which one to buy."

"No," I choked out.

"No, it's okay? Or take it back?"

"No. Just no. This is too much, Fox." I squeezed around Annabelle and jumped out of the truck, reaching back to lift her out after my feet hit the sidewalk.

"Wait, what? What do you mean? I thought you'd be happy about this."

I couldn't look at him right then, so I watched Annabelle as she scampered back up the porch and into the house.

"Avery? Say something, please. I thought we were okay."

"What are you doing?" I blurted. "Why are you doing all of this?"

Fox shoved his hands into his pockets and leaned against the truck. "I'm trying to be a part of your lives."

I'm not sure what I'd expected him to say but, like usual, it wasn't that. I looked up at him, silhouetted in the dusk, all handsome and strong and sometimes not so mysterious, and my heart stuttered a little. "This is more than a grand gesture, Fox."

He pulled one hand free and reached toward me. "It's just a truck. I needed something other than the bike. And you like it. I can tell." He slid his fingers up my bare arm to my shoulder and I stepped toward him automatically.

"I do," I admitted.

"So can I keep it?" His dimple popped and I immediately felt silly. Why was I freaking out because he bought a truck and put in a car seat? *The same reason you almost bolted when he offered to help with your groceries, crazy girl.* God forbid anyone wants to get close to "Most Organized."

"That depends," I said. "Did you buy it from Chase?"

Fox laughed, his full deep chuckle, and I relaxed the rest of the way. "No... They didn't have what I was looking for."

"Then it's fine." He pulled me into his arms and I rested my head on his chest. This afternoon without him had given me a lot of time to think. It had only been a few hours, but I missed him like something essential, like breathing. I knew then that I couldn't truly doubt his intentions. Fox was always here for me, for us. He'd never once let me down. I couldn't imagine he ever would.

As if he could read my thoughts, Fox spoke again. "You don't have to pave the way, Avery. But at least let me follow the map, okay?"

I nodded, stretching up onto my tiptoes to kiss him quickly on the mouth. "A new truck. My dad must be paying you too much," I joked, but I was half serious. I knew his mom was successful, but something told me that Fox didn't necessarily need the cook's job to keep himself in computers and trucks. It was none of my business, but that didn't mean I wasn't curious.

"C'mon," he said, pulling me up the sidewalk toward the house. "Let's do some puzzles and then we'll go for a drive."

∽

Once we'd finally established that we both had feelings for each other, things progressed rapidly. Fox and I went on a handful of dates. Some were with Annabelle and some were not, and I enjoyed them all equally.

The ones with Annabelle were full of laughter and silliness, full of daydreams where I briefly let myself pretend that he was her real daddy and, unfortunately, full of moments when I remembered he was not. Annabelle loved spending time with Fox, and his patience for her was infinite, which was more than I could say for myself at times after a full diner shift and tons of homework.

The dates without Annabelle were exercises in my willpower, because at the end of the evening when Fox walked me to my door and kissed me goodbye, it took every ounce of restraint I possessed not to jump into his arms and request that he carry me directly to bed.

I was currently fighting that exact impulse as we said goodnight after a delicious dinner at a tiny Thai restaurant in Midland. I'd never had Thai food before, and Fox insisted that I start to try other cuisines to prepare me for when Annabelle and I went to New York. You could get anything you wanted there, he said, at any time of the day or night. I considered myself slightly more worldly than the average small-town girl, given the amount of reading I did, but it blew my mind to think that you could get takeout at four a.m. from a variety of restaurants, delivered right to your door. I'd definitely have to take advantage of that during my marathon study sessions. Part of me wondered if Fox fit into that New York scenario anywhere, or if he would want to, but I thought it was too soon to seriously consider.

"Thank you again for dinner," I said, kissing him softly. We were standing on my porch saying the longest goodbye, because between every few words he pulled me into his arms for another kiss.

"I'm glad you enjoyed it." He slid a finger down my cheek.

"More than I thought I would," I laughed.

His dimple peeked out. "You were very adventurous. Not

everyone tries the extra hot curry on the first visit."

"Yeah, that was probably not the best idea I've ever had," I admitted wryly, remembering the mouth-searing burn.

"I have to go," he said suddenly.

I was taken aback by his abrupt statement. "Um, okay. Well, goodnight. Thanks again." I turned to unlock the front door. I'd be home alone tonight, as Annabelle was with my parents at the ranch again. She had a new love of these sleepovers and I was indulging her since it meant a little private time with Fox.

"Avery, wait." He spun me around and wrapped his arms around my waist.

"Fox, I'm confused," I started, but he silenced me with another kiss.

"I have to go because I want to come in, very badly, and when you ask me this time I don't think I'll be able to say no."

"So say yes."

He'd been turning down my invitations to come in after our last couple dates and I knew why. It was getting harder and harder to keep our hands off each other, and the next step in our relationship was looming right before us. Part of me felt insecure about it, wondering if he really felt the way he said he did or if things were getting to be too serious for him. Our relationship was new but we had an easy rapport, which meant hours of conversation about everything and anything.

"I sent you something. Watch it." He kissed my forehead and was gone.

I was still a little stung by his rejection, but the promise of a new video soothed me slightly. Fox hadn't sent me anything lately aside from a couple funny clips of him and Annabelle goofing around. I loved those because it showed how much he let himself go when he played with her, how much he meant to my little girl, how easily and happily she interacted with him. I had a feeling this one was going to be different.

Settling on the couch with my laptop, I logged in and found the clip. The email was titled simply "Avery." I pressed play and the screen widened to show a cloudy night sky. Only a few stars were visible, and the moon peeked out briefly, shining down onto what I recognized as my parents' front pasture, which was visible from the ranch house's porch. This was from the night of the storm. I watched as the scene faded to a glowing fireplace, the dogs enjoying the heat. A song started to play in the background, faint, but I thought it was Brad Paisley. The fire faded and the camera focused to a full frontal of Duke's sleek black head, lying with his nose between his paws. I'd never seen a dog's eyes hold as much warmth, wisdom, and sadness as I did in that shot, but the very best part was in the background, out of focus but very recognizable, was Annabelle's little face, her blond curls tousled as she rested her cheek on Duke's fur.

Annabelle and Duke faded out, and the camera took on a grainy quality as it zeroed in on two intertwined hands, one of mine and one of Fox's. The music swelled slightly and I realized it *was* Brad Paisley, singing about a girl who was his everything. I watched, mesmerized, as Fox's thumb smoothed its way over my skin, tracing the veins of my wrist as he held me close to his chest. Even though only our fingers and a bit of my shirt were visible, I could feel in that moment exactly what it was like to be in his arms. I wanted to be there right now. The camera panned back to another night sky view outside the window and, through a trick of the glass, the fire and the barest hint of our silhouettes were reflected, bringing everything together before fading to black.

I sat for a moment, thinking of a hundred reasons why I should stay put and a million more why I shouldn't, before jumping up and practically running out of the house.

∽

"You should've called. I would've come to you," Fox said when he opened the door.

"You should've known I couldn't wait." I didn't hesitate, I just stepped forward and he caught me. His mouth descended onto mine, and somewhere in the fog of what I would always consider our first *real* kiss, he kicked the door shut and we crashed back against it.

Instinctively, I rose onto my toes, wrapping my hands around the back of his neck and running my fingers through his mane of hair. He took his hands off the door, dragging them down my sides, over my hips, until he reached the backs of my bare thighs under my skirt. My breath caught when he lifted me easily, our eyes locked on each other, and I wrapped my legs around his waist as he pressed me even more tightly against the door. His mouth roamed up under my chin, moving along my jaw with wet, hot kisses.

"Deja vu," I managed to gasp.

"I like how this door looks with you up against it," he murmured into my neck.

"Consider it my new favorite place." I arched and his hands slid up under my shirt, smoothing his way from my waist to just under my breasts.

His lips found mine again, coaxing my tongue to slide in sync with his, and I shuddered into his mouth when his fingers expertly flicked open the clasp of my bra and freed my breasts. If my legs hadn't been wrapped around his waist, my knees would've given out the moment his rough palms slid over my nipples, shattering my nerve endings with his touch.

"Avery." Fox's voice was deeper than I'd ever heard it, raspy and low with the promise of everything his body currently teased.

I felt the solid warmth of his arousal, jerking and pressing tightly against my center. Shamelessly, I tightened my thighs around him and ground into his hips. "I want you," I breathed, twisting his hair into my hands and licking deep into his mouth. "Now."

Fox pulled his face back to look into my eyes, his own hooded and heavy with lust. "Not here," he growled.

In one swift movement he latched his mouth to mine, spun away from the front door, and headed toward his bedroom with my body still wrapped around his. We burst through the doorway and onto his bed, his arms cradling me on top of him and cushioning our fall, our mouths still fused together. The room was dark, with just a soft light coming in through window, and the blankets were rumpled and twisted. The bed smelled like him, like warmth and soap and that unmistakable cedarwood.

I broke away and sat up, straddling his waist. He slid backward to rest against the headboard, propping himself up slightly as he watched me, a half smile on his beautiful lips.

"My turn," I said, pushing his shirt up so I could see his smooth, tanned skin. The muscles under my fingers twitched and his chest rose with a sharp intake of breath as I slid my palms downward to where our bodies met. He sat up quickly and pulled his shirt over his head, throwing it into the depths of the dark room. I leaned into his neck, breathing in – I'd thought about touching him like this forever.

My lips trailed over his collarbone, tasting the saltiness of his skin. I closed my teeth over his shoulder muscle and he groaned, stroking his hand down my back and burying his lips in my neck.

Slowly, I pulled away, reaching for the buttons on my thin sleeveless shirt, undoing them one by one until my unclasped bra was visible. His hands reached for my skin the minute I tossed the clothing aside, cupping my breasts and smoothing his thumbs over my nipples before following with his mouth. My breath caught and I gasped as I felt his erection jump where my core pressed against it.

Automatically I rocked my hips into his and he reacted instantly. The room spun and suddenly I was underneath him, my wrists clasped over my head in one of his large hands while his tongue drew a wet trail from one nipple to the other, pausing to suck and nibble at my skin. I arched up to meet him, loving the sensation caused by his teeth combined with the rough heat of his sandpaper jawline.

His other hand slipped down between my legs as he nudged my knees apart with his own. I spread my thighs willingly, drawing in rapid breaths as his fingers teased over lace before sliding down into my heat. Every muscle in my body tensed with the sensation of his finger deep inside me, and when he added a second one it nearly sent me over the edge.

"Fox," I gasped.

He raised his head from my breast and the look in his eyes took away what little breath I had left. "Your skin is so soft. I want to taste it all." Slowly, slowly, he kissed his way down my stomach, leaving a sheen of wetness in his wake while his fingers continued their delicious, relentless movement. When he released my wrists so he could drag my skirt down my legs and remove his own jeans, I tangled my fingers into his thick hair and pulled his face to mine for another kiss.

His lips covered mine, his tongue swirling around my mouth, then he sucked my bottom lip into his teeth before releasing it quickly and sliding back down my body. I felt his hot breath sweep my inner thigh, closer and closer to my center, and when his mouth joined his fingers I was gone. My gasps turned to moans and my fingers tightly clutched the sheets while he explored the center of my body with his lips, teeth, and tongue.

I was rushing quickly to the brink, my nerve endings screaming with sensation when Fox pulled me back up into a sitting position straddling his lap so we were facing each other. My head spun and I frantically grasped for his shoulder to steady my world as he reached behind us into his nightstand and I heard an unmistakable foil crackle.

Fox supported all my weight, sweeping my hair off the nape of my neck and turning my face to meet his eyes. I could feel his erection throbbing between us, pressed to my stomach, but his hands on my face were calm and gentle.

"Avery," he began, his voice deep with restraint. "I've wanted this since the day we met, but you weren't mine to want."

Between the heavy arousal pulsing through my veins and the lulling drug of his voice, my brain was a tangled mess of lust and what felt suspiciously like love.

"I am now," I told him.

His eyes widened, then narrowed quickly. With one hand he moved my head to bring our lips together, sweetly at first and then with more force, while his other arm lifted me and placed me directly over his shaft. I knew I should take my time but I sank down as quickly as possible, relishing the incredible stretching, craving the feeling of him filling me like his fingers had moments before, but this was so much more.

My eyes closed and I broke our kiss, my head lolling on his shoulder when he rolled his hips against mine. Once I'd recovered from the initial burst of pleasure, my fingers found his hair again and I mashed my mouth to his, our bodies rising and falling together as he thrust up and into me and I came down to meet him.

In a matter of minutes, my sharp whimpers against his lips gave way to cries that I tried to bury in his sweat-slicked shoulder. He held me tightly while started to I clench and shudder around him, shifting to lay me back on the bed. He cupped a hand behind my head, supporting himself on an elbow while his other hand grasped my upper thigh to open me at an angle where he could drive in even deeper, stroking a spot where no one had ever touched me. The waves building inside me were too much to bear, and I cried out his name over and over as the pleasure crashed through my body.

His body stiffened, his thrusts became quicker and he pushed into me one last time, a loud, deep groan escaping his lips as he buried his face deep into the crook of my neck.

I wrapped my arms around his back, sliding my fingers over the slippery, smooth muscles, and waited for our hearts to slow. After a few minutes of lying there together, Fox shifted slightly, trying to spare me the full weight of his body, but I held on tightly and he chuckled, a low rumble that I felt through his chest.

"Don't get up," I pleaded when I felt him try to move again. "Not yet."

He pulled his face away from my neck and I was rewarded with a slow, satisfied smile. "I'm not sure I'm able to anyway."

The idea that I'd rendered this strong, capable, sexy man immobile was incredibly hot, and my core clenched involuntarily. We were still joined, and Fox felt it and laughed. "Again already? You'll kill me," he joked.

"You'll love it," I countered.

"I'll die a happy man."

∽

Fox and I managed to finally roll out of bed hours later, just before lunch. I had to go pick up Annabelle at the ranch, but luckily neither of us had a diner shift that day because every time we tried to put our clothes back on, they just came right off again.

The fact that we both had today off wasn't lost on me – Joy was making the schedule lately and she had a tendency to meddle, but I wasn't complaining. Any free time I wasn't spending with Annabelle was time that I wanted to spend with Fox.

"Will I see you later?" I asked him as I buttoned my shirt for the fiftieth time. "Tonight?"

He raised up onto his elbow from where we'd been lying together on the living room futon couch, trying to watch the same movie for the last few hours. We kept cuddling, then kissing, and then eventually ending up naked, so neither of us had actually seen the movie. I didn't care.

"If you want me, I'll be there," he said.

Even though I knew it was a bad idea to get within his arms' reach if I wanted to get out of there fully clothed, I sat down next to him on the futon. "I always want you."

He sat up further, kissing me sweetly on the mouth. "Then I'll see you tonight."

A thought occurred to me. "Fox... I'm not sure what to do about Annabelle."

His brow creased. "What do you mean?"

"I mean... now that we, you know, and if you stay the night, what if she…" I stumbled.

His dimple popped. "Avery. You're overthinking this. We can find time to be alone, and nothing has to change when I come over. I care about Annabelle, and I want her to be comfortable. We'll take it one step at a time, okay?"

I nodded, feeling better.

He kissed me again, and I felt myself start to melt into him. "Not too slow, right?" I asked, and he chuckled against my lips. "Because we've already done that."

"Get out of here." He got to his feet and pulled me with him. "Before I don't let you leave."

I was still smiling when I pulled up to the ranch and the three dogs ran out to greet me on the porch. Annabelle was right behind them, wearing a towel cape and holding a wooden spoon.

"Hi, Mama!" she cried. "I'm a kitchen fairy! I made cookies!"

I scooped her up into my arms. "That's wonderful! Can I have one?"

She considered my request for a moment. "Did you finish all your lunch?"

Damn it. "No…" I admitted. Fox and I had kind of forgotten to eat.

"Then I'm sorry," she said sadly. "Those are the rules."

"Maybe Grandma will make me a sandwich," I told her. "Then can I have one?"

"Okay!" She danced happily into the house, the dogs at her heels.

"Mom?" I called.

"We're in the kitchen, Avery!" came the reply.

Annabelle and I walked into the kitchen and found my parents sitting at the wooden table having a cup of coffee. I glanced around and saw that Annabelle's cookie adventure was mostly contained, likely due to my mother's obsession with a clean countertop. The aforementioned cookies were resting on a rack near the oven and they smelled delicious. I was definitely going to try and get my hands on one without Annabelle catching me and enforcing her 'no cookies before lunch' rule.

I grabbed a cup and poured myself some coffee before joining them at the table. I had gone by my house to shower and change before I came out to the ranch but my mom gave me the oddest look over her mug, which almost caused me to look down and make sure I'd worn a shirt. My father was oblivious, reading the paper and sipping his coffee.

"How was Annabelle?" I asked them. "She seems like she had a great time." I could hear her in the living room, singing a song about cookies to the dogs. Now was my chance to get up and grab a few before she came back.

"She was a delight, as usual," my mother said. "Why weren't you home this morning?" she asked suddenly. My hand froze halfway to the cookie tray and I spun around.

"What?" Her question caught me totally off guard and I could feel my face pinking up.

"This morning. I called to see if you wanted me to bake an extra batch of cookies for you and Annabelle to take home. I never know what you have to eat at your house."

She was pissed. I could tell by the subtle dig at my grocery shopping practices. I wasn't sure what to say. No part of me regretted the night I'd spent with Fox, but I wasn't necessarily ready to defend it to my parents right at this minute.

"Did you try my cell phone?" I asked, stalling for time to think.

"No," she said. "I called you at home, because at eight a.m. on your day off I couldn't imagine where else you'd be."

"Why were you making cookies at eight in the morning?"

"Don't change the subject, Avery."

"I was out," I said lamely.

"With Fox?" she pressed. "Again?"

I sighed. I was an adult, I had a date, I'd secured appropriate care for my child, and I could do what I wanted. "No, Mom. More like *still*."

Even though I knew it was the answer she was expecting, her face still showed a little surprise. "I see."

"I care about him a lot."

"I'm sure you do," she said, rising to refill her coffee. "I hope the feeling is mutual."

"It is," I said, hating this conversation more and more as it went on. "For the second time, he's not J.D."

"Who's not J.D.?" my dad asked, surfacing from his article.

"Fox," I bit out.

"Of course he's not. Fox is a good man. You're getting closer with him, chickie?"

I nodded, smiling a little at the pleased look on his face.

"That's fine," he said, folding up the paper. "Smart boy. That's just fine."

My mom leaned against the counter, unconvinced. "I'm not so sure."

"Rebecca, let the girl alone."

"I just think Chase is a better—"

I couldn't take it any more. "You think Chase is a better choice? Chase, who cheated on me and lied to me practically since the day he came home? That Chase?"

"What are you talking about?" she demanded. "What happened?"

"Chase isn't the guy for me, Mom. Fox is. Get used to it."

∽

"It happened," I told Heather over the phone the next day.

After I had left my parents' house, Annabelle and I had gone right home and I'd spent the rest of the day cleaning, trying to get out some of my pent-up aggression toward my mother. When Fox came over later that night, I was exhausted, both from not sleeping the night before and my manic episode with the Lysol can.

As a result, I wasn't getting around to spilling the beans with Heather until more than twenty-four hours later. She was bound to be pissed but I knew she'd lighten up once I gave her the lowdown on Mama Kent's disapproval.

"IT DID?" she screeched, and I laughed as I held the phone away from my ear. "TELL ME EVERYTHING!"

"It was…" I searched for an adequate word and then gave up trying to sound sophisticated. "Fucking amazing, no pun intended.'

"Yes! I knew it. He's one of those guys who just looks like–" she broke off. "I mean, not that I was imagining it or anything."

I snorted. "Of course not."

"So what now?"

"What do you mean?"

"Well, what's the plan? Do your parents know it's serious? It *is* serious, right?" she asked worriedly.

"Yes, Heather, it's serious."

"Like, *serious* serious?" she pressed.

"What do you mean?" I asked again, even though I knew. Running Heather around in conversation was one of my very favorite things.

"Like L-O-V-E serious!" she said exasperatedly.

Love. The other night, in Fox's arms, I'd felt something that seemed a lot like love. Of course, it could've been lust, or just a deep, deep appreciation for that rock-hard body that he used so well, but I was pretty sure that it was love. Just like I was pretty sure that the last video he'd made me, the one that had me rushing over to his house and practically disrobing en route, was his way of saying the same.

Love. I loved Fox and he loved me. *Neat.*

"I gotta go, Heather."

"What? Why?"

"I have to do something," I said distractedly. Where were my keys? I wasn't due at the diner until lunch but I knew Fox would be there, cooking on the breakfast shift with Joy.

"You're really strange, you know that?" Heather laughed.

"Yup." *And Fox loooves it.* I smiled to myself.

"Wait, Avery, one more thing before you run off and do whatever you're going to do, which I think I know but I'm not totally sure, so I'll wait for you to call me later and confirm," Heather said in a rush.

"What's up?"

"Chase," Heather admitted. "He knows about you and Fox."

"He does?" We hadn't exactly been keeping it a secret, but we'd gone on most of our dates outside the main streets of Brancher, so I was curious as to how Chase had found out.

"Yes… I guess Kyle's girlfriend saw you two in Midland last week. I heard about it from my mom when she ran into Derek's mom at the grocery store. Anyhow, Chase knows, and probably the whole town."

"Does the whole town know that Chase is a lying cheat?" I asked. "Or isn't that newsworthy? Whatever, I don't care. I gotta go, Heather," I said again. "Thanks for telling me. Love you." I hung up and grabbed my bag.

I blew through the front door of the diner and barely spared a wave to Joy before heading back to the kitchen. When I walked by the pass-through I could see Fox's blond hair, tied back in his favorite bandana, and a small thrill went through me. If my heart ever failed to skip a beat in the presence of that man, I'd be disappointed.

When I stepped through the swinging door, Fox looked up from the eggs he was scrambling and gave me a wide smile. On cue, my heart skipped and I smiled back. "Hi."

"Hey, sunshine," he said. "I wasn't expecting you yet. Hungry?"

"No," I said, coming closer. "I mean, yes. Kind of. What? Not for that, so no, not really. Thanks." I sighed heavily at my bumbling response.

Fox's dimple popped as he glanced up from the eggs again. "We're back to this, are we?"

I came up close to his side. "Fox."

Quickly, he turned the burner off and slid the pan away from the heat. Turning to me, he really looked at me for the first time since I'd come into the kitchen. I knew my eyes were wide and my cheeks were flushed, and I could practically feel my heartbeat rabbiting out of control in my chest.

"What's going on?" he asked, his forehead creased with concern.

"I love you," I blurted. If there was ever a time to be smooth, it was probably now, but that wasn't my style, especially around Fox. "I love you, and you don't have to say it back, because maybe it's too soon and maybe I'm reading into things after the other night, but I don't think so, because I know how I feel." I paused, desperately sucking in a breath of much-needed air. "I really love you."

Fox reached for me, his face more serious than I'd ever seen it. His green eyes burned and his lips parted, offering just a hint of my favorite smile. "I love you, Avery."

Before I could say anything more, he swept me up and his mouth crashed down on mine hungrily. I wrapped my arms around his neck and fully surrendered to the most passionate kiss of my life. Fox urged my mouth open, stroking his tongue deeply, nipping gently at my lips between kisses. I would've let him take off all my clothes and have me on the cutting block but he pulled away after a moment, breathing heavily.

"You have to get out of here," he said, laughing.

"What?" His words registered but my mind was in a daze.

"Remember when we talked about you being a distraction?" he asked, humor flashing in his eyes.

"Yeah?" That was the beginning of the end, the day that Fox admitted he really saw me. After that, I was a goner.

"Now you're a liability. Go, before I cut off a finger or start a grease fire."

"At least you'll know how to extinguish it," I pointed out sensibly.

He laughed again and slapped my butt lightly. "I love you. GO."

"I'm going, I'm going. Want to watch me walk away?" I turned, looking over my shoulder at him slyly. The wry look on his face only made me giggle as I practically skipped out the door. "I love you too."

CHAPTER EIGHTEEN

Since we had a day off together again – thanks Joy! – and we needed whatever work-life separation we could get, Fox and I decided to have lunch somewhere other than The Kitchen. In Brancher, that didn't leave many options, so we eventually settled into a dark booth at Lucky's. It was mainly a bar, but they had a cheeseburger on the menu that probably wouldn't kill you and onion rings that would definitely kill you but were worth it anyway. We got double orders of both, because we liked to live on the edge when it came to simple carbohydrates. Or at least, I did. Fox just liked to eat.

Janie managed to stop ogling Fox and keep it professional while she took our order, which was impressive considering how she had behaved the last time she saw him. After we handed over our menus and she walked away, Fox relaxed against the pillowed booth, draping one tanned, muscled arm across the back. I immediately forgave the free weights I'd tripped over last week in the dark of his apartment.

He caught me staring and grinned. His eyes darted over my shoulder and his expression changed so abruptly, I spun around in my seat and saw Chase coming through the door with Derek and

Kyle.

I glanced back at Fox. His face was calm, observant, and utterly emotionless. I'd come to realize that was his "ready" look. Ready for whatever happened next, which was good because I certainly wasn't.

"We can go," I said quickly.

"Why?" The eyebrow was curious.

"Because… it's awkward?" I ventured.

He shrugged. "Bound to happen sooner or later. I'm surprised it's taken this long, actually." He slid a hand across the table and took one of mine, smoothing his thumb across my knuckles. "You didn't do anything wrong. And besides, we're all adults."

I barely had time to remark that Chase might not, in fact, be an adult, before I heard snickering and a couple of loud coughs coming from the direction of the bar. I turned my head to find all three of them blatantly staring at us, especially Chase, whose gaze seemed to be honed in on my hand intertwined with Fox's. My first reaction was to blush and feel guilty, but then I realized Fox was right. Brancher was a small town, we were all adults, and I hadn't done anything wrong. Let them childishly stare away.

Fox shifted slightly, bringing my attention back to him. I still felt like an animal in the zoo, but Janie showed up with our plates and I busied myself piling ketchup onto my burger and rings.

Fox watched me for a moment before he spoke. "Can I have some or should I grab another bottle?" he asked.

"What? Oh, sorry." I looked down at my food and realized I'd doused almost my entire meal absentmindedly. "I like ketchup?"

"No one likes ketchup that much," Fox countered.

"I do," I said confidently, feeling much more relaxed as Fox and I picked up our usual banter. "In fact, it's my favorite condiment."

"Good to know," he grinned, his dimple showing. "I'd peg you for a barbecue sauce girl."

I handed him the bottle and took a bite of onion ring. "Nope. Sure, it's tangy but way overrated. Ketchup is complimentary and it doesn't overpower." I gestured with my half-eaten ring. "Even in large quantities."

"I see," Fox smiled. "You have some complimentary on your face." He reached over to brush my lip with the tip of his finger.

His skin met mine, and there was a loud crash from the bar, like bottles breaking. I whipped my head around and saw Chase getting to his feet, a mess of broken glass on the floor around him. The few other patrons in the bar turned curious glances his way as he brushed the spilled beer from his clothes and started toward us.

Fox got to his feet instantly, obviously intending to intercept Chase before he reached our booth, and that caused Derek and Kyle to lurch forward also. I dropped my onion ring in defeat.

"Well, well, well… What do we have here? The lovebirds on a little date?" Chase smiled snidely. He looked around Fox to where I still sat in the booth.

"Hello, Chase," Fox said evenly. "Derek, Kyle." He acknowledged the other two men with a head nod. They seemed surprised at Fox's cordial greeting and returned it uneasily.

"Avery? You can't say anything to me?" Chase was still speaking to me around Fox, and I mentally rolled my eyes before responding.

"How are you, Chase?" My voice was as polite as I could make it.

Chase slapped his knees and started cackling like my inquiry was the funniest thing he'd ever heard. Kyle and Derek looked at each other with confusion before joining in hesitantly.

"How am I? How am I? That's a great question, babe. I'm doing fucking wonderful!" Chase swayed slightly where he stood, causing me to wonder if he'd already been drinking even though it was barely noon.

A muscle in Fox's jaw started to work when Chase replied, and I could see his body language change. He went from a casual stance to a more guarded one and sidestepped slightly to put himself directly in between me and Chase.

"That's good, man," Fox said. "We're going to get back to our lunch." He didn't make a move to return to the table, though, or turn his back to Chase. From behind him, I could see his shoulder muscles tensing, and my palms started to sweat. A beat went by, and then another, with the two of them just standing there staring at each other. Chase looked away first.

"Sure, Fox. You go on ahead," Chase nodded, backing away with his hands up. "Enjoy my leftovers."

Most of my favorite 80's movies used the beloved record-scratch sound effect at one point or another. You know, the one where someone says something so outrageous that the whole scene abruptly screeches to a halt? Chase's last dig was definitely deserving of such a moment. I watched the aftermath play out in slow motion: Chase's shitty grin, Fox's furious face, and Derek and Kyle's sudden call to attention. We had the focus of the entire bar at this point, and unfortunately I wasn't sure whose side they'd be on.

"You'd better go, Chase," Fox said slowly. "Before we do something we'll both regret." His voice was too even. He was more scary when he was this calm.

Derek and Kyle stepped up behind Chase, ready to finish whatever he started. I bit my lip nervously, trying not to draw any attention. The last thing I needed was Fox distracted because of me.

"I regret *nothing*," Chase spit.

Fox's jaw twitched again but he remained silent.

Out of the corner of my eye, I saw Lucky himself lumbering across the room from his office, Janie at his heels.

"Take this shit outside, assholes," Lucky rasped. He smacked the floor with the old baseball bat he was currently using as a cane. "I don't care who your daddy is, Dempsey. Nobody gets blood on my bar."

Chase shrugged. "Whatever, old man. We were just leaving." He gestured to Derek and Kyle.

Lucky turned his gaze to Fox. "You done too, Backdraft?"

I stifled a nervous giggle at the expression on Fox's face. It was a cross between incredulous and irritated, but it broke the ice instantly and, before I knew it, Chase and his minions were heading out onto the bright sidewalk and Fox had settled himself across from me in the booth once more.

A few moments passed while I pushed my ketchup-covered food around on my plate, and when the overall tension in the bar seemed to ease, I glanced up at Fox.

"Maybe we aren't all adults," he admitted.

"I hate to say I told you so, but..." I trailed off, shrugging. My heart finally returned to its normal rhythm once Fox's jaw unclenched, and I naively hoped that Chase would get over his bruised ego before we next saw him.

"He's not going to let this go." Fox was reading my mind as usual. "At least, not anytime soon."

"I'm afraid you're right." Chase seemed especially upset this afternoon, and I hated to think that eventually he and Fox would have a real confrontation.

Fox reached across the table to take my hand again. "I'll talk to him. Don't worry." His brow creased for a second. "Did Lucky really call me Backdraft?"

A real laugh burst from my lips at the sight of his annoyed face, and then his dimple popped and suddenly everything was okay again.

∽

"Annabelle, slow down!" I complained as she tugged on my hand. "We'll see everything, I promise."

Annabelle stopped obediently and waited for me to pull my wallet from my purse at the ticket booth. The county fair bustled all around us, lights flashing, rides spinning, and delicious smells wafting from every direction.

"I want to see the pigs!" she cried. "And go on the Ferris wheel! And get some cotton candy!"

Fox already had cash out and was exchanging it for what looked like an obscene amount of game and ride tickets. I poked him in the side and waved the wallet that I'd finally managed to procure.

"I have money," I protested.

"Great," he said. "Use it to buy yourself something nice. I'm taking my girls to the fair." He swung Annabelle up to perch on his shoulders and took my hand. "Let's go!"

I laughed and shook my head. "Where to, Annabelle?

"The piggies!" she cried, pointing to the livestock barn.

I had been worried that the incident with Chase earlier today would put a damper on our evening at the fair, but Fox never mentioned it after we left Lucky's. I was still irritated at Chase for acting like a bully and trying to call Fox out when in reality he was the one who'd been in the wrong, but I tried to brush it off so we could have a good time.

After we saw the animals, Annabelle wanted to play games, so we headed over to the fairway where all the carnival games were lined up on either side.

"Which one should we try first?" Fox asked her.

Annabelle scrunched up her face as she considered. "That one!" She pointed to the ring toss.

Fox let her go through about a billion tickets all down the row before he took over, switched games to the bottle-breaking booth, and quickly brought home the bacon in the form of what else: a stuffed pig.

"How about we all go on the carousel?" Fox suggested.

Annabelle picked her horse and insisted that Fox buckle the pig in with her. "You sit here, Mama!" she said, pointing to the horse on her left.

"What about you?" he asked me. "Need a little help?"

I grinned at him as he slid his hands around my waist and tightened the seatbelt. His fingers brushed over my thigh and we locked eyes just as the ride started to spin.

"Aren't you going to grab a horse?" I asked him.

"I think I'm fine right here."

When we got off the carousel, I wasn't sure if I was dizzy from the up-and-down motion of the horse or the way Fox's eyes hadn't left mine until he had to unbuckle Annabelle and gently lift her to the ground. She looked so happy, walking and holding his hand, clutching her prize. I knew I'd remember this night for a long time.

"Mama, I'm going to name my pig Wilbur, like the story," she said, referring to the picture book version of *Charlotte's Web* I'd bought for her.

"Wilbur is a great name," I told her.

"He's sad, though," she said.

"He is?"

"Yes, very sad," she said mournfully, her head down.

Fox glanced at me questioningly and I shrugged. You never knew with Annabelle. She had a very active imagination for three years old.

"Why is he sad?" I couldn't wait to see where this was going.

"He really wants some cotton candy."

Fox gave me a side eye and I tried not to laugh.

"Well, we can fix that. I'll go get us some, okay?" he offered.

"Yay!" Annabelle cried. "Wilbur will be so glad!"

Fox gave me a kiss on the cheek. "I'll be right back."

I nodded, and he walked away toward the brightly lit concession stands.

"Let's go on the Ferris wheel while we wait for Wilbur's snack, Annabelle." I gestured to the group gathered outside the smaller kid's version of the popular fair ride.

"Okay!" she said excitedly.

We approached the operator and I handed him two tickets.

"You have to ride in the same bucket with her," he said, looking us over with a bored expression. "She's too little to ride alone."

"Avery!"

I heard someone call my name close behind me, and when I turned around, I was face to face with Chase.

"Twice in one day… to what do I owe the honor?" he slurred. "Where's your boyfriend? Lose him already?"

"This isn't the time or the place, and you know it. If you want to talk, we'll do it privately. Later." I felt Annabelle clinging to me, hiding behind my legs, but I didn't want to turn my attention away from Chase and his volatile mood.

"I can't believe you'd lie down for him so quickly, Avery," Chase said angrily. "After all you put me through? How patient I was? How I waited for you even though I had plenty of other offers?"

"I'm sorry, what? You waited for me? Is that what you call what you were doing at that girl's house? WAITING? You really are an asshole, Chase. Leave me alone." I moved to brush past him, but he caught my arm.

"Don't walk away from me! You're making a huge mistake, you stupid bitch. Fox isn't here to stay, I promise you that. You'll come running back to me and I'll just laugh at you this time." Chase's handsome face was twisted, ugly, as he sneered at me.

I wrenched my arm out of his grasp. "Please don't hold your breath. And you know nothing about Fox, so shut your mouth!" Almost involuntarily, my hand flew back and I slapped his face.

"DAMN IT!" he roared.

Out of the corner of my eye, I could see Fox loping toward us. The next few seconds were a blur. In his drunken rage, Chase kicked the gate, then reached out and yanked the emergency handle of the carnival ride, bending the rusty metal and sending the kiddie Ferris wheel to an abrupt, screeching halt.

I heard a thin scream and then "MAMA!" and my heart skipped two beats. I whirled around, looking for Annabelle at my side, but she was gone. Frantically, my eyes skipped over a dozen children in the immediate vicinity until I heard her voice again.

"MAMA!"

Looking up, I saw Annabelle at the top of the Ferris wheel, where the jarring motion of the ride's stop had caused her to slip out of her bucket and fly forward. She was now dangling half-in, half-out of her seatbelt, her little arm bent at an impossible angle as she tried to hang on, her sneakers scrambling for purchase on the rusty metal. I could see a small trickle of blood starting to run down her cheek.

"ANNABELLE!" I screamed.

"MAMA!" she cried. "MAMA!"

Fox was at the Ferris wheel in an instant. The ride wasn't full, and luckily all the other children were in lower buckets and could safely get out. Their parents rushed around, plucking them from the seats and herding them out the gate, but I couldn't tear my eyes away from Annabelle as she hung more than twenty feet in the air. My heart had restarted and was beating triple time as I hopped the gate and ran to stand below her. My mother hurried to join me and we clasped hands, our argument forgotten.

"What happened? How did she get up there?" my mother asked. Guilt flooded me immediately. While my focus had been on Chase, Annabelle had snuck onto the ride alone.

"ANNABELLE!!" I cried again. "Hold on!"

"MAMA!" she sobbed. Tears were running down her face as she gripped the side of the bucket. "Mama, help!"

My father and Fox were desperately trying to restart the wheel to swing it down and bring Annabelle to safety but the broken handle wouldn't budge, and Fox ran over to me.

"Fox! She's hurt!" My legs were shaking and I felt powerless. I couldn't believe I'd allowed myself to be so careless, and now Annabelle was in danger.

"Avery, listen to me. She's caught in the seatbelt, and she can't fall from where she is because she'll hit that support pole. I have to get to her before the seatbelt gives out. I'm going to climb up and get her, okay?" He held both of my arms and spoke firmly. "We're going to get her down, Avery. I promise you she will be okay."

I was trembling, on the verge of a total breakdown, but I looked into his eyes and nodded.

"Annabelle, baby, hold on! Fox is coming to get you!" I yelled to her, trying to keep my voice calm.

Out of the corner of my eye, I saw a crowd had gathered, and I was sure someone had already called for help, but I knew the fire truck wouldn't get here fast enough to reach Annabelle. She'd already slipped a few more inches. My heart was beating out of my chest but I kept calling out encouragement to her, telling her what a good girl she was and how well she was doing. It was torture listening to her whimper and cry, but I kept my voice as steady as I possibly could.

Fox had started his ascent when we heard another rusty metal creak, and one of the buckets came loose right beneath his feet. Swearing, he looked up at Annabelle and jumped to the ground. He met my father's eyes for a moment before he spoke, and my dad nodded grimly.

"I can't reach her. I'm too heavy for this broken-down wheel and I'm afraid it's going to come crashing down."

I started to cry in earnest. "What? No! She can't hold on!"

"Focus, Avery. You have to do it. You have to get her. You're almost seventy pounds lighter than me, and the ride will hold you. Climb up there, pull her back into the bucket, unbuckle the belt, and then let her drop down on the other side. I'll be there to catch her." Fox's face was gentle, his voice firm, just like that day in the storm. He was good at saving us.

I didn't stop to think, I just looked up at Annabelle and started to climb. Never was I more thankful for those hours of mandatory high school gymnastics than as I pulled myself from bar to bar. Precious seconds ticked by as the voices below me got farther and farther away, but I focused on her little tearstained face and her fingers gripping the side of the bucket.

I could hear Fox in the background and vaguely registered him following my movements underneath the wheel as I picked my footing. The wheel was fairly simple to climb, but the metal was rusted and the entire ride jolted as I moved upward. When I finally reached the bucket, I pulled myself inside.

"I'm here, Annabelle! Mama's here! I've got you, baby."

Quickly, I slid my arms under her and pulled and we fell back into the bucket, where I immediately unbuckled the broken seatbelt. The crowd below let out an audible sigh. She was limp and crying but she was whole.

"Oh Annabelle! I'm so sorry!" I sobbed. Her entire life had flashed before my eyes on that climb. From infancy to first steps to yesterday, I relived it all in a few seconds.

"Mama!" she sniffed, holding me tight. "I'm sorry, Mama."

"It's okay, baby. You're okay," I soothed her.

"Avery!" Fox called. "You have to hurry. Put her over the side and I'll catch her. I'm right here."

I looked down, feeling dizzy. Now that I had Annabelle in my arms, I was reluctant to release her. I kissed the top of her head and squeezed her close to my chest, my whole body trembling. I trusted Fox to catch her, I just wasn't sure if I could bear to let her go.

"Now, Avery!" Fox's voice was urgent. I heard the creaking metal of the old wheel, and my panic renewed itself. Leaning as far out of the bucket as I could, I held tight to Annabelle's torso and prepared myself.

Fox was standing right below us, his arms out. "Drop her, Avery! You have to!"

I took a deep breath and let go. It seemed like she fell for a full minute but it was only seconds until Fox's arms closed safely around her.

"I've got her!" he shouted. "She's okay!" Fox immediately passed Annabelle to my father, who ran with her in his arms to meet the arriving EMTs, my mom right behind him.

"Fox!" I called. "How do I get down?" I tried to block out the distance between myself and the ground, but my adrenaline was waning and I felt weak and tired.

He considered for a brief second before answering. "Come down the same side you dropped her. I'll be right underneath you."

The pig. Annabelle would want me to get the pig. I stuffed Wilbur halfway into my pocket and put one leg over the side of the bucket and started to descend, my hands still shaking. Going down blind was a lot more difficult than climbing up to my frightened child.

"That's it, you're doing great," Fox encouraged.

I took another deep breath and felt around for my next

foothold. I'd only made it about three feet when the old wheel started to shudder and heave. Terrified, I glanced over my shoulder and saw I was still far from solid ground.

"Fox, it's collapsing!" I cried. The bar I was standing on detached from the main structure, and my feet started sliding downward. I gripped the pole above me as hard as I could but my hands were clammy and slipped on the metal.

"JUMP, AVERY! Jump! I'm here!" Fox yelled.

One of my hands slipped from the pole and I made a split-second decision. *Just get clear of the wheel*, I thought. Heaving myself backwards and away from the ride, I trusted Fox to catch me in my haphazard fall.

When my body collided with his, we both went down, but his arms cradled me and he shifted, protecting me from the worst of the impact. I wanted to lie there for a minute and catch my breath, but Fox got to his feet quickly, urging me to stand. The wheel was making horrible sounds, metal creaking and snapping, and we were directly underneath it. It was a dangerous place to be and we didn't have much time. I let Fox drag me up, my hipbone protesting where I'd fallen, and he quickly tugged me away from the broken Ferris wheel.

We turned around just in time to watch the ride collapse in on itself from its own weight.

CHAPTER NINETEEN

"I'd like to keep Annabelle overnight for observation, Ms. Kent." The young doctor consulted his clipboard. "The head trauma is obviously more concerning than her dislocated shoulder. There's only a slight concussion, and I'm certain she'll make a full recovery, but at her age it's better to be safe than sorry."

Four hours later, my hands were still shaking and I couldn't get warm. Was it me or was the hospital hallway freezing? *Concussion, concussion, concussion.* The word rattled and swirled around in my head, making me nauseous. I pulled Fox's fleece-lined hoodie tightly around me and shoved my fingers deep into the pockets. "Of course, Dr. Stone. Whatever you think is best."

"I'll put in my notes that she'll be released around noon tomorrow, barring any complications. You and your husband are welcome to stay in her room tonight," he said, gesturing at Fox through the window to where he sat on Annabelle's bed.

I didn't bother correcting him. Sue me, I liked that he referred to Fox as my husband. It was a small pleasure on this incredibly fucked-up night. "Thank you."

"Just ask the nurses for any extra pillows or anything you need. I'll be back to check on Annabelle in an hour or so." He flashed a warm smile at me before reaching for his buzzing cell phone and scanning the message. "The hospital administrator just informed me that the police have arrived. They'd like to ask you, and me, a few questions." His brows knit together as he read the screen. "Apparently it cannot wait."

"What? The police are here?" I'd anticipated having to deal with the police when we decided what to do about the liability of the carnival company, but not until then. Then it dawned on me. Chase. That cowardly asshole. He took off when we realized Annabelle was stuck on the ride. I hadn't told the first responders why the Ferris wheel had collapsed, but maybe someone else had. There were plenty of witnesses at the fair, and the police must've gotten at least part of the story.

"We're to meet them in a conference room on the third floor," Dr. Stone said. He gave me a sympathetic glance. We'd filled him in on the logistics of what had happened, in order for him to treat Annabelle accordingly, but the look in his eyes told me he understood it was not just an accident, it was personal. Ferris wheels didn't fall down every day, obviously. "They want to speak to your husband and parents as well. Is there someone else in the waiting area who can stay with Annabelle while we deal with this?"

"Yes, of course. My best friend is here, and my aunt. They'll sit with her while we're gone."

Heather and Joy had rushed to the hospital immediately when they'd heard the news. I was lucky to have them both in my life as a constant source of support, especially since Annabelle's birth. Joy had even stopped at my house and picked up some clothes for me and things for Annabelle, including her pajamas and her baby doll.

"Okay then. I'll see you on the third floor." Dr. Stone got into the elevator as I opened the door to Annabelle's room.

In spite of the circumstances, my heart burst into a million happy pieces when I saw Fox and Annabelle snuggled up in her hospital bed. Her little head, complete with a large white bandage, rested on Fox's chest as he read her a Fancy Nancy book that Joy had stuffed into our overnight bag, and the arm without the sling clutched her baby doll tightly. *Concussion.* My heart beat in time with the syllables. I shoved my guilt aside and smiled at them.

"Hi, Mama." Annabelle sat up. "Fox is reading me Fancy!"

"That's so nice, baby," I said, my heart still stuttering as I took in the vision of my precious daughter and the completely surprising man next to her. Fox met my eyes and his beautiful mouth turned up at the corners just slightly. Once again, the intensity and depth of his look took my breath away.

"Fox," I began, shaking my head slightly to clear my thoughts. He chuckled, and I gave him a half-annoyed glare. He knew exactly what he did to me at all times. Including right now, which was getting my mind off her bandage and her sling, and into the gutter. Because he loved me and Annabelle. And he wanted to take care of us. And he didn't want me to worry, ever, about anything.

"Fox," I tried again, firmer this time. "They want to see us on the third floor."

His forehead creased as his brows lifted. "Who?"

"P-O-L-I-C-E," I spelled, not wanting Annabelle to understand. She was old enough to know that uniforms and badges were serious, and she'd been through a lot today already.

His eyes flashed. I knew it was taking every bit of his self control not to hop on his bike and go looking for Chase, but his concern for Annabelle's well-being trumped his anger. For now. I just hoped the police found Chase before Fox did, for Chase's sake. Between the attempted uneven bar brawl and Annabelle's accident, Chase was no friend of Fox's anymore. A less loyal man would've dismissed Chase a long time ago, but even Fox had his hard limits.

"Bells, I have to get up, okay?" My heart lurched again when he called Annabelle by her nickname. "Mama and I will be right back."

"Auntie Heather and Auntie Joy will come sit with you while we're gone, baby," I said to her. "We're going to get more pudding." I hated to lie, but I was also actually planning to find more pudding because Fox had eaten all of mine earlier.

"Okay! Chocolate please, Mama." Annabelle smiled.

Fox swung his legs off the bed and shoved his feet into his

unlaced boots. He stood, stretching his arms above his head. His long-sleeved thermal shirt rode up just barely over the waistband of his jeans, exposing lean, tanned muscle. Warm, tingly sensations ran through me as I thought about his chest without the shirt altogether. I looked away. *Entirely inappropriate, Avery,* I told myself.

Fox kissed Annabelle's cheek. "We'll finish Fancy Nancy when I get back, okay?" Annabelle nodded sleepily and curled up with her thumb in her mouth.

The door opened and Heather popped her head in. "Hi dollface! Auntie Joy and I thought it might be fun to watch a movie while your Mama's gone." She stepped into the room with Joy right behind her, taking in Annabelle's drowsy eyes and thumb-sucking.

In an aside to me, she said "Your daddy told us y'all had a little interview to get to." Rolling her eyes, she continued. "I can only imagine what strings will be pulled in regard to those consequences."

Unfortunately, I knew she was right. While I didn't expect to see him with a long sentence for what was definitely a thoughtless, drunken mistake, Chase had endangered quite a few people tonight, my own child most of all. *Concussion,* my heartbeats reminded me. He should sit in a cell for a while and know that.

But with his family's influence in the county, I'm sure he'd get a slap on the wrist and nothing more. If Annabelle had been severely hurt, no judge or jury would be able to curb my crusade for justice, and luckily that wasn't the case. I'd love to see him in a superbly degrading community service situation, but I knew even that outcome was doubtful. Regardless, God help him the next time we were face to face.

"Is he all right?" Heather whispered to me, nodding toward Fox, who had an intense look as he watched Joy chat with Annabelle. Not just angry but fierce, with the wheels turning full speed. He did a good job smoothing his expression for Annabelle's benefit but didn't bother to mask it when she wasn't looking.

I frowned. "No. He wants to find him."

Heather's eyes grew wide. "Bad idea."

"No kidding." My head pounded. I needed caffeine, or a sedative, or a vacation, or a time machine to rewind today and avoid this mess altogether.

Heather gave me a quick, one-armed hug. She smelled sweet, like the sugar cookies she'd doled out to the kids from her concession booth at the fair.

"How 'bout we all cozy up and watch that *Tangled* movie you like so much?" Joy held up a portable DVD player. I was touched again by how thoughtful they both were.

Heather and Joy squeezed onto the bed, Annabelle between them. They looked a little cramped, but happy. I tucked Annabelle's special blanket over their laps and kissed the tip of her nose. Joy started the movie, and Annabelle was immediately engrossed in the drama of Rapunzel and Flynn Rider, although her big eyes drooped with fatigue. I glanced at the clock and saw it was after ten p.m. Of course she was tired. It was hours past her bedtime and she'd been through a traumatic experience, first on the Ferris wheel and then again when she was poked and prodded upon her arrival to the hospital.

How had I allowed this to happen? And when would it really be over? Bumps and bruises would heal, but what about the drama outside these hospital walls? *And how could I make sure it all ended here, before more people I loved were hurt?* My breath caught as I considered the ramifications of small-town gossip and good ole boys' loyalty. I had to nip this in the bud, now, before it all blew up in my face.

"We'll be back soon," I said softly, taking Fox's hand as we left the room.

∽

In the elevator, I turned to Fox.

"Tell me what's going on in your head." I slid my arms around him. Under my hands his muscles relaxed slightly, and he exhaled.

"I'm sorry, Avery." His turbulent green eyes met mine.

"What for?" I asked, surprised.

"I'm so angry," he bit out as he broke my hold, his fury renewed. "I don't give a shit how drunk he was! It doesn't matter! He was fucking stupid and reckless, and he put those kids in danger tonight. Annabelle... any of them could've gotten really hurt." His broad chest heaved, and he moved to lean against the wall of the elevator, clenching his fists, the muscles of his forearms bunched and tight. "This was about me and him, and no one else. I'm so sorry, Avery. Annabelle is in that hospital bed tonight because I let this get out of control. I should've taken care of it earlier, at the bar." His eyes were on fire.

"I'm angry too. But it's not your fault. Chase went off the handle. And I know what you're thinking. At least, some of it," I amended, as he raised an eyebrow skeptically. "But we have to let the police find Chase." I moved close to him again, until our chests touched and he bent to rest his forehead against mine. "Promise me you won't go outlaw, okay? I need you here with us."

I hated to play the clingy card, but I knew it was the only thing that would keep him close. I had to keep it together for Annabelle, and Fox on the hunt would be the straw that broke me.

Fox looked over my shoulder for a moment, lost in thought. A muscle in his jaw worked furiously even as his gentle hands came up to my sides.

"Okay. I promise. For now." His lips brushed mine, his arms encircling my waist and pulling me up tightly against him.

Any thoughts I had about Chase or the police went directly to the back burner of my mind as Fox's warm mouth skimmed over my lips, coaxing me to open and let him in. His tongue traced the curve of my lips before sucking my tongue into his mouth slowly, and I melted against him, allowing him to support my entire weight as he explored my tongue with his own.

He took all his worry, and mine, and put it into that kiss, hoping to erase the events of the day with low whispers of love as his nose skimmed up my jawline, his hot breath tickling me as his lips found the hollow behind my ear and slowly worked their way back to my mouth. I vaguely heard the mechanical ding signaling our floor, but I was lost in Fox.

The elevator doors opened, and Fox reluctantly released my mouth with a final nip to my lower lip. I opened my eyes and was embarrassed to realize we had an audience of three wide-eyed nurses. Fox nodded his head to them politely.

"Ladies." His shy smile made him even more endearing, if possible, like a sweet little boy who got caught with his hand in the candy jar. *My* candy jar, specifically.

Mortified, I turned fifteen shades of red and grabbed his hand, tugging him out of the elevator. *Concussion, concussion,* my heart stuttered, refreshing my guilt. We quickly walked down the hallway to the conference room but not before I heard one of the nurses sigh to her friend.

"Wow," she murmured.

From the expansion of his grin, I knew Fox heard her too. As we walked, I thought I noticed a slight hitch in his gait and immediately my mind flashed back to falling into his arms from the top of the Ferris wheel, and then us crashing to the ground... his leg. *Oh no.* Was there more damage? How badly was it hurting him?

Fox saw me glance down and pulled me to a stop just outside the doors. "I'm fine. Don't worry. It's nothing."

My entire brave facade crumbled under the reassuring look on his face. "Shit, Fox, your leg! I didn't even think. You caught me, and Annabelle, and..." Tears welled up in my eyes again. "You're hurt too. Both of you are."

"No, sunshine, I'm okay. I'll be good as new in a few days. Please don't cry," he murmured into my temple as he pulled me against him. He smoothed a hand down my back. "I just need a little rest and a good stretch. I'm slacking on my PT lately... been a little distracted." I could hear the smile in his voice and then his fingers lightly tapped my butt.

I looked up into his confident face and tried to push my anxiety back down from where it bubbled in my throat. I'd never met a person who knew himself and his body better than Fox, so I decided to take his words as truth. These days he radiated health and self-assuredness, and his positive demeanor was a calming balm on my frazzled nerves.

His expression changed two seconds later, however, as we entered the meeting room and found the police chief, two officers, my parents, and Dr. Stone waiting for us. His guard went up, his shoulders squared, and his eyes sharpened. I felt his tension radiate down through his fingers, and when I rubbed my thumb soothingly over his, his face didn't register the contact.

Fox wasn't just angry. He was furious.

"Ms. Kent, Mr. Fox, I'm sorry for pulling y'all away from Annabelle tonight." Chief Barnes met my eyes briefly as Fox and I settled into the empty chairs, a sympathetic look on his worn, wrinkled face. It didn't really surprise me that the chief got pulled into this case, especially given our close-knit county, but I was a bit surprised at how fast the whole thing had mobilized. The last name Dempsey really meant high profile. "This won't take but a minute and then we'll get out of your hair." He gestured to one of his deputies who began recording our statement on the iPad in the middle of the table.

"We're here to discuss the accident involving Annabelle Kent, on the evening of November tenth, at the Ector County Fairgrounds. A malfunction on the Ferris wheel rendered it inoperable, causing the minor child Annabelle harm and injury as a passenger on the ride," the chief stated for the recording, consulting his notes.

Fox stiffened next to me when Barnes mentioned Annabelle.

"After the ride malfunctioned, the child's mother, Avery Kent, climbed the wheel to retrieve the child, before the wheel's collapse. The first responders at the scene noted Annabelle's potential concussion and dislocated shoulder, transported her to the hospital, and she was admitted, where Dr. Eric Stone confirmed the injuries and treated her as needed," Barnes continued. "That is our official report thus far. Now, I'd like to ask y'all a few questions to fill in the gaps."

❧

After Barnes and his deputies left the room, I slumped down in my chair, cradling my head in my arms as I rested them on the table. The interview went exactly as I'd imagined it would. Not enough evidence, witness accounts pending, unable to confirm Chase's whereabouts at the time of the accident, no permanent damage done. I was welcome to try and sue the carnival company for faulty equipment and allowing Annabelle on the ride in spite of the height restriction, but no individual criminal charges were to be pressed by the county in regard to the incident.

But he knew. Every weathered line on Chief Barnes' face told the real story. His hands were tied, his department was funded largely by Dempsey philanthropy, too many politics were involved, and there was nothing he could do. He looked at me with a combination of guilt and compassion and told me they would look into it, but we both knew nothing would come of any investigation. My stomach churned with disgust and disappointment. Just another reason to get the hell out of Brancher as soon as possible, away from the long reach of the Dempsey association.

My parents were talking softly with Dr. Stone when I stood up suddenly and shoved my chair back. I was sick of tiptoeing around this town like I had done something wrong. My sweet baby was in a hospital bed with a concussion, all because I'd dared to try and find happiness after confronting my lying ex-boyfriend about his infidelity. Chase had cheated on me, and yet I was the one being punished by the entire county.

"Avery, where are you going?" my mother asked as I strode toward the exit.

Fox jumped up from his chair, close on my heels when I slammed open the heavy metal door and burst into the hallway, nearly running into Janice Dempsey as she walked from the hospital cashier's office to the elevator.

"I knew it!" I cried. "I knew you were here somewhere. This police interview had your name written all over it," I said, making air quotes when I spit out the words 'police interview.'

"Avery," Janice said calmly, giving me a slightly condescending once-over. "How nice to see you, unfortunate circumstances aside."

"Are you kidding? Nice to see me? You've never been glad to see me, not once in my life. I'm sure you're ecstatic that Chase and I broke up, as am I, but he almost killed my daughter tonight, so excuse me if I don't share your enthusiasm for our not-so-coincidental meeting," I fumed. I felt Fox come up behind me, his presence rock steady and reassuring, even though I knew his hold on his own temper was tenuous.

Janice met my eyes coolly as usual, but I saw something different in her gaze this time. "I'm afraid I've severely underestimated you, Avery, and that's become very apparent to me in the last few months. You're a strong woman and an excellent mother and, for those reasons, you're correct. I'm glad you're no longer dating my son."

For a moment I was shocked, and then I found my voice. "I'm sorry, I don't understand. You don't like me. You never have."

"That's not true, my dear. I used to tolerate you, because I thought you were good for Chase. He needs a woman who will let him be and turn the other cheek when he strays or lets her down. He's too much like his daddy's side, you see, weak and easily influenced. I was hoping firefighting would give him a little backbone, some integrity. But he's the same as he ever was. And you, Avery, are not." Those cool eyes met mine again, and now I recognized the difference. She was looking at me with something very similar to respect.

"You don't know me." The direction of this conversation was beyond disturbing.

"On the contrary. I know you very well. You're a mother doing whatever it takes to protect her child. As am I." Her gaze sharpened.

There was the Janice I knew. "My baby could've died tonight."

"You're correct again, and for that I'm very sorry. I wish nothing but the best for you and your little girl. You and I both know that is not my son, and I'm happy you realized it sooner than later. But he is my son, and I am his mother, and I will do whatever it takes to protect him and keep him out of jail. Period."

That woman's spine was made of cold, hard, bitchy steel with a side of dictator. "So that's it? He endangers a group of children, causes injury and chaos, and drunkenly drives away? It's good to be a Dempsey," I remarked darkly.

Janice ignored my sarcasm. "I've taken the liberty of covering Annabelle's hospital bills and any further expenses she might accrue in outpatient care or physical therapy. The cashier's office will provide you with a receipt. I'm also prepared to offer you a cash settlement, seeing as you likely won't get a penny from the carnival company."

"I don't want your money!" I cried. "I want Chase to leave me alone! I want to go back in time and erase this nightmare from my child's memory." I wrapped my arms around myself and shook my head. "I don't need you to buy me off. I don't want anything to do with any of you."

"I knew you'd say that." Janice regarded me thoughtfully. "That's why I've already placed the money in a joint trust for you and Annabelle, with you as the executor, for incidentals, her college fund, or any other needs that might arise. My lawyer will be in touch with the paperwork."

Before I could respond, Fox cut in. He'd been silent through this entire exchange, and his voice was rough as he addressed Janice.

"This isn't over. Between me and him, it isn't over."

Janice turned her gaze smoothly, without an ounce of surprise. "Mr. Fox, contrary to what I'm sure is popular opinion here in Ector County, I have nothing but the utmost respect for you and the selfless work you represent. My daddy was a soldier, a hero, and the best man I've ever known. I was hoping for some of the same to rub off on Chase after he insisted on public service instead of football, but I'm not sure that's been the case. You saved my boy's life once, and I trust that you won't take it now."

Fox's gaze was steady, pensive, as she spoke. "I'll find him before the police do."

"I don't doubt that for a minute. But I also know, after you're finished beating on each other, you'll deliver him to my doorstep mostly intact. I don't think Chase is innocent here, and I'm more sorry than you know for what happened to Annabelle. What's between you and Chase is no business of mine. I know you're a good man, Mr. Fox. Put the fear of God back into my boy, and protect what's yours. I would expect nothing less." With that, she turned on her heel and continued down the hall.

Fox and I watched her walk away in slow motion and, after she entered the elevator, he turned to me, a strange expression on his face.

"Is it wrong that I'm not sure if I hate her or almost... like her?" he asked.

I laughed bitterly. "Ten minutes ago, I would've said you needed your head examined. But after that conversation, I'm conflicted too."

CHAPTER TWENTY

When Dr. Stone finally released Annabelle in the late afternoon of the following day, I couldn't wait to get home and try to put the last twenty-four hours far behind us. My parents and Heather were on hand to help me and Fox get Annabelle situated on the couch with fluffy pillows, snacks, coloring books, and cartoons. Joy sent her love and promised to come by with fresh pie after she finished her diner shift.

Once everyone left, and it was just Fox, Annabelle, and me in my little cottage, I excused myself from the living room and went straight down the hall to the bathroom. Fox glanced up curiously as I passed, but luckily Annabelle was distracted by the Disney channel and didn't notice my abrupt exit or the expression on my face. I was sure that Fox did, but he let me go without comment.

A sob hitched in my throat as I slid down the wall next to the closed bathroom door. *Just five minutes,* I told myself. *You can have five minutes to lose your shit, and then you have to pull it together and go be a mother and a girlfriend and a student and everything else. You are allowed five minutes of weakness and then it's business as usual.*

And so I sat on that cold tile floor in my cramped but cheerful bathroom, and I cried. I cried for Annabelle and everything that could've happened but didn't. I cried because I wanted so much for her and wasn't sure how I was going to make it work, and because she'd given so much to me already by making me her mama.

I cried for Chase, because yesterday was the final death of a complicated relationship that made up half a decade of my life. I cried for the man I thought he was, and for the man he turned out to be.

I cried for Fox, and his poor leg, his impeccable timing, and his beautiful, generous soul that I wasn't sure I deserved. And I cried for me, because I needed to, and because it was silly and naive to think I didn't, even though I prided myself on always keeping it together no matter what.

When my five minutes were up, and I was determinedly mopping up my mess of a face with a wad of tissues, there was a soft knock on the bathroom door.

"Avery? Are you okay?" Fox's voice was low and gentle.

I gave my face one last swipe and opened the door. Fox was standing in the doorway, one arm bent and braced on the frame, the other raised to knock again. His gaze swept me quickly, and when he reached my tearstained face and red-rimmed eyes, his expression changed from confusion to worry.

"What's wrong? Are you sick?" He stepped into the bathroom and quickly gathered me into his arms.

"No, I'm not sick. I'm just… it's been a long couple of days," I said into his shoulder. His T-shirt felt smooth and cool against my hot cheek.

Fox exhaled as he rested his chin on the top of my head. "I'm so sorry you had to go through this. But it ends now. I will never let anything happen to Annabelle, or to you." He pulled back and took my face into his hands. "I love you."

I stood on my tiptoes to press my lips to his. "I love you too. And thank you. For everything."

"You were so brave, way more than you give yourself credit for." Fox looked serious. "You did it, you climbed up there all on your own."

"You knew I could. Your faith in me got me to the top of that wheel and got us both down." I repeated to him my one coherent thought from those first panicked minutes after we'd realized Annabelle was stuck on the ride. "You're always saving us."

His mouth quirked up on one side. "Just returning the favor, sunshine."

∽

I'd barely finished putting Annabelle to bed and stepped out into the hallway when there was a knock at the door. Expecting Joy, some warm berry pie, and maybe even a little ice cream to go with it, I jogged to the front door and threw it open.

"Avery, wait–" Fox came bolting from the living room, his face concerned, but it was too late.

I stepped back with shock when I saw Chase on my doorstep. My head spun and I felt rivulets of ice coursing through my veins. And then I lunged, pushing Chase backward a few steps until he was on the sidewalk.

"You fucking asshole!" I screamed, heedless of the neighbors. My fists rained down on Chase's arms and chest, landing blow after blow as I half-sobbed, half-screamed the phrase over and over.

Chase did nothing to protect himself or to restrain me, he just took the beating for about thirty seconds until Fox pulled me off him and moved me back through the doorway. I stood there, my chest heaving, and glared at Chase.

"Get inside, and stay there! Please, Avery." Fox's voice was angry but controlled. "Please."

I was out of breath, hysterical and exhausted, but I did as Fox asked. The look in his eyes was pleading toward me, but murderous when he turned his gaze on Chase. I knew better than to argue with Fox when his eyes looked like that. I nodded and moved to shut the door.

"Avery," Chase started, his voice raspy. "I'm so sorry. Is she... is she okay? My mom said she was okay." He looked up at me from the bottom of the porch, his expression hooded and sad.

"She will be." I took a deep breath, trying to keep my voice steady. "Don't come back here, Chase. I don't ever want to see your face again. EVER!" I slammed the door and immediately burst into tears for the second time. Today, I deserved more than just five minutes of crying. I was going to give myself another ten.

∽

Two minutes into my ten, I was sitting against the front door trying to ignore the raised voices outside when I heard another car pull up and a woman's angry shout.

"Do not make me get the shotgun out of my truck, Chase Dempsey! Get on out of here now!" Joy had arrived.

I quickly opened the door and ushered her in.

"What's happening?" she demanded, taking in my freshly tearstained face and shaking hands. "What's he doing here?"

I glanced out the window, and it took all of my willpower not to freak out again when Chase and Fox got into Fox's truck and drove away, but I figured it was better that whatever happened between them took place in a location other than my front lawn.

"Fox wants to talk to him," I said. "We weren't expecting him to just show up, though. At least, I wasn't."

I thought back to how quickly Fox had reached the door when Chase knocked. His boots were still on, even. Maybe I was the only one who hadn't thought Chase would visit tonight.

"I'm going to check on Annabelle real quick, and I'll be right back. Make yourself at home, okay?"

"Sure, darlin'. I'll make us a pot of coffee to go with the pie. I don't know where those boys got off to, but I know neither one of us will sleep until Fox comes back."

It was nearly three a.m. when I finally saw Fox's headlights in the driveway. I'd given up on sleeping alone in my bed, and instead pulled an old afghan off the back of the couch and settled in to watch a few rerun episodes of *Friends* while I waited. I'd considered polishing off the rest of the pie but decided I might need it to help digest whatever situation presented itself upon Fox's return.

Joy had gone home around midnight, under protest, but I knew she had to work the early lunch shift at the diner the next day, and no one wants a drowsy waitress overfilling coffee into their lap. She left in a flurry of kisses and promises that I'd text her as soon as I heard anything, good or bad.

I was just sending that dutiful text when Fox came through the door, looking tired and a little dirty. He kicked off his boots in the hallway and stopped when he saw me lying on the couch, the TV flickering in the semi-darkness.

"I wish you hadn't waited up," he said softly, coming closer.

"You knew I would." I could barely make out a hint of a bruise forming on his cheekbone, but other than that he looked fine. I wondered briefly if Chase could say the same, and then decided I didn't care.

He laughed once. "You're right. I did."

I sat up and scooted over to make room for him so he could sit next to me on the couch. "What happened?"

"I did what Mrs. Dempsey asked me to. I returned him mostly in one piece." Fox ran a hand through his hair. "When it came down to it, when it was just about me and him, it didn't go as either of us expected."

I waited patiently as Fox gathered his thoughts. He shifted toward me so we were facing each other on the couch and took one of my hands in his, idly skimming my fingers with his knuckles.

"There's something that happens to you when you go through an experience like the situation where we met," he said, referring to his time with Chase in the Forest Service. "Suddenly life or death actually means life or death, in the most real way possible. Everything else sort of pales in comparison." Fox looked up from our hands and gave me his quirky half-smile.

"It probably sounds strange, but I try to remember that. I hold on to that feeling every day. It helps me, it centers me, to keep that perspective close." He kissed my knuckle, the one that was scraped from my climb. "Chase forgot."

I shook my head, trying to take it all in. Chase forgot, and my beautiful, complicated, sometimes intense but always noble firefighter reminded him. And although he didn't say it, I knew it wasn't mainly with his fists. Beyond the territorial nonsense and the pride, Fox and Chase shared a bond that was fractured but never completely broken.

"Where is he now?" I asked.

"At home." Fox paused. "He's stone-cold sober and nursing a black eye and a busted lip, but he'll be all right."

I raised an eyebrow, and he shrugged.

"He told me he was genuinely sorry about endangering Annabelle, and I punched him twice in the face. It was a reflex." Fox grinned, and then his face turned serious. "For what it's worth, I believe him."

I nodded slowly. "I believe him too, but that doesn't change how I feel. I don't want him in our lives." My mind flashed back to the defeated look on Chase's face when I pummeled him with my fists on the sidewalk.

"I know, sweetheart. He has a lot to figure out, and he needs time to do it, and probably a little professional help." Fox stood up and raised his arms over his head, his back to me. I admired the way his broad shoulders bunched and contracted under his shirt even as I yawned, but watching him stretch like a lazily powerful lion definitely perked me up a little. He turned and reached for my hand to pull me off the couch.

"C'mon. Let's check on Annabelle and then try to get some sleep."

Neither of us made any mention of Fox going home tonight, and I was glad it wasn't up for discussion. I wanted him here. I let him help me to my feet, and we headed down the hall to peek into

Annabelle's room. Satisfied that her breathing was even and steady, I led the way into my bedroom.

When we crossed the threshold, I turned and paused just inside the room. Fox stopped short, a briefly confused look flitting over his handsome features. "Did you forget something in the other room?"

I reached up, running my hands down his chest softly. I shook my head no, my heart pounding as I touched him. We stood like that for a moment, breathing each other in, before I grasped the hem of my oversized T-shirt and slipped it off. Dropping it to the floor by my side, I looked up into Fox's eyes. The moonlight streaming in from the window backlit my body, and I registered Fox's change of expression as he stared at me. His eyes narrowed, his lips parted, and his hands reached toward me.

I slowly moved toward my bed until the back of my knees hit the mattress. Fox came to me like a magnet, his hands smoothing over my hips and waist, touching and whispering over my body. His mouth followed his fingers, leaving a hot trail on my bare skin. I slid my hands under his shirt, my palms skimming over his abdominal muscles on their way to his chest. He pulled back for a brief second, reaching behind him to pull his shirt over his head, and then his mouth latched onto mine.

He kissed me slowly, thoroughly, taking his time while all of my nerve endings danced and exploded under his touch. My legs started to buckle and he held me up, supporting my back as he gently lowered me to the bed. My hands found his belt, and I fumbled for a second before it gave way. Finally free of the last barrier between us, he came over me, supporting himself on his forearms so as not to crush me with his weight.

I couldn't get close enough, and he laughed against my mouth as I tried to pull him down on top of me, craving the skin-to-skin contact. "Slow down, sunshine. I'm right here."

His lips skimmed over my jaw, down my neck, to my breasts, where he nudged a nipple into a hard peak before taking it into his mouth. I ran my hands through his hair as he swirled his tongue around and around, drawing small sounds of excitement from me. The stubble from his jaw rubbing on my sensitive skin only heightened the pleasure until I thought I would burst from the growing pressure between my legs.

"I need—" I gasped. I couldn't finish the sentence before his mouth was on mine again, his strong callused hand replacing his mouth at my breast. He kneaded and plucked my wet nipple, sending shockwaves through my body down to my center. I spread my legs wide and he shifted to cradle himself between my thighs, the tip of his erection just brushing the exact spot where I wanted friction.

Fox's tongue stroked the inside of my mouth in deep, slow licks that kept pace with his hand at my breast and pressure at my core, until the sensation was too much for me to handle. I broke our kiss and turned my head, exposing my throat to his lips and teeth as I strained to raise my hips and bring him inside me. A deep, delicious groan rose in his throat as his mouth pressed hotly behind my ear.

"Fox, please—" My hands ran desperately over his lean back muscles, pressing him closer.

"Look at me, Avery." His hands came up to hold my face gently. The teasing motion of his hips stilled and I came back down to earth briefly. When my eyes met his, something shifted, just like it always did. In one swift motion, he pushed forward, so deep it forced a cry from my throat, which I muffled in his shoulder as I held him to me. Our movements were beautifully in sync, our breaths catching and holding together as he moved inside me, and in a moment of clarity between the pleasure I thought that nothing had ever been this good for anyone but us.

Fox's murmured endearments at my ear let me know that he felt the same. "I love you, Avery. I'd do anything for you."

Even though I was supposed to be the writer among us, I had no words for what I was feeling. So instead, I let his strong hands and stronger promises caress my skin and fill my heart and my ears while we burned brighter than ever, and held each other until we cooled.

⌒

Three days later, Chase Dempsey once again 'prepared to disappear from Brancher. This time his departure wasn't heroic, or dramatic, or even widely discussed. Word on the street was that he was simply going to Lubbock to manage the Dempseys' second car dealership, which was stagnant and in need of a resurrection.

I knew better, of course. In spite of myself, I was almost touched that Chase would sacrifice this town for me, that he would up and leave a place that worshipped him just so I could have some peace. At once I felt it was both too much and not enough.

I recalled Fox's comment about Chase potentially needing professional help, and the more I thought about it, the more it seemed likely. Even through my anger, I hated to think of him suffering. I'd loved him once, a hopeful, childish love perhaps, but there was still a place in my heart for the boy he used to be.

"Are there resources available to help him?" I'd asked Fox out of the blue the day before.

He looked up from his reading, curiously. This was an almost picture-perfect replica of the weekend morning I'd daydreamed about all those weeks ago. We were both reading, relaxing on the couch while Annabelle set up a tea party for her dolls, and Fox was deeply engrossed in a thick nonfiction novel about World War II, but he set the book aside and faced me.

"Yes. But he has to want help." Fox looked off over my shoulder briefly, his eyes clouded. "It's a sensitive topic, one that unfortunately comes with a bit of a stigma."

Fox's expression cleared, and he looked back at me but didn't seem inclined to say anything further. On impulse, I took his hand into mine and squeezed.

"You can tell him it's okay. He'll listen to you." I wasn't intimately familiar with the hierarchy but I knew that Fox felt a responsibility toward his crew, even out of the wilderness, and that seeing Chase clearly suffering was difficult for him, especially in light of recent events.

"I already did. It's up to him now."

∽

I saw Chase's move to Lubbock in a new light after that, a fresh start for him too, where he could be semi-anonymous and hopefully get himself back on track. I was still so furious at him for what he'd done and how he'd treated me, but I had to take his current mental state into consideration and open my mind to forgiveness.

After a lot of thought, I decided to see him one more time before he left town. Fox was cooking at the diner, and I left Annabelle with my parents before I started the drive out to the Dempseys' spread. My heart beat nervously as I turned onto the long driveway leading to the house. I thought about all the times I'd been down this road, both years ago and then as recently as a few months past.

Chase was sitting on the wraparound porch when I pulled up, as though he expected me. He got to his feet quickly, and his eyes never left mine while I parked and got out of the car. I could see the bruise on his face and the swollen lip as I got closer. We met halfway between the driveway and the porch steps.

"Hello, Avery." His voice sounded sad and far away. "I didn't think you'd come."

I shrugged. "I didn't either."

"Do you want to come in, or sit down..." He trailed off, realizing he'd gestured to the porch swing where we'd spent time as a high-school couple.

"No thanks, I can't stay," I said softly. A sudden surge of sadness overtook me, and I had to look away from his serious face. I kept my gaze down on my boots, toeing a loose rock from the driveway's gravel.

"Okay." Chase seemed resigned. "Look, I–"

"Chase, we–" I said at the same time.

We both stopped.

"Go ahead, I'm sorry," Chase said.

"No, you first."

He took a deep breath. "Avery, I am so sorry. I know I can be a total jackass sometimes, in fact, probably most of the time, but you have to believe me when I tell you that I would never intentionally do anything to hurt you or your daughter." Chase's voice was gruff with emotion.

"Everything got so out of hand," he continued. "I was hurt and angry, even though I had no right to be after what I did to you, going behind your back with that girl. But then a few weeks later, when I found out you'd been seeing Fox, I just lost it." He shook his head sadly. "And then, on top of trying to pick a fight with Fox, I went and did this. I'm sure you can never forgive me, but you have to know how damn sorry I am."

I decided to say what I'd come to say before my throat closed up completely. "I don't know if I can ever forget what happened to Annabelle, how you blindly and drunkenly put her in danger, but I can forgive you. I can forgive you because I know that while sometimes you are incredibly self-absorbed and have no awareness of how your actions affect others, you are not a bad person. This person you've been lately, that isn't really you. I know you didn't want to hurt us." The lump in my throat was rising out of control, and I desperately tried to swallow it back down.

"I messed up. I know that. I could never forgive myself if Annabelle wasn't okay. Thank you for coming, hearing me out, and for what you said. I'm going to miss you, both of you." He took a half step toward me uncertainly.

I followed my instinct and stepped into his arms. We hugged for a long minute, him holding me close but not too tightly, and when I pulled back, he released me immediately.

"I hope you find whatever it is you're looking for, Chase." It sounded clichéd but I meant it. Since his return he hadn't seemed settled, and I wanted that for him.

Chase nodded. "I have a lot of shit to figure out," he said, echoing Fox's words from the other night. "I thought I could come back here, pick up where we left off and be the prince again, but it's not working." He sighed. "I want you to be happy, Avery. Really. We both know I wasn't the guy to make it happen. I wanted to be but trust me, you deserve better."

"Better like Fox?" I asked, curious to hear his response.

"Yeah," he said, smiling ruefully. "As much as I hate to admit it, exactly like Fox."

CHAPTER TWENTY-ONE

"**A**very?" my mom called from the office. "Do you have a minute?"

I'd just put on my coat to go pick up Annabelle, but I glanced at my watch and saw that I had extra time. My mother and I hadn't spoken much in the couple weeks since the incident at the fair, aside from updates about Annabelle's condition. I was still irritated about her opinion on Fox, and I didn't have much else to say on the matter. But I was raised to be polite, so I grabbed my purse and headed in her direction.

"What's up?" I asked, coming in and taking a seat on the old couch across from the desk.

"How's Annabelle?" Routine ice breaker.

"She's fine. I have to go get her at school in a little bit," I said, indicating that I couldn't stay long.

"Of course," she nodded.

We sat looking at each other awkwardly for a moment, and then she sighed. "I owe you an apology about Fox. He's not like J.D., not at all, and I see that now."

"Thank you," I said, knowing how hard it was for her to admit she was wrong. "I appreciate that."

"You have to understand, Avery," she continued. "It's the hardest thing in the world to watch your beautiful, headstrong, independent daughter make choices that you don't agree with. I can't stand to see you hurt or struggling. And so I have opinions."

"Lots of them," I remarked dryly.

"Lots of them," she agreed. "You'll understand when Annabelle is older."

I groaned. "Luckily that's a long time from now." I couldn't even imagine Annabelle as a teen, much less a full-grown, sassy adult. I wondered how long she would still want to wear a princess crown everywhere she went.

Her smile turned a little wistful. "It'll go by in a flash."

I checked my watch. "I have to go, Mom. Love you."

"Love you too, sweetheart."

I ran out the door to where my car was parked out back, pausing to see if I could catch a glimpse of Fox through one of the upstairs windows. He was scheduled for the dinner shift tonight, and I was kind of surprised that he hadn't come down earlier before I finished my last tables.

I was unlocking the sedan when a big, shiny, black SUV pulled into the lot and Fox hopped out of the backseat. *What the hell?* He waved to whoever was still inside and turned to jog up the stairs to his apartment, when he saw me standing there staring.

"Hey!" he called, heading in my direction.

"Hey yourself," I said warily. Who was in that SUV? It looked like a chauffeured car. And why was Fox wearing a collared shirt and very expensive-looking slacks?

He bent his head to kiss me, and for a couple seconds I forgot all of my questions. I stepped closer into his warmth and wrapped my arms around his waist. He even smelled different, less like the cedarwood and more like a cologne I didn't recognize.

"Glad I caught you," he said, pulling away slightly. "Want me to come by after work with pie?"

"I'm not sure," I said in what I hoped was a flippant tone. I thought I might die from curiosity right on the spot, but I was determined to see if he mentioned the large elephant lurking in our conversation.

He took a step back and surveyed me for a second, shoving his hands into his pockets and leaning against my car. "Do you have something you'd like to ask me?"

"What? No. Why?" I didn't sound casual at all, more like slightly frenzied and accusatory, but I tried to play it off.

"My family is in town, Avery."

His family? Suddenly, everything clicked. His family. That explained the car, and the nice clothes, and maybe even the cologne. "Your family?"

"Yes, my mother and Lucas. We had lunch in Midland. They showed up unexpectedly this morning."

I exhaled. Maybe I was still a little gun-shy due to extraneous circumstances. "You didn't know they were coming?"

"Not a clue. Savannah Miller typically does what she wants, when she wants." His words were spoken with a great deal of affection toward their subject, and suddenly I couldn't wait to meet her.

Fox read my mind because his next words were exactly what I wanted to hear. "I want you to meet them, maybe dinner tomorrow night? They're staying in Midland for a few days."

I quickly ran through my schedule in my head. "I'd love to meet them, Fox. Tomorrow is fine."

"Great. We'll bring Annabelle too, okay? My mother insisted on meeting you both."

"She did?" I asked, surprised. *What had Fox told her about me, about us?* A warm feeling settled into my chest.

"Of course she did." He bent forward again, capturing my lips with his own and sending a chill down my back. "I'll see you later. I love you."

"I love you, too." I got into my car and watched as he turned and ran up the back stairs to his apartment.

I was going to meet Fox's family.

I was going to meet *Fox's family.*

I whipped out my cell phone and dialed. "Heather? I'm picking you up in half an hour. We're going shopping."

∽

I gripped Fox's arm tightly with one hand and Annabelle's little fingers in my other as we navigated the stairs to the lobby of the Midland hotel. While I was absolutely certain it wasn't the nicest hotel in which Savannah and Lucas had ever stayed, it was definitely the most luxurious that Midland had to offer.

We were dining in the hotel's restaurant tonight, and I was especially looking forward to sitting under the beautiful stained-glass lamps and trying their signature martini. I practically knew the menu by heart already because "Most Organized" and her best friend Google had stayed up late last night doing research in order to be extra prepared.

My stomach fluttered with nervous butterflies as the waiter led us to our table and I got my first glimpse of Fox's mom and brother. Savannah left her seat and came around to the front of the table as we approached, her chic black dress swaying gently as she moved. I saw that she had Fox's exact eyes, almost too green to be real, and his blond hair, although hers was a bit more highlighted and fell to her collarbone in pretty waves.

"Hello, son," she said, smiling warmly as she turned a cheek to accept Fox's kiss.

Lucas came up behind her, and for a moment I was struck by the resemblance between him and Fox. Lucas had darker blond hair and hazel eyes, but they both had the height and the broad shoulders. I was sure that every woman in the restaurant was looking our way, and probably a few of the men too.

"Mom, Lucas, this is Avery and Annabelle Kent."

"Avery, it's wonderful to finally meet you," Savannah said, taking my hand in both of hers.

Her genuineness put me instantly at ease. *So, so different from my interactions with the Dempseys,* I thought.

"It's a pleasure Avery, Annabelle," Lucas said in his deep voice that was so like Fox's.

"I'm so happy to meet you both as well," I said. "This is my daughter, Annabelle."

"Well, hello, Annabelle! That is a beautiful dress," Savannah told her.

"Thank you very much," Annabelle said. She tugged on my hand. "Fox's mama is pretty!"

"I love her immediately," Savannah laughed. "Shall we sit?"

We ordered drinks and appetizers while Savannah told us all about her Dallas exhibit. I learned a little more about what Lucas did also, as his company provided security services for Savannah's travel and the ground transportation of her paintings during the tour.

"Mom won't put them on a plane," he explained dryly, and Fox half-laughed, half-coughed into his drink.

"They want to crate them haphazardly and shove them down into the bowels of the aircraft," Savannah said disgustedly. "I can't allow it."

"You're the boss." Lucas' half smile around his glass was so like Fox's when he took a sip of his scotch.

Fox snickered but Savannah ignored him. From what I knew of Fox, I assumed she was used to the constant banter between her sons.

"I wish you could come to Dallas so we could spend Thanksgiving together," she said, changing the subject beautifully. "Beckett said you're all working that day, though?"

It threw me for a minute to hear her refer to him by his first name but I recovered quickly. "Yes, every year we do a free meal at the diner for anyone who doesn't have a place to go."

My parents had started that tradition when they first took over the restaurant, and it was my favorite day of the year. Typically we got a lot of young ranch hands, the occasional group of oil riggers, some elderly folk, and often a few families that were having a rough time. Throughout the day, our regulars would trickle in with extra food from their own tables – someone always "accidentally" made a double batch of biscuits or too many pumpkin pies – and it turned into a real party atmosphere with kids running around and everyone laughing and talking.

This year, my dad and Fox were planning to cook eight huge turkeys, and they'd been talking strategy for the past few days. No matter where we ended up next year, I knew I'd come back for Thanksgiving at The Kitchen. It wouldn't be the same anywhere else.

"That's a wonderful thing your family does," Savannah remarked. "I miss those intimate things about a small town."

"My mother is from Washington state," Fox told me. "Up near Vancouver."

"Very rainy and cold, but I loved it," she said, a faraway look in her eye. "After I met Carter, we traveled all over, but the Pacific Northwest still calls to me. Of course, I'm spoiled and used to the beautiful California weather now!"

I smiled at her as I tidied Annabelle's area at the table. She was quiet as a mouse, chewing on a breadstick and listening to us talk while scribbling away in her coloring books contentedly. I smoothed her hair and kissed the top of her head. When I sat back in my chair, I saw Fox looking at me, an odd expression on his face. I raised an eyebrow at him and he smiled at me, a new smile I hadn't seen before, almost a cross between proud and wistful.

Savannah didn't seem like she missed much, and I could tell that she definitely noticed our exchange. I felt Fox's hand slide onto my thigh under the table, just high enough to make me wish it was even higher. I would never get enough of that man, never ever.

"So you're cooking now," she said to Fox with a sly grin.

"Is it so unbelievable?" he laughed.

Lucas smirked. "It is to me."

"Not at all." Savannah speared Lucas with a stern look, but the amused expression on his face didn't falter. "He can do anything he sets his mind to, Avery, and he has. Early admission to UCLA, top of his class in paramedic training, Hotshot crew leader at a young age…" she trailed off.

Fox looked around the room uncomfortably and I didn't know what to say. We didn't discuss his firefighting career much these days and it suddenly felt like the most important thing in the world. *What was he thinking? What were his plans? Did they include us?*

Annabelle picked that minute to break the ice as she piped up and asked when our food would arrive.

"Soon, baby," I told her. "Have another breadstick."

"Tell us about graduate school, Avery. It sounds terribly exciting." Savannah changed the subject again with ease.

"Well," I began. "I applied to NYU and now I'm just waiting for their response."

"Waiting is horrible, but you'll love New York. How fun, to be young in that city! Have you ever been?" she asked.

"No," I said. "Not yet. I was planning on taking a trip out there once I got my acceptance."

"It's one of the greatest places in the world," she said. "We loved traveling there when the boys were young. There's always plenty to see. Of course, there's the garbage and the traffic and the noise, but that's all part of what makes it New York City." Her eyes sparkled as she spoke.

"It sounds amazing," I agreed. And a little overwhelming, but in a good way.

"Lucas has offices in New York, so I still find myself there frequently. Did you know that?" she asked me.

"No," I said slowly.

Fox and Lucas exchanged an indecipherable look that piqued my curiosity, but neither of them said anything. Suddenly Fox's enthusiasm about my potential enrollment at NYU made a little more sense.

"Carter – their father – and I visit him and then stay in Manhattan for the weekend. There's always something to do – galleries, shopping, theatre. I know you'll be busy with your studies but you have to find time to enjoy the city."

"I will," I assured her.

"Good," she said, satisfied. "By the way, Beckett – your father is sorry to have missed you. He couldn't get away from his consulting work."

"Yes, the General sends his regards," Lucas said wryly, and Fox laughed even as Savannah shushed him good-naturedly.

Waiters appeared and presented our plates with a flourish. The food was delicious, and Annabelle ate all of her chicken and even a bit of her veggie medley, so I promised her we'd have dessert.

∽

I was halfway through my cheesecake when Savannah cleared her throat and all four of us looked over to her.

"Beckett," she started. "I had an interesting thing happen the other day."

Lucas' body language immediately changed and suddenly he looked distinctly uncomfortable.

Fox raised an eyebrow at her as he took a bite of cake. "Oh?"

"Yes, I got a call from McDaniels and Sloane. Apparently they've been trying to contact you, and after no luck they got a bit worried."

I glanced quickly from Fox to Savannah to Lucas, trying to read between the lines of their conversation. I wasn't sure who McDaniels or Sloane was but I could guess. Not many people were referred to by last name only, so I assumed they were former colleagues of Fox.

"I told them not to worry, that I'd just spoken with you and you were fine," she continued. "I gave them your phone number again to be sure, but they said they'd already left messages."

Fox pushed his plate of cake away. "Thanks," he said shortly, but without heat.

Savannah said nothing, just studied him as she stirred her cappuccino. I got the distinct impression that Fox knew exactly which unreturned messages she was referring to, but neither of them planned to elaborate on the issue.

"Of course," she said finally.

Lucas signaled the waiter and there was a heavily silent moment while our coffees were refilled and no one said anything. Fox changed the subject, another impeccably smooth transition that must've been spoon fed to him as a child, and we began discussing the driving conditions between here and Dallas like the previous awkward conversation never occurred.

My mind was in overdrive even as I nodded and smiled. *Why would Fox be avoiding talking to his friends? Wouldn't he want to stay connected, especially if he was planning to return?*

The constant stream of questions flowed through my mind as we said our goodbyes to Savannah and Lucas and thanked them for the delicious dinner.

"You're quite welcome, Avery." She kissed me once on each cheek. "I am so happy to finally meet you and see that you're every bit as lovely and charming as Beckett said, if not more."

Lucas leaned in to brush his lips against my temple. "Don't worry so much," he said in a voice so low that only I could hear him. "You're the end result in all of his equations."

I stepped back and looked at him curiously. "Thanks," I said softly.

"And you, precious baby," Savannah hugged Annabelle tightly. "Thank you for coming and showing me your pretty dress and for this beautiful drawing." She held up the crayoned paper Annabelle had given her. "I know just where I'm going to hang it."

Annabelle beamed, and my heart felt full. So this was what it felt like to be approved of by your boyfriend's family. I could get used to this.

⁓

"They loved you both," Fox said in the car.

"They're great," I said sincerely. "Your mother is so lovely. It was a wonderful dinner."

We'd bundled Annabelle into her car seat in the truck, where she fell asleep almost immediately, and were currently on our way back into Brancher. Fox put a low blues channel on the stereo and cranked the heat and, between my full heart and full stomach, I was tempted to take a doze myself.

I was so comfortable that I nearly forgot about the conversation regarding Fox's colleagues, but it came rushing back to me all at once, along with a new feeling of something close to dread. As much as I didn't want to push this issue because I was afraid of what he would reveal, I had to know.

And then there was Lucas' comment. I felt like he was telling me the truth, that Fox was considering us in all of his decisions, but that still didn't make anything any clearer.

"Fox, why haven't you called your friends?" I asked softly.

His face was shadowed by the dim dashboard lights in the cab of the truck so I couldn't completely make out his expression, but it looked like a combination of sad and conflicted. "I don't know."

"Will you consider it? It sounds like they really miss you." *This is what I should be encouraging him to do,* I told myself. *Don't be selfish. He needs this.*

He glanced over at me for just a second before turning his eyes back to the dark roads. "Yes."

I reached for his free hand and slid it into my lap, closing both of my smaller hands around his large one. "Good."

CHAPTER TWENTY-TWO

My head was presently crammed full with too many stanzas of poetry so I wasn't entirely sure but it sounded like there was some sort of alarm coming from Fox's lap.

"Is your tablet ringing?" I asked.

Fox tapped the screen and amusement settled over his face. "It is. Excuse me."

We were sitting on the couch, recovering from our marathon Thanksgiving at the diner the day before while Annabelle played with her stuffed animals and I tried to catch up on some homework. Fox was in the middle of sending emails to his parents and his brother, trying to firm up plans for the holidays. We were hoping to see them at some point before the New Year, either here in Texas or maybe even in California.

The idea of the California trip was monumental to me, because not only did it mean I'd meet Fox's entire family, but it also sort of cemented our status as a real couple. We hadn't discussed the Forest Service or my graduate school plans lately, and while that was mostly due to major mental avoidance on my part, I hoped naively that everything would just fall into place.

I watched curiously as he got up and headed toward my

bedroom with the tablet. There could only be a handful of people who would be trying to video chat with him, and from the look on his face I had a pretty good idea of who it was. Minutes ticked by and I heard the low murmur of his voice and the occasional deep chuckle, but I was too far away to really make anything out.

Part of me wanted to sneak over and listen at the door, but the other, more sane, part of me knew that eavesdropping on Fox's conversation was not only childish but also incredibly rude. He didn't make a habit of hiding things from me, so I needed to trust that he would share when he was ready.

"Avery, can you come in here for a minute, please?" he called from my room.

Maybe he was going to be ready sooner than I thought. I stepped over Annabelle and headed down the hallway nervously. He met me in the doorway with bright eyes and a smile that verged halfway between a smirk and a grin. Taking my hand, he led me over to my desk where he'd propped the tablet, and I saw two men in T-shirts grinning back at us from the screen.

"Well, well, well..." one of them snickered good-naturedly. "I can see why Foxy has been MIA for so long. Hello there, darlin'."

The other man gave him a hard shoulder nudge. "Shut up, McD."

Fox shook his head, raising his eyes to the ceiling. "Jeremy Sloane and Trey McDaniels, this is Avery Kent. Avery, these are two of the most irritating people I've ever met."

I laughed and sat down when Fox pulled out my desk chair. He grabbed the ottoman and sat next to me so he could see the screen. "Very nice to meet you."

"Likewise, sweetheart. Thanks for taking good care of this idiot while he hopped around on that bum leg," McDaniels said.

"It was my pleasure," I said giving Fox a cheeky side-eye.

Sloane burst into laughter. "I like this girl, Fox." He turned to me. "Are there more of you? Where is this little town?"

"She's one of a kind, she's all mine, and you probably ran a GPS on me the minute we started this call, so stop pretending like you don't know."

"Glad to see your sense of humor didn't get shredded along with that leg, Foxy," McDaniels teased.

I blanched momentarily at McDaniels' choice of words, but it was fairly accurate. Fox put everything he had into his physical therapy. The scarring on his leg was intense, and although he'd spent a lot of time building up the muscle that he'd lost, it was still a very evident former injury. He'd had a few setbacks, but the man was very nearly a machine. Now when he ran, instead of the minute wobble, he was completely fluid and fast. And there was definitely no denying his strength.

"Now Avery," Sloane began, changing the subject. I focused my attention on him gratefully. "Fox tells us that he's been cooking at your family's restaurant. I'd like to know, how many people have been poisoned so far, approximately?" He kept his face entirely straight and I laughed when McDaniels couldn't do the same.

"He's actually very good!" I protested. "No hospitalizations as of yet," I said, glancing over at Fox.

"Well, I can't believe it," McDaniels said. "You had a hidden talent and you never told us. Where were all my fancy-ass omelets and roasts and shit?"

Fox shrugged. "You'll eat anything, any time. I only cook for those who appreciate me."

"Pack your knives and your blender or whatever, asshole, and get back to work out here. You're whole now, and we miss your ugly face."

I think McDaniels intended his comment to be offhand, but it had the opposite effect. My heart jumped into my throat, Sloane gave him a dirty look, and Fox sat back, running both hands through his hair. A long ten seconds passed while we all tried to look anywhere but at each other.

"It's not that simple," Fox said finally.

"We know," Sloane responded quickly. "McD has a big mouth."

"I do," McDaniels agreed. "But I meant it."

Fox shifted stiffly on the ottoman, and I felt distinctly

uncomfortable being a part of this conversation. I made a move to get up and excuse myself, but he put a hand on my shoulder. "Don't go."

"I should let you—" I began.

"Please stay." Fox looked directly into my eyes and I felt my insides unclench a little.

"Shit, Foxy, I didn't mean to start anything," McDaniels said. "I just said the thing that we've been thinking since you medevacked out of here. When's Fox coming back?"

"I know," Fox said.

I had to hand it to McDaniels – he had the balls to say what the rest of us had been dancing around for months. It was out there now, the big question.

"We just want to know, man. We've all been there, felt it. Sometimes it's hard to remember how you got here, or why." Sloane looked down for a moment and then raised his head. The transparent conflict on his face was brief, but I caught it.

The night that Fox had been injured, the Hotshot crew lost a firefighter and a young camper. Fox told me that everyone had a hard time after that, because the loss was exponential – one of their own along with someone they were supposed to protect. Fox couldn't go back to work immediately because of his leg, but the rest of the crew – Chase included – did. When they grieved, they did it in full fire gear.

"You want to do something else? Make movies or whatever? Open a restaurant, have some cows... I dunno, farm some shit?" McDaniels sat back. "Do it after, when we're old."

My mind flipped ahead forty years, to me and Fox relaxing on a porch somewhere, maybe even here in Texas. I wouldn't be opposed to coming back someday, maybe closer to a big city, and retiring with some land of our own. But McDaniels had a point... we had time to do that when we were older.

Fox opened his mouth to say something, then closed it.

"Just think about it," Sloane said.

Fox glanced over at me and nodded, his eyes softening. "You

guys will be the second to know."

⌒

I flipped through a rack of sweaters listlessly. I thought that driving out to the big mall in Midland to start some Christmas shopping would be a good idea, but I was too distracted.

Fox and I hadn't discussed our conversation with his friends, but we needed to. I'd thought about it constantly for days, wondered what Fox was thinking, made pros-and-cons lists in my head for various scenarios, and basically just obsessed about the entire situation. For me, it boiled down to one simple thing: I couldn't be the reason that Fox didn't continue the career that was so very important to him.

I knew part of him wanted to stay and part of him couldn't wait to get back, but I didn't know which part was currently winning, and it didn't really matter. He'd come here with a goal, and I had no intention of derailing that. He alluded to the fact that his hesitation was multi-faceted, but I had to take myself out of the equation. I was here for him no matter what.

"Find anything for your dad?" Fox came up beside me and startled me out of my thoughts.

"No," I mumbled.

"Let's take a break," he suggested.

We walked out of the department store without buying anything and headed toward the food court. The mall was already decorated for Christmas and probably had been since before Halloween. Tinny carols played over the speakers and I could see Santa's Village all set up over by the west end. I'd have to bring Annabelle here one day soon so she could see him and give him her Christmas list.

At the edge of the food court, Fox stopped and grabbed me around the waist, pulling my back against his chest and resting his chin on top of my head.

"We have an important decision to make," he said.

"I– I know." Fox caught me off guard but I supposed now was as good a time as any to have our serious conversation.

"I just don't know what to do," he mused.

"Me neither." I wished I could see his face and try to read exactly what he was thinking, but he held me tightly against him and I couldn't crane my neck far enough to look into his eyes.

"Part of me wants to go for barbecue, but then another part of me says why not Chinese? It's a tiny food court in a West Texas mall, what could possibly go wrong?" Fox said sardonically.

Chinese? What the hell was he talking about? "Um."

He spun me around so we were facing each other. "Avery? Aren't you hungry?"

"Oh right." *He was talking about food, you idiot,* I thought. *Not life choices.*

Fox's mouth quirked up on one side as he looked down at me. I always had the feeling he knew exactly what I was thinking, especially when I was flustered. "So? Chinese or barbecue?"

"Both?"

"That's my girl."

We filled our trays with an array of questionable-looking items, grabbed a couple drinks, and headed to one of the laminate tables in the center of the food court.

"I think the Chinese barbecue pulled pork really ties everything together," he said, surveying the food spread out in front of us.

"Absolutely," I laughed.

"Who's left on your list?" he asked me, digging into his mashed potatoes.

I pulled the slip of paper from my pocket. "Well, my dad. And a few more stocking stuffers for Annabelle. At some point I have to assemble the Barbie castle and hide it somewhere," I said thoughtfully.

"You picked it out, I'll put it together," Fox said. "Since you wouldn't let me buy it."

"You got her five dolls," I protested.

"The princess castle is nothing without the princesses."

"You'll spoil her." I leaned forward to kiss his lips.

His eyes flashed hot for a moment as I pulled away. "She loves me."

"You're the most important man in her life," I agreed. "You and my dad."

"I'm in good company then." He paused. "But… someday she might want to know her biological father, and I'd have to adjust." His voice grew rough when he referred to J.D.

"That would bother you?" I asked softly.

He steepled his fingers together. "Selfishly, yes."

"Why?"

"Because the only way she isn't already mine is by blood." He smoothed a hand over his mouth and chin. "And there's nothing I can do about that."

"You think of her that way? As yours?" My heart was doing its skippy beat thing again.

"As ours," he said. "You are mine and she is ours."

I didn't know what to say. Sometimes he knocked every coherent thought right out of me. He knew that I couldn't have more children; we'd had that very important discussion after our first time together when I told him I was on permanent birth control. The fact that he would refer to her as ours made me feel like he was honestly fine with it.

"Is that okay?" he asked when I didn't respond.

"It's better than okay."

He smiled into his chow mein. "Good."

It was such a sweet moment that I wanted to let it settle, but instead I blurted out the only other thing that was on my mind. "Fox, you have to go back to the Forest Service. You have to be a firefighter again, a medic. That's what you do, you help people."

I knew it was true the moment I said it aloud. Fox was too strong and brave and smart to give up everything he'd worked for. If he was being selfish in wanting to be Annabelle's father figure, I was being selfish in wanting to keep him here with us.

He stared at me, his chopsticks forgotten. "I know."

"You do?"

"Yes." He pushed the food aside and reached across the table to take my hands. "I wanted to tell you, but today didn't seem like the time."

I shook my head. "It doesn't matter."

"Anything that concerns the two of you matters to me."

"We can't be the reason you don't continue your career. You would never let yourself keep me from grad school," I pointed out.

"I can go back almost anytime this spring, first to Washington probably, then wherever we're needed, maybe Alaska or Montana. I need to commit to stay through the summer, through fire season."

Washington. Alaska. Fire season. I swallowed quickly and looked away. This is what Fox needed to do, and I'd be damned if I stood in his way.

"I have something for you," he said suddenly. "An early Christmas present."

"Fox!" I cried. "It's like two weeks away!"

He smiled and pulled out an envelope. "Here."

Curiosity had me almost snatching it out of his hand. "What is this?"

"Just open it." He sat back in the hard plastic chair and watched me intently.

I slipped a finger under the flap and carefully opened the envelope. Inside were three small slips of paper, and for a moment I had no idea what they were, but then it registered. Application submission receipts. University of Washington, UC Berkeley, and UCLA. Fox had submitted some of my finished grad school applications, the ones I'd completed but never turned in, partially because I didn't have the money for the fees and partially because the idea of multiple rejections on top of money wasted was enough to give me hives.

I looked up from the envelope to Fox, my eyes bright. "You didn't."

"I want us to have options, Avery. If your heart is set on New

York, I'll be back in the fall and that's where we'll go. Lucas offered me a partnership in the security firm, so we'll be all set."

"He did?" Lucas' comment about Fox's equations suddenly made sense.

"Yes, but if for some reason NYU doesn't work out, or it isn't what you want, we can go to California. I can work with him there, or join a fire house just about anywhere. After my season is up, wherever you land, we'll be together. We'll decide together."

Fox smiled at me, and my heart felt like it was pumping double speed.

"Avery? Are you still with me? I know this is a lot."

"I'm glad you're doing this," I said sincerely. "But is one season enough? What about Sloane and McDaniels? They'd be getting you back just to lose you again."

"I need this. We both know that. I can't leave things the way they are now without another run, or it'll always be unfinished business for me. The way I left can't be the way I go out. I owe my crew that much. And myself," he added.

"That's what I mean!" I protested. "You owe it to yourself to focus on your career."

"It was never just a job to me, Avery." His voice was low and serious. "It made me feel something when nothing else could. It gave me purpose, defined me."

"And you want to give that up?" I was incredulous. "Why?"

"I'm not giving anything up." Fox's green eyes caught mine and held. "I'm gaining everything I've ever wanted."

"Fox, I–" His words left me without any of my own.

"We will make it work," Fox promised me. "Please don't worry."

"I'm not worried, not about us."

But I was worried. I couldn't help it. We knew we wanted to be together, but I still didn't know what was going to happen. There were so many variables – Fox's upcoming departure, my grad school applications. Nothing was concrete, and it scared me. "Most Organized" liked things to be just that, organized.

CHAPTER TWENTY-THREE

I threw myself into Christmas preparations with an almost maniacal fury, seeing as it was one of the few things I could control in my immediate future. I wasn't sure where any of us would be next year – I couldn't expect a response from grad schools until February, and Fox had a spring and summer of wildland fire and rescue ahead of him.

On Christmas Eve, after Annabelle was in bed and Fox and I had eaten all of the cookies she left out for Santa, we curled up together on the couch to watch my favorite Christmas movie, *Scrooged.*

"I can't believe this is your favorite holiday film," Fox said when Bill Murray suggested stapling antlers to the tiny reindeer mice. "It's disrespectful to the classics, like *How the Grinch Stole Christmas* and *A Christmas Story.*"

"Whatever," I said, poking him in the ribs. "It's a cult classic."

"If you say so." He turned slightly so he could wrap his arms around me and nuzzle my neck.

"Mmmmm..." I said, closing my eyes. I could watch this movie any old time.

"Avery?"

"Hmmmm?"

"We need to talk."

Way to kill my buzz. I opened one eye and saw that Fox's face was serious. "Okay." I reached for the remote and turned the TV off.

"I love you," he began.

"I love you, too," I said, leaning forward to kiss him. His lips teased over my mouth and I opened it, inviting him in, but he pulled away.

"I have to say this." Fox searched my face for a reaction before he continued. "I never planned on being here this long. But then I saw you. I wanted you from the minute I stepped off that damn bus." His eyes drilled into mine, reminding me of every night we'd spent together, every touch, every breath. I couldn't remember a time before Fox. He'd seeped into all aspects of my and Annabelle's life and enriched it. She and I were a great duo, but he made us a family.

"I wanted you, too," I whispered.

His dimple flashed for a brief second and he looked pleased, but then his expression turned serious again.

"I knew I wanted you, but I also wanted what was best for you and Annabelle, and I wasn't sure that was me. But as time went on, Chase kept hurting you and taking you for granted..." he trailed off. His voice was even but his knee jiggled as he sat, a sign of his agitation.

"The two of you were beyond my comprehension. I never imagined a life like this, a family. I knew I could be what you needed. I could be that for you. I wanted to so much. And just like that, my plans changed."

He took my face into his hands and stared deep into my eyes.

"You think I haven't considered everything, and I have. I've thought about it from every angle, every scenario. I'm done thinking. I'm going to be thousands of miles away from you two, and I need to know you're okay. More than that, I can't imagine my life without you, and I don't want to, ever. I love you." He paused.

"Marry me."

"Fox, I—"

"Don't think, Avery. We think too much. Don't ruin it."

"It was always you," I said, my voice stronger. A beat passed, and it seemed like the air stilled then crackled with anticipation. The calm before the storm.

"Marry me," he said again, and in that moment I knew there was only one answer.

I nodded, and the look on his face made my heart feel as though it would burst. "Yes."

∽

The light of Christmas morning dawned on me and Fox wrapped up tightly together in my bed. I knew there was a good chance Annabelle would awaken soon, but I couldn't help myself as I ran my bare foot down his calf. My skin craved the contact and I gave in every time.

Fox cleared his throat huskily. "I have so many things I want to say to you, but I don't know where to start."

My heart skipped at the raw emotion in his voice. "From the beginning is always a good place," I said gently.

His beautiful mouth turned up at the corners just slightly. "You are my beginning. I don't think I lived before you and Annabelle. I just existed."

I wasn't used to this side of him, this vulnerable, open side. Fox always let me in, he always made me feel like I wasn't alone, like he could do anything and move mountains and be right there exactly when I needed him. But at his core he was the observer, quiet and often withdrawn, an introvert in the true sense of the word. This was a new level, a direct tap into his soul that I still wasn't sure I deserved but I desperately wanted.

"What do you mean?" I asked.

Fox had accomplished so much in the twenty-six years before I met him. I knew he'd seen some horrible things and been faced with countless difficult choices, but he'd also helped people and his work made a difference. He was educated, and not just through formal institutions. He'd taught himself to be strong and resilient, loyal and dedicated. As corny as it might sound, to me he was the definition of a hero.

"You've been a bigger part of my rehabilitation than you could possibly know," he said.

"Your leg was more than halfway healed when you got here," I protested.

"I'm not talking about my leg. I'm talking about my head."

"Your head?"

"When you told me I was good at saving you, and I said I was just returning the favor – I wasn't kidding."

"I don't understand."

He smiled and smoothed a hand down my bare back, and I desperately wished I could turn back the clock a couple hours and give us more time together in this bed, but I knew Annabelle would be clamoring to open her presents any minute.

"Get dressed, sunshine," he said, slipping out from under the covers. I watched his perfect naked ass amble over to the dresser and pull on a pair of boxer briefs, then sweatpants.

"Ugh, do we have to?" I said, half-jokingly. Christmas morning with Annabelle was really fun, but so was Fox.

"Yes. There's something I want to do, and we can't be naked for it."

I sat up and felt around for my robe, intrigued. Slipping it on over my shoulders, I turned to Fox expectantly. "What?"

"Nope," he said. "Less naked than that."

"Okay, okay," I grumbled, getting out of bed and grabbing some pajamas. I slid the flannel bottoms up over my hips and threw on a long-sleeved thermal shirt. "Is that better?"

"Yes." He leaned forward and kissed me deeply. "You're perfect."

Normally I would've laughed since I had total bed head and

sleepy eyes, but there was something about the sincerity in Fox's voice that stopped me. I watched as he reached into the pocket of his coat hanging in the closet and extracted a small velvet box.

"I wanted to do this the right way last night, but you were already in my arms and I got carried away," Fox said.

My heart sped up to an alarming speed when I saw the box, and tears swam into my eyes when Fox got down on one knee in front of me.

"Now is good," I whispered.

"I love you endlessly, Avery, forever." He flipped open the box to reveal a gorgeous round diamond, set in platinum with tiny diamonds encircling the center stone and trailing down the band. "I'll take whatever you'll give me and I'll make it into a beautiful life for us. Say you'll be my wife."

I looked away from the ring and into his eyes. He could've had one of Annabelle's plastic baubles in there and my answer would've been the same, just as it was last night. He was exactly what I needed and what I craved at the same time. "Of course I will."

He slid the ring onto my finger and stood, gathering me into his arms. I raised my face for his kiss, drinking in the way his eyes swept over my lips before he settled his mouth onto mine.

"Mama! Fox! It's Christmas!" Annabelle called from her room.

We broke apart, laughing, and rested our foreheads together. Fox pressed another kiss to my hair. "I'll get her."

I sat down on the messy bed and gazed admiringly at my ring. I was getting married. Not only was I getting married, but I was marrying Fox. This was turning out to be some Christmas already, and it wasn't even eight a.m.

After we had breakfast and Annabelle demolished the living room in a storm of wrapping paper, we called my parents to give them the good news. It turned out that they both already knew, as Fox had asked my father for his permission before buying the ring.

"I would've asked you anyway," he admitted after I hung up, their congratulations still ringing in my ear.

"Rebel."

"Just persistent."

"Should we call your parents?" I asked.

"Let's talk for a second first," he said. I glanced over at Annabelle and saw that she was completely absorbed with her new Barbie princess castle. I'd have to explain it all to her eventually, but for now she had no idea what was going on and it was easier that way.

"Okay." I snuggled into his side and stuck my hand out to look at my ring again. Yes, I was in love with the man who gave it to me so the ring itself didn't matter, but damn it was pretty.

"You like it?" Fox asked, a small smile on his face.

"I love it," I told him.

He kissed me softly, just barely brushing my lips with his. "Good."

"So what did you want to talk about?"

His body language changed slightly to a less relaxed position. "I need to leave by the beginning of February."

My heart sank but I nodded. "So soon?" I knew it was happening but I'd hoped we'd have more time.

"Let's elope."

"What?"

"Let's elope. Or a quasi-elopement. What about Lake Tahoe? We can bring everyone – Annabelle, your parents, Heather, Joy. My family can meet us there. What do you think?"

I tried to wrap my head around everything he'd said in the past few minutes. February, elopement, Lake Tahoe. "I don't know."

"What's wrong? Did you want a big church wedding? I'm sorry, Avery. I didn't know." Fox took my hand in his. "We can wait. I just thought–"

"No," I said.

"No?"

"I don't want a big wedding. I just want you and me and everyone we care about in the same room. Lake Tahoe sounds wonderful. Let's do it."

CHAPTER TWENTY-FOUR

O n New Year's Day in Lake Tahoe, I prepared to walk down the aisle to marry Fox in front of a small audience of our family and friends. I couldn't believe that Fox had managed to mobilize the entire event and the travel accommodations so quickly, but he'd promised me a winter lake wedding, and he was set to deliver on that promise in full.

"You look beautiful," my mother said, coming up behind me as I took a last look in the mirror. "Your daddy and I are very happy for you."

I turned and saw tears in her eyes. "Thanks, Mama."

Heather bustled into the room carrying my bouquet. "It's time! Are you ready? You look so pretty!"

I looked down at the fitted antique lace dress I wore and smiled. I had gone to the nearest bridal store the day after Christmas and, as luck would have it, the only dress I wanted to try on fit as though it was made for me. Even Heather, my toughest critic, had approved immediately. We'd picked out a creamy champagne-colored dress and shoes for Annabelle and we were done. Fox took care of everything else.

My father appeared and offered his arm. "Let's go, chickie."

If you asked me to describe my feelings as I walked down the aisle to marry a man who was already so intricately a part of my life that being with him was as natural as breathing – well, maybe I just did. The ceremony and vows were a blur, but I distinctly remember promising to love him all the days of my life, which was a given. Fox's thumbs smoothed over my hands as we pledged our love forever, and when it was all over and we'd slid the rings onto each other's fingers and he'd dipped me into a kiss that raised a whistle from Joy, he scooped up Annabelle and we headed into our tiny reception.

After a delicious dinner, the small band pulled out their instruments and began to play.

"Let's dance, Mrs. Fox," he said, taking my hand.

We swirled out onto the dance floor and I rested my head on his shoulder. "This is perfect."

"You're happy," he said in a low voice, more of a statement than a question.

"Beyond happy," I told him. I raised my head and looked into his eyes. "I love you."

"I love you, Avery." The music picked up speed and he spun me around. I crashed back into his arms, laughing.

"My family loves you too," he said.

"Even the General?" Fox's father was more than a little intimidating, but at the rehearsal dinner the night before he'd hugged me warmly and welcomed me to the family. I saw where Fox got his height and his serious face, but his dad was on the next level.

"Especially the General," he confirmed. "He has a weakness for blondes with big ideas."

We looked over to where Carter Fox had Savannah wrapped in his arms as they swayed to the music. I saw Joy and Henry, her longtime beau, and my parents on the dance floor as well, Annabelle in my father's arms. I raised an eyebrow at Heather when she spun by with Lucas. I loved Lucas because he reminded me of Fox, just a little less intense and even more inclined to the occasional wry observation.

Fox noticed them too and laughed. "That could be a good match. He really liked her cake." He nuzzled my neck. "Let's go."

"What? Now?"

"It's our party. We can leave whenever we want to."

He grabbed my hand and pulled me down the hallway, not stopping until we were in the elevator. We zoomed up to the third floor bridal suite – complete with overwhelmingly stunning views of the lake – locked in an embrace. I came up for air as the doors opened. There was something about Fox in an elevator that was just so damn appealing.

Fox unlocked the door and swept me up into his arms, carrying me inside as I laughed and draped myself against his neck. When he set me down, I kicked off my shoes and ran over to the windows immediately to look outside. Lake Tahoe was my new favorite place. We'd have to come back here soon.

I turned and saw Fox sitting on the bed, looking at me. He lounged back on the duvet and for a moment I just stared at him, casually comfortable in his tuxedo, his bow tie untied and his hair slightly mussed. His dimple looked even better now that I was married to it. My husband was beautiful.

My husband. It would take me a while to get tired of hearing that, even if it was only in my head.

"Why don't you come a little closer?" His low voice carried easily across the room.

I was already moving toward him before he finished speaking. The lace of my dress whispered and rustled as I approached, his eyes tracking my every movement. When he stood we were just inches apart, and I was sure that he could hear the accelerated beat of my heart when he reached for me.

"Close enough?" I asked him.

"Not yet."

I placed my hands on Fox's waist to steady myself as his hands skimmed across my skin, his fingers caressing my collarbone and slipping over my shoulder blades before finding the gown's hidden zipper and gently tugging it down in one even pull. The dress slid to the floor to puddle around my feet, leaving me in only the ivory lingerie I purchased especially for today. Fox's eyes widened briefly then narrowed as he took me in.

"Better," he said, cupping my face in his hands and kissing me deeply.

I reached up and pulled a few pins from my hair, sending it tumbling down around my shoulders. He quickly shrugged off his tuxedo jacket, followed by the rest of his clothing, and then we were wrapped around each other again. The room darkened as the dusk of twilight crept through the panoramic windows, but Fox's eyes burned into mine even in the low light.

His kisses were like a drug, slow and deliberate, numbing my thoughts and heightening my senses until I was wound up so tightly that I was shivering in his arms. Our lips touched once more, briefly, before his head dipped and his mouth moved down my neck to my collarbone, lower and lower until he bent to kneel in front of me. I reached behind my back to undo the hooks on my silk corset, but he pushed my hands away gently.

"Let me."

His fingers twisted the metal clasps easily, and the corset fell away from my body. I shuddered again as the cool air hit my bare skin, but Fox smoothed his palms over my torso and I warmed beneath his touch. My eyes closed involuntarily when his lips followed his hands, and I gasped as he bit my hip then softly sucked on the same spot.

Slowly, he kissed his way over my stomach, and my hands found his shoulders, kneading the muscles underneath. A low groan came from Fox's throat when I reached the back of his neck, tangling my fingers in his hair and scraping my nails delicately over his scalp. My breath caught when he grasped either side of my silk and lace panties and dragged the material down my legs.

Before I could lift a foot to step out of them, he hooked his hands behind my knees and pulled gently, urging me back until I was fully lying on the bed. I tried to shift and bring him with me, but he held me in place and didn't lift his head as he kissed up the side of one thigh and then the other and I gasped again, clutching his hair in my fingers.

He raised his head and the look in his eyes sent electricity racing across my skin. In one swift move, he surged up and forward onto his elbows, so we were chest to chest, his hips between my thighs and his hands in my hair. He tipped my chin up with his thumbs so we were eye-to-eye.

"Beautiful," he breathed. "You're so damn beautiful."

"I love you, Fox." My voice hitched a bit on his name.

"Always, sunshine. Always." His shoulders flexed as he started to move, and then the room spun and I was swept away.

EPILOGUE

FOX

Somehow my best days have a way of turning into my worst.

The day I saved those kids turned into a nightmare with lives lost.

The day I first saw Avery, I realized she was with Chase.

The day I felt like we had moved forward, we almost lost Annabelle.

The day I married Avery, in the back of my mind I knew I would be leaving.

And the day before I was coming home... well... it's just *black*.

PLAYLIST

"A Thousand Years" - Christina Perri

"I Hope You're the End of My Story" - Pistol Annies

"Colder Weather" - Zac Brown Band

"Anthem" - Alana Yorke

"Tennessee" - The Wreckers

"Have a Little Faith in Me" - Joe Cocker

"Fireproof" - One Direction

"More Than Anyone" - Gavin DeGraw

"Gone, Gone, Gone" - Phillip Phillips

"Walkaway Joe" - Trisha Yearwood

"Ready to Run" - One Direction

"Merry Go 'Round" - Kacey Musgraves

"Mama's Broken Heart" - Miranda Lambert

"I Will Wait" - Mumford & Sons

"Simple Man" - Lynyrd Skynyrd

"Don't You Wanna Stay" - Jason Aldean & Kelly Clarkson

"Hear Your Heart" - James Bay

"Good Girl" - Carrie Underwood

"Everything Has Changed" - Taylor Swift & Ed Sheeran

"Heart of Dixie" - Danielle Bradbery

"She's Everything" - Brad Paisley

"Famous in a Small Town" - Miranda Lambert

"Ain't No Sunshine" - Bill Withers

ACKNOWLEDGMENTS

I t would not have been possible for me to write this book without the following people:

My husband, who knows my completely true self and always has my back no matter what. Taking a chance on us was the very best thing I ever did. Thank you for letting me be me, embracing my crazy, and loving me in spite of it all.

My daughter, who teaches me daily about wonder, patience, and laughter. I love you. Thank you for coming into my life and changing it in the most wonderful way. This is my first step in showing you that the scope of your accomplishments are limited only by your imagination.

My mom, who has always believed that I could do anything I ever wanted, even when I wasn't sure I could. Thank you for your unconditional love and support, your unfailing optimism, and your incredible example of what it takes to carve your own path.

Jenny, my editor, my sounding board, and my best friend of almost thirty years, who always holds my hand when I need it and talks me down off the ledge when the situation warrants it. Thank you for believing in me and this story, and your willingness to go on this journey together. I could not have done it without you.

Ben, who is a constant source of love, support, humor, and friendship. The best thing I ever got from the internet was you. (And those boots I got on sale from Amazon.) I love you. Thank you for helping me realize the opportunity I have to see how big my life can be.

Nicole, who kicks ass and motivates while still always keeping it real. Thank you for showing me that change is not only possible but achievable, and for encouraging me to take that first step and cheering for every milestone after that.

Evan & Ty, who have infinite patience and generosity not only with their time but also with their willingness to share experiences. Thank you.

Jessica, who is always there for me and encourages my creativity. Thank you for being an amazing friend and especially for helping me navigate this crazy job called motherhood.

Sarah from Okay Creations, who took a vague idea and made it into something beautiful. You unlocked a life achievement for me the day I saw my name on the cover of this book. Thank you.

My family and in-laws, who are forever supportive. Thank you for allowing this book to take me away from gatherings, phone calls, and thank-you notes that I probably forgot to write. I love you.

My friends, who are used to my big ideas and still get excited every time I share something new. Thank you for not laughing at me, for believing I could do this, and for buying the book. You guys *did* buy the book, right?

My internet/blog/Twitter community, who have been there for me since that random day in 2007 when I decided to start Clever Girl Goes Blog. The ultimate compliment you've given me is taking the time to read something I've written, because I've so incredibly enjoyed reading your work over these years. Thank you.

COMING DECEMBER 31ST, 2015

The **HEY SUNSHINE** Trilogy

continues with

NIGHT FOX

All he wants is to remember her…

How much strength does it take to move forward when history seems determined to knock you down? And how do you find the path to redemption when you don't even recognize your own life?

AVAILABLE ON AMAZON.COM AND WHEREVER EBOOKS ARE SOLD

ABOUT THE AUTHOR

Tia is a Southern California hairstylist, a former English Lit major, and blogger-turned-author. She was the voice behind the now-retired personal site Clever Girl Goes Blog, and her work has been featured on numerous forums including Open Salon and Hooray Collective. She believes in eyeliner as a defense mechanism, equal rights, and Marc Jacobs. Her favorite things include One Direction, story time, and the overzealous use of punctuation. When not writing and reading, she binge-watches only the best (subjective) TV shows. She lives in San Diego with her husband, daughter, and tiny dog. Stay updated on her upcoming projects by visiting her website at tiawritesbooks.com.

15102749R00168

Printed in Great Britain
by Amazon.co.uk, Ltd.,
Marston Gate.